Beautiful
Horseflesh

Beautiful Horseflesh

A Novel

Karen S. Bennett

Apprentice House Press
Loyola University Maryland

First Edition

Hardcover ISBN: 978-1-62720-317-3
Paperback ISBN: 978-1-62720-321-0
Ebook ISBN: 978-1-62720-251-0

Design: Paige Akins
Promotion plan: Sarah Ford
Managing editor Kelley Chan

Author photograph by: Raleigh Desper, LLC www.raleighdesper.com

Published by Apprentice House Press

Apprentice House Press
Loyola University Maryland

Apprentice House Press
Loyola University Maryland
4501 N. Charles Street
Baltimore, MD 21210
410.617.5265 •
www.ApprenticeHouse.com
info@ApprenticeHouse.com

In Appreciation

With sincere appreciation to Georganne Hale, vice-president of racing development for the Maryland Jockey Club, for her authoritative information from racing horses' lip tattoos to how a horse is assigned a gate placement at the track. I thank her for hosting me at her office of the Laurel Racetrack and her readiness to answer my many questions.

I thank Jonathon Friedland, my Baltimore go-to guy on baseball cards.

My thanks to Sally Whitney, Sherry Morrow, and Teresa Cook for their reading and editing at various stages of the book's progress.

Contents

Foreword

Yes, the book deals with the sport of kings. And its main character is a strikingly handsome piece of horseflesh. The riveting drama, on the other hand, is all too human and complicated.

Every step in this narrative of striving and peril has its subplot. Each carries an element of portent. The overlapping story lines might be difficult to manage by a less adroit story teller. The reader becomes, appropriately, more eager for each new perilous step.

The almost too perfect Bumble B arrives in Florida for her maiden race with an undertone of mystery—or worse.

High spirited, for sure, but Bumble is a bit more than that. Her trainer demands too much control. He drinks too much. Has eyes for the training track's 16-year-old daughter. Luis, the 18-year-old brother watches the drama unravel in front of his discerning eyes. Luis wonders what is the mystery with Bumble's hind feet.

All of this plays out beneath Patrizia Smitt's family's pressing financial concerns. The bright, adventurous daughter finds her way into dangerous territory. Concerning enough without the added potential of her own attraction to the trainer. Luis is ready to make almost any sacrifice for his sister and super-stressed mother. His concerns lead to near disastrous decisions—very unlikely key ones if the reader forgets his youth.

The final unfolding, in which all the questions are answered, is handled deftly. One decision the author has made—one or two, adds to the story's credibility making the rest of this human drama all the more believable, and effective.

Bennett tells her story with abiding concern for the language. Cars and trucks turn onto the farm in "full rumble." Horses run with unnerving speed or "gambol" to their destination.

Of the well observed scenes, there was this one: "Pale rags of Spanish moss hanging from the distant trees blended into the morning's mist hugging the ground. The smudges of chestnut and black Thoroughbreds, stretching their legs, ran neck and neck. The dark specks of the riders hunched forward, backsides above their saddles, creating an image as if from Degas's brush. The horses scorched the track.

Fraser Smith is a reporter and editorial writer for *The Baltimore Sun*, and a reporter and commentator for WYPR in Baltimore, Maryland. He's the author of *Lenny, Lefty and the Chancellor: The Len Bias Tragedy and Search for Reform in Big Time College Basketball, William Donald Schaefer: A Political Biography, Here Lies Jim Crowe: Civil Rights in Maryland* and *The Daily Miracle: A Memoir of Newspapering*

Chapter 1

FLORIDA

April 1999

Day two of spring break from Palmetto High School was in full bloom, as were the orange trees in the side orchard. Patrizia Smitt and her children, high school senior Luis, and sixteen-year-old Miranda, pushed away from the midday Sunday dinner.

"Okay kids, let's get on with the preparation for the Maryland horse. Miranda, Honey, please put the chocolates into the refrigerator before they melt, and the Easter eggs too. Then get with the dishes. Luis, you'd better get out to the barn for the finishing touches."

Patrizia leaned in to gather plates and heard the predictable response from her truculent daughter, "But Mom, I want to run." Miranda whined and screeched her chair away from the table.

"Randa, you have this whole week of vacation to shatter your previous records. Dishes now." Patrizia turned, waved her hand backwards over her head and started from the kitchen.

Luis flashed a brotherly "ha-ha" look, crossed his eyes at his sister and followed his mom from the kitchen.

The kitchen wall phone jangled. Patrizia intercepted the phone, said a few quiet words and stretched the cord over to Luis. "For you." Her eyes smiled as she mouthed, "A girl!"

Luis's eyebrows shot up and his lower lip poked out at the unexpected call. He grabbed the phone and turned from the family. Mother and sister stood shoulder to shoulder, witness to Luis's first call from a member of the opposite sex. He bent his head to his knees, providing more privacy, pulling into the hallway, already at the limit of the phone's cord. "Oh, hi! Ashley! Happy Easter to you, too. We're finishing up." He puffed a nervous bonhomie laugh and said, "I can't talk right now. You know, family witness. How 'bout I call you later? Yeah, Miranda has your number." He mumbled a few more words and hung up, then laughed aloud. "Wow! I can't believe it. That was Ashley calling me."

Miranda looked up from loading the dishwasher and responded in singsong, "Luis-y has a girlfriend."

"Just shut up Randa. The only reason you have a boyfriend is because Baxter's probably scared to death to break up with you. You'd break his knees if he even smiled at anybody else."

Patrizia stopped her hurried exit to consider Luis might get a girlfriend before college. "One girlfriend now, but once in college, it's girls, girls, girls."

Miranda shrugged and delivered her wisdom. "It gives him a date for the prom." She pushed the ON button of the dishwasher and, self-satisfied with her job, crossed her feet and leaned back against the appliance.

Patrizia asked a mother's question. "What's Ashley's last name?"

"Sousa."

"What kind of name is that?" Her hands came up in the universal palms up questioning posture.

"American."

"No, I meant …"

Luis smirked. "What's more American than the name of the composer who wrote "Stars and Stripes Forever?"

Defeated, Patrizia exhaled, letting her hands slap down to her sides.

Miranda said, "She's got all that wild curly hair. She may be blond, but she's not pretty. I think she skipped a grade back in elementary, so she's only seventeen. Too young to drink. Anyway, she seems too geeky for you."

"Come on Randa. Smart's a good thing. Maybe not for you. She's in the top ten in our graduating class. You're jealous."

The attentive mother asked the requisite, "Where's she going to college?"

"Duke. Look, Mom, we haven't even had the first date. I'll get back to you two if I get a first date. Okay?"

Patrizia resumed her trip to the barn, "Ummm-hmmm."

Out in the barn, Smitt's Water Walk Farm's three employees would be going home to a late Easter dinner. Kirk and Jose finished stacking and squaring bales of straw and raking the paddock, while Big Russ hosed the floor of the water walk area, insuring the bath in the hydrotherapy tub was glitteringly fresh. All effort was directed at making the filly from Maryland's horse country comfortable. The barn never looked better.

Mr. Prescott, the owner of the horse who was at this moment making her way to Smitt's Water Walk Farm, faxed his signed contract for a week of boarding. In the margin, he wrote in a thin hand a few words about his horse's exceptional speed and need for especial care and coddling before the upcoming Sterling Bridle Stakes Race at Tampa Bay. He was certain the purse of $200,000 would be his.

Patrizia, the farm and family's CEO, joined Luis, whistling as he mucked Donkey Boy's stall. She leaned over the fence listening to her son's excited commentary on the upcoming visit from the "horse to beat" at the big race next weekend.

Luis yammered on, "You said this horse unofficially broke some Belmont Stakes records on her home track? I wonder if she's already raced, or are we going on the word of the owner?"

Patrizia answered, "We'll know if she already has a lip tattoo."

"How about I borrow your computer and look up some of this stuff."

Patrizia nodded. "I don't know if she's raced yet, but he mentioned her speed in the contract. Mr. Prescott said he doesn't want everybody in Florida betting on his horse. Could put a big dent in his winnings, so keep a lid on it, my son."

Luis agreed, pulled his Mets cap from his head and wiped his forehead with his forearm. Returning to the task of sweeping up the donkey's stall he said, "I can't believe that Maryland horse is coming here. Dad was sure right.

Think about it, they picked our farm because of our water walk. Oh man, he'd be so proud."

The widowed Patrizia Smitt put her forehead against the flat plane of Donkey Boy's forehead and rubbed his ears, knowing her son would overhear, "All this fuss reminds me of when the children were little and Santa Claus was coming to town."

Luis glanced at his watch again and looked up to see Miranda, in her running shirt and shorts, dash past the barn's open door. "There goes The Streak. She sure can train for track when there's work to be done around here."

"She'll be back. We have a week of work ahead of us. She'll get her share." Patrizia pushed her damp bangs from her forehead. "Phew, what a scorcher. I hope the horse and driver are traveling in air conditioning. Luis, I know this is vain of me, but as long as we're trying to impress these fancy out-of-towners, why don't you get out of your dirty baseball shirt and get shined up a little before they arrive. You know, first impressions, et cetera."

Luis looked down at his soiled, worn-out number one Mookie Wilson pin-striped baseball shirt. "Yeah, I guess you'd have to be a New Yorker or dad's age to know who Mookie Wilson was. Okay, I'm going. Besides, if the trainer is from Maryland, he's gotta be an Orioles fan. Booo, American League."

Patrizia didn't answer. She ignored what she considered baseball's quackery, the plethora of trivia and its many intricacies. The subject, however, had been bonding glue between her late husband and her son. She answered, "In a second I'll get dolled up too." She made an unsuccessful attempt at twisting a long tangle of hair back into her loose pony tail. Luis propped the road apple pan and broom against the inside wall of the barn and hustled to the house to change clothes.

While Luis's head was still cocooned in his newest, whitest shirt, and his elbow was poking straight up, he heard and felt the deep rumble of a heavy truck and trailer. He yanked the shirt over his chest and ran to his window to be rewarded with the view of a rich-looking, pale green truck toting a horse trailer maneuvering next to the barn. Flourishing lime green script on the trailer's side panel told of the filly's home in Prescott Acres, Long Green, Maryland. "Ah, Dad, I wish you could see this."

The new boarders from Maryland arrived a few hours early, catching Patrizia still in her old, sleeveless plaid work shirt. Barney, the basset, trotted back and forth, supervising, and barking instructions. Patrizia leaned to scratch the dog's ear as he took his protective position next to his mother's leg and banged his tail on the ground. "Yes, Barney, I see the truck. Wait 'til you see who's inside."

Luis shot from his room, bounded down the steps, out the door, off the porch and arrived at the side of the truck as the driver slid from the front seat.

Cue the background music, Bud Coleman looked like an advertisement for a man's cologne. He was slender, tanned, well-muscled, in a lime green shirt with Prescott Acres printed on his left chest, and the palest ring of perspiration under his arms and a faint damp patch on his back. He said, "Phew, whatta long ride. When I passed a string of palm trees all lined up so pretty next to the highway, I knew

6

I was in Florida. Glad we're here at last." He bent forward and rubbed both upper legs then stretched. He pressed his spread hand against the small of his back.

Embarrassed that she hadn't had time to spruce up, as soon as Patrizia introduced herself and her son, she spun off to her office. "Let me get those keys to your bunkhouse," and she was gone.

The handsome man pushed up his cap and squinted at Luis and asked, "So, are you part of the circus? I saw the sign at the turnoff from the main highway."

Luis laughed, "Oh, no, that's in Sarasota, the winter headquarters, up the road a bit. But another three hundred yards would have taken you to one of the horse acts for the circus. That's the sign you saw. The sign is on their property. They sure would have been surprised to have a racing Thoroughbred arrive from Maryland. But *we're* expecting you. Let's get your horse out of the trailer. She must be ready to walk around too."

The farm's employees grouped around the tail end of the air-conditioned horse trailer. They watched the hopeful filly, arriving for a week of using the water walk, resting, and acclimatizing to Florida's heat, before the Sterling Bridle Stakes Race next Saturday.

The elegant young horse was hands-off to everyone except for Luis and her trainer, Bud Coleman. The Smitt's farm workmen whispered among themselves, nodding, and in general, approving of the Thoroughbred. Big Russ pointed to the detail of the pale green travel wraps on the horse's lower legs. The men smiled and clapped their hands as the magnificent horse was backed from the ramp into the bright sunshine. A welcoming waft of orange blossom fragrance spirited among the cluster of men and beast.

"Watch her feet. Careful, there she goes, careful, careful." Bud Coleman stood at the bottom of the ramp and waved his Prescott Acres baseball-style cap, directing the capable eighteen-year-old, Luis Smitt. Barney wagged his tail and backed from his supervisory position as he watched the majestic horse.

Coleman stretched out his hand and sounding like a politician said, "Gentlemen, I give you Bumble B, the next winner of the Sterling Bridle Stakes Race." More appreciative applause.

Luis looked up from Bumble B, "This is one beautiful piece of horseflesh." The sun sparked light on the horse's dark glossy haunches and on the muscles rising and falling on her black satin withers. Her noble head bounced up and down, shimmering her thick mane. Luis said, "She looks like she's been varnished. She looks like Black Stallion from the movies."

Coleman flicked a piece of hay from his pant leg then stood tall and gloated, folding his arms across his chest. He rocked back and forth on his tasseled loafers and ran his appreciative gaze across the gleaming dark body and long legs of his trophy. He reached to the horse's head and tied a loose bandana around her eyes. "She can be flighty," was his explanation.

Luis asked, "Shall I walk her to the stall with her eyes covered?"

"Yeah, keep 'em covered 'til you get 'er in there. This girl can dance."

Luis called over his shoulder as he ambled the horse past the trainer, "We're going down to number seven. It's the roomiest."

Coleman laughed, "Seven. Should be good luck." He re-tucked his shirt tail into his khaki pants and followed the boy and horse to stall number seven.

Luis said in his new, deep voice, "If she runs half as good as she looks, we have ourselves a filly who doesn't need a low gate number to win. Looks like a real winner." He led the horse through the aisle with four stalls on each side. "Come on, you black beauty. There you go, girl. You're something." Luis sounded like a proud father, his hand on the horse's flat cheek. He clicked his tongue and spoke in a practiced, low, reassuring tone to the horse. The filly whinnied and reared. Luis grabbed the bridle and clip-clopped Bumble B to the most distant stall.

Donkey Boy, in apartment number one, lifted his head and trumpeted a message. Luis pointed. "Donkey Boy is either welcoming your horse, or warning my prize horse, Paley's Comet, over here in stall three. We also have a permanent young palomino boarder, Gingerfoot, in stall number four. Luis continued with the tour. "We have a small paddock, straight through those doors, and a field between the track and the orchard. Our track, with a new gate for four, is next to the road you came in on."

Coleman followed, his cap pushed high on his head with the bill poking straight upwards. He tucked his thumbs behind his belt buckle with a B on the silver square as he scanned and took stock of the new digs. Luis led Bumble to her stall, closed her in and stood back. He reached an upturned hand toward the horse to indicate Bud could now remove the horse's blindfold. Coleman stepped in to stall seven and flicked the bandana from Bumble's eyes. Tired of the blindfold game, the horse swung her head side to side. Her muzzle hit Bud's back, knocking his cap from his head. He laughed. "She's young." He snapped his cap from the floor, and ducking to avoid another swipe of the horse's head, leapt from the stall.

Luis laughed to himself when he noted how focus-driven the trainer's rapid exit was from the horse. Coleman regained his dignity as he perused the antiseptic-washed stall, glanced at the straw bales heaped by the door leading to the paddock. He ignored the bibbed, black and white cat's overture, rubbing against his pant leg.

Luis saw the cat's flirtation and said, "That's Tuxedo and the calico is Fleabag, his wife. And this is our barn dog. His name is Barney—obvious, huh?"

Coleman did not react to the joke, but cooed. "Well, would you look at this handsome basset." Bent in half, pressing his nose to the black leather nose of Barney, he abandoned all effort of appearing as the elite, exclusive horseman from Maryland. Coleman started to straighten up, but succumbed to the dog's brown eyes. He bent back to the dog and said, "Young man, you'd better check my luggage when I leave because I might have to steal this handsome pup."

Coleman scanned the property but was distracted by the ground-thumping, tail-wagging dog. He stopped to laugh out loud, and bent to rub Barney's ears. "How old is this wonderful puppy dog?" His voice was as high as an old lady's when talking to her precious kitty.

Luis answered a business like, "Three." His arms crossed his chest and he leaned back on one leg as time ticked on. The new trainer straightened, clicked his tongue and tapped the side of his leg for Barney to accompany him on the continuation of the tour of the barn and paddock. Barney joyfully obeyed, his brown ears swinging wide.

Coleman fingered the bridles, leather reins, and nylon webbed halters hanging on the wall. "Only eight stalls for all this track and your water treadmill?"

"Most of our water walk business is for horses that come in a few times a week or every day. Those are our 'Dailys,'" Luis answered. "Dad named the water exercise area the water walk, but it's the same as aqua-therapy or hydrotherapy. You know, physical therapy for horses."

Bud nodded. "Do you have the above ground, circular tub or the ditch type? You'd think I'd know, but Mr. Prescott, the boss, made all the arrangements. Why would *I* need any information? *I'm* the lowly trainer."

Luis ignored the disgruntled tone and launched into a salesman's pitch, "We have the stainless steel walled ditch with a down ramp to the ten-foot long treadmill, with two jets per leg. Then, of course, the up and out ramp. The horses seem to love it. When dad was a kid he used to exercise his father's horses in the Gulf of Mexico tide a few miles from his home. Great exercise without stressing the knees. Well, you already know." Luis continued, "Luckily, we don't have to go to the gulf to exercise. Did you want

Bumble B to get in a little water treadmill workout this afternoon after your long ride down here?"

"Nah." Bud answered. "I'll start first thing tomorrow, but I'll want strict privacy." Coleman answered. "You can see she's a high spirited horse, and she'll do better without other horses around and without a lot of people making noise, slamming doors, dogs barking, trucks coming and going," Coleman answered.

A frown grew on Luis's forehead in response to Coleman's negative description of the farm. He was surprised by the visiting trainer's strict rules, but Coleman was the paying customer, so Luis answered, "Yes sir, Mr. Coleman. Anything you say."

Bud Coleman, making a show of looking around, said, "I see you're still using leather bridles instead of nylon."

Luis turned to excuse this un-modern feature and said, "Yeah, my dad insisted on leather bridles. It's the one thing he was stubborn about."

Coleman interrupted, "Your dad, is he still around? You said he *was* stubborn about leather bridles."

Luis was unprepared to discuss his father's recent death but returned a succinct, rehearsed answer, "Dad died of a blood disease in '97." Not one to linger on the uncomfortable, he recovered, "But we have a lot of newer, lightweight saddles, and some rubberized leads. He wasn't willing to trade in the old leather bridles. In time we'll replace them with the nylon. Mom sees no reason to update. Unnecessary expense." As soon as Luis mentioned 'expense' he wished he could take it back. He did not want this man with this rich horse to suspect there were money problems at Smitt's

Water Walk Horse Farm. Luis jumped in, "Leather's so smooth and it smells so good, doesn't it? And besides," he laughed, "in a few days you'll have won Tampa Bay's Sterling Bridle Stakes Race. No more leather or nylon bridles for this winner." Glancing up, Luis pointed to the tack room door, changing the subject. "And mom keeps a refrigerator of bottled water, Dr Pepper, Mountain Dew, you know, pop or maybe you call it 'sodas' inside the tack room. Did you notice the wall phone by the barn's front door? The important numbers are tacked up right next to it."

The telephone jangled, as if indicated in the script, as Patrizia reentered the barn. She lifted the receiver, smiled at Mr. Coleman, then directed her eyes to the floor. "Oh, hi Baxter. No, she's running. Okay, I'll tell her you called. Luis is busy settling our new Thoroughbred from Maryland. Gotta go. Bye, Baxt."

Patrizia had piled her auburn hair into an attractive loose bun on the top of her head with short tendrils of hair curled around her face. She had slipped into a shin length, full skirted denim dress which brushed the top of her everyday cowgirl boots. Her lipstick was a glossy coral, and in all she had made a stunning transformation in fifteen minutes.

Patrizia handed Mr. Coleman the keys to his cabin and turned to go. His eyebrows went up when he regarded the shined-up Mrs. Smitt. Patrizia did not miss the fleeting gesture. Her cheek dimpled. Bud pocketed the keys, nodded his appreciation and turned to Luis. "Do you think you could do something to muffle that loud jangle?" He pointed his thumb backwards toward the phone. "I mean, I'm afraid my horse will have a fit every time that phone rings."

"Sure, we can manage that," Luis answered. Coleman strutted a bit. He chewed a piece of straw as he moved about the barn.

Luis asked, "Are you ready to see the horse's own little Florida swimming pool, right out here behind the barn?"

"Nah, later. Need to get my gear now." Satisfied with his sizing up, Coleman started toward the trailer, parked in the shade of the barn. He turned to Luis. "Oh, and how far are we from Tampa Bay Downs?"

"About an hour. We have an interstate across Tampa Bay and another highway over land to the same address, either route, an easy ride."

"You'll muck the trailer too, young man?"

"Yes sir. Call me, Luis."

Coleman called "Hey, Luis," and threw the truck keys, and turned to the truck's cab.

The keys clacked into Luis's senior ring, like iron filings to the magnet. He returned to the barn, feeling capable and grown, and trusted by the new boarder.

Miranda dashed into the barn. She caught her breath, then gasped at the sight of the imposing black Thoroughbred. Bumble B shook her head and mane, without obvious reason other than to entertain the girl, then reared back.

"Oh, Louie, she's magnificent." Miranda was breathless after her daily two-mile run. "I was turning around down at the mailboxes, ready to head back when this great big, fat, fancy horse trailer almost ran me off the road." She mopped her face with a corner of her high school's track team tee shirt and absentmindedly snapped her bra strap

14

flashing her coral fingernails. "Who's the gorgeous guy in the lime green shirt?"

"Bud Coleman. Bumble B's trainer. He's getting his gear out of the truck's cab. Seems too good looking for a trainer, huh?" He bent closer to Miranda. "Mom almost choked when she saw him." He laughed. "He sure doesn't look like any trainer we ever saw here or even over at the circus." Luis elbowed his sister. "You should have seen her dash out of here after introducing herself. Coleman got here early and Mom still looked a wreck. I had to laugh." He looked behind, belatedly thinking to see if his mother or Coleman could overhear him. Seeing neither, Luis continued, "Speaking of good looking, how do you like this fine equine specimen? But, Randa, Mom'll kill ya if you get too close to that horse. Bumble's like royalty and she's jumpy. But isn't she spec-*tac*-ular and grand? I can't believe we're housing and training her until the race."

Miranda stood back to view the whole horse. The kicked up straw caught the sun's beams and gave a dusty halo to Bumble B's smooth black musculature. "Beautiful horseflesh."

"Yeah, that's what I said." Luis leaned on the doorway's upright, admiring the filly. His eyes glowed with awe and pride. "After the race, our sign could say, 'Smitt's Stables, Bumble B Slept Here.' Should be real good for business."

"That's true, but mom's little newspaper article mentioning the Maryland horse coming here didn't hurt." Miranda picked up Tuxedo and rubbed his whiskers. She buried her face in his fur and added, "Especially if she wins."

The trainer's voice boomed from behind the teens. "Oh, she'll win alright. Look at her!" He laughed and pointed to Bumble. The Smitt kids spun to see Mr. Coleman walking toward them. He held up his duffle.

Luis waved, "I'll be right there to help out. By the way, Mr. Coleman, this is my kid sister, Miranda."

Miranda was preparing to say the standard and polite, "How do you do," when Bud stepped toward Miranda. "Well, goodness me, aren't you the prettiest filly I've ever seen?"

Miranda drank in the man and blushed to her scalp. She made a quick, "Hi," wave and backed from his steamy stare to stand behind Luis's shoulder. Bud leaned sideways from his waist to get a longer look at Miranda. She dipped a shallow curtsy.

Bud laughed and said, "Charming," and turned to exit. He looked over his shoulder for one more, not subtle, look at Miranda.

Miranda elbowed Luis. "Quit the 'kid sister' routine. I'm not an eight-year-old, skinned-knees-kid stupidly tagging behind you."

Luis looked around at his sister and threatened her over his shoulder. "Sorry Brat. But, Randa, no touching. No kidding. She's no pet pony." He ran ahead of Bud to escort him into the bunkhouse.

Luis flipped the light switch at the door. Bud entered the furnished cabin and thudded his duffle to the floor. Both inhaled the woody scented knotty pine paneled walls and fragrance of the evergreen tree shaped deodorizer hanging on the kitchen window's latch. Coleman scanned the room. "This looks comfortable," he said, nodding to the black, dial-front telephone next to a small tablet and a cup of pencils and pens on the square Formica kitchen table. "Thank your mother for me."

"The phone's got to be a collector's item, but it works." Luis turned his hand toward the sturdy bunk beds on the far wall. No explanation required there. "So here's the kitchen corner. Pots and pans are in the closet. Mom wants you to be comfortable. If you need anything, call or come to the porch. If we can't hear your knock, call out and come on in. Mom's office is in the back of the house. That's good if she wants quiet, but bad if someone is calling her from the porch. Maybe you'll want to rest or walk around the field, the track and barn after that long trip. So, welcome Mr. Coleman. I'll get back to mucking the trailer. Call if you need us." Luis hustled to the barn for the pitchfork and water hose. He hurried through the dirty work, all the while rehearsing what he'd say on his return phone call to one Ashley Sousa.

Coleman stepped to the bunkhouse porch. He pulled his Prescott Acres visor to the bridge of his nose, shading his eyes which, unobserved, drank in the youthful feminine beauty of Miranda as she walked from the barn to the house. "Cute mom. Cute sister. This assignment's getting better and better," he said as he rubbed his chin.

Chapter 2

TRAINING

Luis's alarm ripped him from sound sleep. His heart leapt when he remembered the soon-to-be-famous Bumble B from Maryland was waiting in *his* barn. "Thank heaven for spring break." He scrubbed both hands through his brushy new short haircut and smiled at the acceptance letter to the University of Miami taped to the U. of M. poster on his wall. "Okay, you Hurricanes, I'll be with you in a few short months." He jumped from bed, dropped to his morning exercise of thirty-five rapid-fire push-ups saying "Ashlee-Soo-sa, to his rug with each up and down. He ended his regime with an unself-conscious gorilla pounding of his chest accompanied by a loud growl. He looked at the old Mookie Wilson poster and the display cabinets holding his most valuable baseball cards and asked, "How'm I looking? Good enough?"

Not waiting for an answer, he noticed a pink envelope, along with a postcard advertisement for four tires for the price of three at the dealership in Palmetto, on the floor behind the trashcan. He glanced at the two-week-old date on the pink envelope with the letterhead of Family First Radiologists in Palmetto. "Mom's gonna kill me." He ripped opened the large envelope and recognized this was yet another in a series of letters threatening to take action if the amount shown on the bottom of the letter was not forthcoming. He looked at the amount of the payment due for radiology services for his father's lengthy battle with cancer. "Oh no, Mom's gonna flip when she sees this. I can't believe medical bills are still coming in."

Luis snapped his orange and blue Mets shirt from his top drawer, passed his window and halted. His mom was standing next to the paddock. Luis checked his watch against the electric alarm clock to confirm that the time was six fifteen. He watched in disbelief, because there she was, last-out-of-bed Mom, dressed in a light green top, her hair pulled into a jaunty pony tail. She leaned against the paddock's railings with her best booted foot propped on a cross beam. Mr. Coleman, in his lime green Prescott Acres shirt rode Bumble B into view from behind the barn. "Oooh, so that's the reason she's out of bed so early." Luis nodded and smiled as he watched the pantomime.

Coleman was seated tall and neat, on Bumble B. He looked like a movie star, and so did Bumble B. Luis's mom's whole face was smiling up at Bud Coleman. Even the special occasion's dimple in her cheek was back. The trainer, holding the reins next to his breastbone, was laughing and showing Bumble, dancing her in tight circles. Coleman pointed to both Patrizia's green shirt and his own with the Prescott Acres logo. She bounced her pony tail, waved and backed away, retreating to the kitchen. Luis never thought about his mom with a man before, but right down there, before his eyes, was the evidence. Mom liked Mr. Coleman.

Coleman reined his horse's head and trotted out, behind the barn to the track. Luis shook himself from his stupor. "Holy … What time does this guy get up? I guess this is what a Thoroughbred does, huh?" He pulled on his jeans, socks and work boots and jumped over his flopped open book bag and was gone from his room.

As Luis blew into the kitchen his mom held out a baseball magazine and a thick envelope. "Here's the set of cards you were waiting for. I signed for them on Saturday at the post office, then stuck them in my purse and forgot all about them. Sorry, Luis-o."

"I'm sorry too. I found this bill on my floor a second ago. Guess it fell out from between the pages of my last baseball magazine. Sorry, I made it even later."

The mother and son swapped mail. Patrizia looked at the radiology bill, groaned and stuck the envelope on the windowsill with other folded, dusty mail.

Luis grabbed his mother's offering and ripped through the envelope. "At last! It's Kranepool and Harrelson. That'll complete the 1970 Mets team. Great." His attention was on his cards for a second. He looked up with worry on his face. "Did Coleman say anything about me being late?"

"No, honey. You aren't late. He was up early, showing off his horse, and I was batting my eyes at him, doing mental math, spending the money we'll get for his famous horse living with us. Bumble B will be your tuition money for sure. Oh, and good old Mr. Prescott stuck a note in with his first half of the payment that said if Bumble B wins the race, he'll give me a tip of one thousand dollars. Terrific, huh?" She blew air from her puffed cheeks. "I hate to think so much about finances, but dammit, it's expensive to run a horse farm. The water walk will be all paid off by August.

21

They won't dig it out and take it away if I'm late with a payment. That leaves the bill coming due for the four-place race gate. We'll make it, but," she poked her thumb over her shoulder at the stack of unpaid hospital invoices, "can you hear them calling? Luis, promise me you'll stick to the college plan, no matter what. Get away from the farm. Be a lawyer like you always wanted. Make a living like Baxter and Penny's mom. Be something real, Luis. You know, a career, not a job. Get real pay, including insurance, a real vacation. Like normal people. I'm sure Baxter will get a good career."

"What's that supposed to mean?" Luis asked. "Baxter's not like me. He doesn't love horses. He doesn't even *like* them. Can't imagine why. Makes me wonder why we're friends. The guy's a geek. You know, calculus and chemistry. Weird."

Patrizia continued, "I'm glad you love horses, honey, but there's no money in horsing around." She threw her dish towel at Luis and changed the subject. "Randa said Penny and Baxter's mom got a new Cadillac SUV. Who ever heard of a Cadillac SUV?" She clinked the flatware into the drawer and smiled up at her son. "I guess Counselor Blackerby must be raking it in in her own practice."

Luis answered, "Yeah, divorce pays." With a lilt of wonder in his voice he said, "Baxter says the SUV is a righteous pristine white, an Escalade!"

"Escalade? Never heard of it, but, geeze. Must be nice. Where is Baxter going to college? Princeton? Brown?"

"Don't know yet. But, you're still convinced I'm going to go over the wall to join the circus, aren't ya, Mom?" No answer. "I'm saddling Paley's Comet. Maybe Coleman wants to run Bumble B this morning."

Luis expertly peeled a blue Easter egg, stuffed it into his mouth, and dashed from the kitchen. He hollered back through his half eaten egg, "Hey, Mom, let's get Gingerfoot into the water walk this afternoon, how 'bout it?"

As Luis exited, Miranda arrived in her electric pink sleep shirt. A growling lion was jumping through a red hoop with the circus's logo written across her chest in red bubble lettering. Miranda twisted her fingers through her sleep-pressed hair, and yawned. "Why are you up? And you're dressed. Did you forget we don't have school today? It's not even seven a.m. and here I am, standing upright in the kitchen on Monday of spring vacation, and worse, so are you." She leaned into the open refrigerator, and rooted around for some yet undiscovered magical breakfast choices. "Oh, great. I still have some chocolate bunnies and coconut eggs to eat, and marshmallow chicks too."

Patrizia watched her daughter until her patience was at an end. "Not the best breakfast choices for a committed runner. For heaven's sake, Randa, have an Easter egg, or maybe a biscuit. Choose something and close the refrigerator door. There's nothing new since last night when you and Luis poked around for sandwiches."

Miranda shot an early morning glare at her mother, then returned her attention to the contents of the refrigerator. She put a hand on her hip and dug in for a studied, contrary, good long look, lit by forty watts. The black and white cat do-si-doed between her legs as a reminder that he too would like some delicacy.

"Did you mention to Luis that that vet, Dr. Stanley Horse-something called about maybe buying Paley's Comet?" Miranda flaunted her inside information to her mother.

"The vet is Dr. Stan Horsham. And, no I didn't tell Luis, and don't you say anything either. I don't want him to worry about that horse. I still haven't heard back from the vet. But, I mean it Kiddo, don't you dare say anything to Luis."

"Wow, Dr. Horsham, the horse vet. An easy name to remember. Anyway, are we talking big money, huh? Besides, quit calling me 'Kiddo.' I'm almost seventeen."

Patrizia ignored the reminder of Miranda's birthday, half a year away. She chastised, "Miranda, I'm not kidding. You be quiet about Paley's Comet."

"Okay, okay." She carried butter and strawberry jam from the refrigerator and kneed the refrigerator door shut. She swore when the cold butter crumpled the biscuit in her hand.

"And on to a different subject, dear daughter, did you get the extra set of mandolin strings for Wednesday night's practice, or do I have to mail order a new set?"

"Got them. I'm ready." Miranda surprised her mom by charging, "So what's with you and the hunk on the super horse?"

Patrizia self-consciously brushed the few strands of hair across her forehead. She leaned into the small mirror and touched her scalp. "Hummm, need to touch up those roots already. I got everybody's attention this morning, didn't I?" She shrugged. "I thought it would be good business to schmooze with the new tenant, that's all." She blinked, unconvinced by her own argument.

"Yeah, right, with your pale green pullover and ponytail. Cute, Mom, real cute. You and the trainer, both in matching green shirts. You two looked like backup singers to the main act. Anyway, how *could* you? He looks way too young for you, and besides, Dad's been dead only a year."

"Two years, one month and thirteen days, Miranda." Patrizia looked to her watch and finished, "Do you need to know how many hours and minutes?" Her voice cracked. "Not that it's your business, young lady, but I'm old enough to flirt, *if* and when I choose. And about the trainer, I didn't ask, but I doubt he's younger than I am. I was thinking of the business." Patrizia turned to the kitchen windowsill, busying her fingers with the curtain's ruffle, and hiding the hot tears that flooded to her low lashes.

Miranda, prickling from her dressing down, pushed her empty chair to the table and backed from the kitchen. "Uhhh, well, okay Mom. I'm gonna get dressed and go for my run now."

Patrizia wiped her eyes, rinsed her breakfast cup, and hung the handle on the mug tree. The phone rang. Patrizia changed her tone from her recent annoyance with her daughter to a more tuneful, "Hiya Betina. You're up early. Okay, let me write that down. Country Steppin Tavern, this Friday night. No, Miranda can't join us, even as a musician until she's eighteen." The proud mother covered the receiver and leaned back to check the stairs to see if her daughter could overhear. "Yeah, she *is* good, and she talks about joining us. Someday. Okay, see ya at seven, Friday night."

Patrizia walked to her office replaying the phone call. "How lucky that my beautiful, headstrong, opinionated daughter is agreeable to playing in a band with her old mom. Miranda'll give new meaning to Betina's Country Cuties." She smiled and passed her music stand, which until the last year held classical orchestral parts for first violin. Patrizia was becoming one of a few local, famed fiddlers. Country fiddling was fun, and an easy transition for a past music major. She touched her violin lying in its purple velvet lined case. A small square of yellow chamois, glued to a block of golden transparent rosin nestled next to the flat waxed paper bag of new violin strings. She lifted the bow hanging from a metal arm of the music stand, adjusted the string's pegs, then skated the rosin across the bow. She pinched her violin between her left shoulder and chin and played a series of complicated scales. "This is good for my heart. Luis has his horses, I have my violin, and Miranda has her attitude. Three for three."

Within the hour, Miranda trundled down the stairs and, not seeing her mom, called to the air, "Mom, I'm going to run now. Be back soon." Not waiting for a reply, she ran out, off the porch and onto the dusty lane. She paced toward the main road as always, picking up her speed in exchange for not increasing the distance. The heat, unusual for April, was too hot to do a long run on the baking, semi-shaded roadside. "Maybe I should start running on the horse track when the horses aren't using it. Nope. No shade. Boring."

Miranda jogged her usual trek to the mailbox at the end of Smitt's Lane. On the turn to start for home, she pivoted toward the car horn tap-tapping a familiar "Shave and a Haircut" rhythm. Baxter was driving toward her on the main road. She continued to jog in place and waved to the boyfriend. He poked his head out the smoothly lowering window and made a pitiful rendition of a wolf whistle. Miranda bent forward with her hands on her knees, caught her breath and laughed. "Wow, Baxter, this is your new car? Solid, baby." She reached into his window and ruffled his white blond hair. "This is one big ass vehicle."

"Come on, get in."

"Aw no, Baxt. I'm all sweaty. Your mom would skin both of us for me being dirty and sitting in her new car."

"Hold it. I have a plastic bag in the back filled with all the stuff I took out of our old SUV. Look, here's the raincoat we keep under the seat. Come on." Baxter pulled into Smitt's Lane and spread the raincoat on the seat. "How about a quick ride in my new chariot, m' lady? A little buzz around town, perhaps?"

Miranda couldn't say no. While stepping up into the front seat, her shin scraped on a roadside stick jutting into the open door. "Yeeouch!" She pulled her leg backwards and stepped into a thorny bush. "Owwww! This is a booby trap. My leg!" She pulled herself up and jumped into the relative safety of the sparkling, all white Escalade to have a better look at her injuries.

"What happened?" Baxter asked with sincere interest in his girlfriend's injury. He quickly turned his attention to the blood on her leg. "Oooh, wait. Be careful. Don't drip blood onto the carpet."

Miranda rolled her dark brown eyes. "You know, Baxter, let me out. I can walk home. We'll do the drive another time."

He grabbed for her arm. "No, no, I couldn't let you walk home all bloody. You know, your temper is almost as bad as your brother's. Stay there." His face pinked up to his blond roots with his bossing. He swung his arm to the bulky, large bag in the seat behind him. "Hold it. I have to go through that bag. I saw those tissues last night." He hopped from the driver's seat to open the door behind him. "Still bleeding? You holding up over there, Randa?"

"Still bleeding. At least the gnats and the no-see-ums haven't discovered me yet. Never mind, Baxt. I'll walk home. Keep your mom's new car clean."

"Wait. Miranda, here they are, Mom's emergency zip bag with antibiotic ointment and bandages." He hustled to her open door. "Let me see that leg. Oh, you've got scratches on both legs."

Baxter saw he had permission along with the obligation to touch and soothe her legs. He held her bare, muscular, and now dirt-and-blood-speckled leg. She watched his head bent to the task of dabbing and cleaning, and watched his eyes taking in every freckle and each scratched insult to her legs as he wiped, compressed, and followed with a thin distribution of ointment. At intervals he petted her and said, "Awww, there that's better," or other comforting words with cooing, and ended by kissing her knees.

She teased, "I bet you planted that sticker bush right there so you'd have an excuse to pet my legs. Cagey, Baxt."

"Yeah, but the plan started way back before the sticker bush, with coaxing my mom to buy a white car with white upholstery."

"Thanks Baxt, for the drive-to-town offer, but Mom's expecting me back to do some stuff around the old plantation, but I'd appreciate a ride home. You can show Luis your new car. That'll be fun, huh?"

Baxter agreed and drove his lady to the Smitts' porch. Big Russ, Jose, and Kirk appeared from various corners of the farm to admire the new SUV, as they had admired Bumble B the day before. They arrived like hungry bees training in on bright blossoms. Luis appeared fenderside and reached to touch Baxter's shoulder. "Wow, Baxt. This is quite the trophy! I never heard of an Escalade before."

Baxter stood taller, placed the flat of his hand on the hood, ready to give the sales pitch. "This SUV won't be on Florida lots 'til July at the earliest, but Mom knows people. If you think I look proud, you should see her." He smiled and stroked the SUV in one long perambulation.

"Baxt, if you weren't already on your way to law school, I'd say you had a career in car sales."

The somewhat envious Luis Smitt inspected the Escalade, then after a polite amount of time spent with Baxter, he headed back to his chores and turned to check Paley's Comet, his personal Escalade.

Despite that Miranda had relinquished her position next to Baxter's elbow, showing the new car gave him an enjoyable fifteen minutes of fame. He drove home, a proud young man, almost a college student.

Chapter 3

MIRANDA'S DRIVE

Back at home, Miranda ministered to her scratched and scabbed legs and slinked into skinny brown jeans and boots, and reported back to her mom. Patrizia had not yet cooled after her daughter's earlier inappropriate remarks. "Miranda, I need you to get about twenty bales of hay before lunch. They still owe me a balance of last month's paid ton. If Johnson's Feed and Seed doesn't have enough, maybe you can go to Gigante's to see if they have a few extra bales we can buy. I spoke to Hank last season. He offered me bales if I got low. Take the truck with our decal, in case Hank's not there and you have to beg from another employee. Okay? Miranda, I'm talking to you, okay?"

"Yeah, great. Maybe I'll pick up Penny for company and her help loading the bales."

"I'm serious, Miranda. When I said no boyfriend, no passengers, and no radio for the first two months after the new license, I meant, *No*body. The guy at Feed and Seed will load the truck bed. It's his job, for heaven's sake."

Miranda chewed a yellow sugary marshmallow chick without acknowledging her mom's admonition. She turned her shoulder and approximated a 'get real' stare, then sat to page through her newest copy of *Cosmopolitan* magazine. Her foot bobbed and petted Tuxedo under the table.

Patrizia rolled her eyes, a communication staple popularized by her daughter, then returned to her office.

Miranda touched up her glossy lipstick in front of the small decorative mirror by the kitchen door. She pushed at her straight black hair, unbraided and loose in celebration of school vacation, hooked her purse from the hat rack, slammed the screen door and sauntered to her mom's truck. She twirled the keys on her finger, manufacturing a casualness not yet earned.

Miranda opened the truck door, climbed up and onto the worn-out bench seat, shoveled her backside into a comfortable position, then adjusted the seat to be closer to the pedals. She looked out to all directions, then, in secret, she switched on the radio. "Un-Break My Heart," one of her mom's old favorites finished and went to an advertisement. She abandoned the hokey oldies station in search of her favorite rock music, which provided mind-blowing dissonances at eleven in the morning. Miranda reflexively turned the volume to a crackling whisper. She took a square of bubble gum from her purse and worked the pink powdery surface to a slippery, sweet mouthful of joy. Emergency brake released and she was on her way to the feed store. She stretched to the rear view mirror and smiled at the comely teen behind the wheel.

Miranda drove to the end of the lane, rolled down the windows feeling competent and happy with her driving responsibility, like a real adult. She worked her tongue around the artificially enhanced, strawberry flavored bubble gum while bobbing her head to the music, designed to singe. Down the lane and away from her mom's supervision she twisted up the radio's volume. She waited for a short parade of local traffic to buzz past, then accelerated onto the road as a big pink bubble popped, grabbing onto a few loose hairs and stretched across her nose, catching her eyelashes in the rubbery mask.

Without slowing the truck she yipped and swerved to the right. She cried, "Oh no!" from under the burst bubble. Whining and pinching at sticky strands, she blinked and twitched her face to loosen the gum. Her hands pulled from the steering wheel to correct the gum-stuck hair. She reprised her cry as the raised scrubby berm raced to meet the front fender of the Smitt's Water Walk Farm truck. She jammed the brakes.

The truck skidded to an abrupt stop on dry weedy ground and rocked front and back. Her forehead and nose met the steering wheel. "Oh crap, what a day!" She sat up straight and watched a long string of gum stretch from her nose to the round, flat horn pad. Her blaring, forbidden music was magnified now that the noise of the Smitt's truck's engine and the turbulence of the wind through the open windows were quieted. She moved her foot from the brake to straighten the truck, and twisted off the ignition. "Shit, I hope Mom doesn't drive by and catch me."

She took a few deep breaths, repositioned the mirror and gasped at her reflection. She had a slight rosy bump above her left eyebrow, swollen but not black and blue. "First the sticker bushes, now this." She tweaked at the bubble gum beads and strings of pink gum, and peeled a wide piece, like scalded skin, from her face. "Damn. That hurts.

Ouch, ouch!" Her face pulled to an astringent twist. Tears gathered. "I'm such a failure."

Two trailer trucks blew by her left side. One pumped his air horn, causing her to jump in her seat. She clapped her hand to her pounding heart, then burped. "Uhhh, I hope I don't throw up. That was close."

She rolled the bubble gum into a ball, and poking her hand through the driver's side open window, left-handedly threw the wad overhead, aiming for the passenger side weedy field. She clicked on the turn signal and rested a moment listening to the turn signal's satisfying regular ticking sound. She assumed a parochial school, erect sitting posture, made a silent prayer and pulled onto the road. "What's that scraping sound? Oh God, I'll die if I injured the truck. I can't take it." She pulled back to the apron, hearing and not able to discern the reason for the unwelcome sound. She swore, put on her emergency blinkers, and hopped out to inspect the under carriage of the truck. She gasped, "Hallelujah!" at discovering a beat up, empty plastic gallon milk bottle wedged under the front bumper. She kicked the culprit free. With a few tears threatening to spill over she whispered, "Driving. What a bother!" Tears dried as she concentrated on getting back into the mainstream of the highway. She took a deep breath and looking to the thin, high strips of clouds, said, "Thank you, God, for not much traffic and for not letting Mom's truck get hurt. I promise to do better." She switched the radio station back to her mom's musical choice and turned the radio off. "That was close." Repentant, she was off to Johnson's Feed and Seed. She braided her thick ponytail to hide the remnants of bubble gum in her hair while the men loaded the hay.

Patrizia walked from the barn after taping a small piece of cotton to the ringer of the barn's phone, at Luis's suggestion. She indicated with her scissors, "That should muffle the noisy ring." Luis grunted agreement as he struggled to hoist a fifty-pound bag of feed into the barrel on wheels. Moments later Patrizia sat at the picnic table on the porch and sipped at her coffee awaiting Miranda's return. The careful mother was on hand to snoop-ervise to see if her daughter, who sometimes did not follow instructions to the letter, had picked up Penny despite the strict injunction.

Returned from a successful trip to Johnson's Feed and Seed, Miranda bumped into the yard. Her speed created a danger to any furry or feathered beast who happened to be walking or pecking the ground between the house and barn. She circled the yard, corrected for speed when she spied her mother on the porch, and looking over each shoulder, backed to the barn's open double doors.

Patrizia retreated to the house, wincing at Miranda's unfinessed, novice's stop. The truck bed was filled with hay bales, radio was off, and no passengers hopped from the cab. She didn't read any significance in that Miranda's hair was now braided, but noticed and wondered at the large wad of pink bubble gum stuck to the truck's roof above the passenger door.

Miranda watched Bud Coleman walking across the barnyard, swinging a water bucket in time with his swagger. The heretofore official eighteen-year-old boyfriend, Baxter, big brother to Penny, her best friend, was fading into a pale, fuzzy memory. She stuck out her chest, made more attractive by the silver piping dipping up and down across her bodice, and flashed a quick look into her rear view mirror. She licked her lips and patted her tight jeans and jumped from the truck. Bud descended on her. "Can I help you with those bales, Little Lady?"

Miranda recognized the offer as flirting, but was unprepared with a clever rejoinder. She was surprised that he seemed to be interested in "little old me." Maybe he flirted with all the girls, like the guys in school. Miranda smiled at Bud and shrugged her shoulders in a little involuntary flirt. She batted her eyes and was unable to control her flushing neck and cheeks. She choked out, "No need to help. That's okay. Big Russ and Jose are here to unload the truck and do work around here. Mom actually pays them to work. They saw me drive in and they'll be here in, like a minute." She dismissed the idea of the unloading work with a flip of her hand. She tilted her head in a way she had practiced in front of the mirror. The high school senior boys were charmed by the head tilt. Her ready, wide smile was well practiced and gleaming, now that her braces no longer fenced in her teeth.

Bud leaned in to her. "So, Randa, I hear that a circus horse act is your neighbor. Your mom said you go there for feed or straw sometimes? Wondered if you'd take me along sometime." He smiled at her as if he contemplated eating her for lunch, finishing off by licking his thumb and each finger.

Miranda blushed and looked down to her boots. She took a breath and looked up to Bud Coleman's handsome face. "We got straw yesterday and hay today. But I guess we could go for some other reason. They call us every now and then for an emergency. Like, last year one of their non-show horses had a foal right after a hurricane. Their foaling barn had suffered some storm damage, so they brought their mare and foal here. And that's how Mom is in with one of the big guys over there. We help each other out." Miranda wanted to brag about her mom's association with circus people, but at the same time didn't want Bud to be interested in her mom.

"I'd love to go over with you for any excuse you can come up with. Maybe I'll ask your mom."

"Oh no. You don't have to ask her. I'll take you. We can say you want to look at their colt. If Hank Gigante is on duty today, he'll show you around. I'll try to take you as soon as the men get the bales out of the truck bed."

Bud slipped his hand down her bumpy brown braid and said, "That would be fine, Randa."

Miranda's hair stood up on her arms at his closeness and that he called her by the family's nickname for her. In a nervous, unanticipated gesture, she applied a slip of lip gloss to her lips, pulled in a flash from her back jeans pocket, and smiled up at him.

Not one to miss the electric signals shooting between Mr. Coleman and her daughter, Patrizia called from the porch, "Miranda, honey, I need you in the house right now." She knew without looking that Miranda would be screwing up her mouth at the instruction. Perhaps her daughter's rebellious behavior would be evidence to the trainer that Miranda was still a kid.

Patrizia went into the laundry room for guaranteed privacy. Miranda tromped into the kitchen and called to the empty room, "Mom? What couldn't wait?"

"I'm in the laundry room. Come on in and close the door, please." Patrizia held a large blue bottle of fabric softener and silently, repeatedly pounded the plastic bottle into her palm, practicing the proper words.

Her rude daughter entered the small room and looked up from the floor to meet her mother's accusation. "So, what's all the cloak and dagger?"

"Number one; you know the circus people don't want strangers poking around over there. And number two, Randa, he's too forward with you. You're *waaay* too young for him, yet he keeps after you. He should know better. In particular, because I'm standing right where I can see and hear him." Patrizia handed towels to her daughter, and indicated with a nod of her head for the teen to start folding. She matched up socks as she spoke. "I know you'll think I don't understand, and I'm interfering, but you need to avoid that man. He's trouble."

Miranda's mouth formed a teasing *O*. "What's this? A talk about the birds and the bees?" She laughed. "Mom, you're jealous."

"Trust me, honey, I'm not jealous. But, he's too familiar, too forward with you. He's already calling you by our family nickname for you and that's bold, and I don't like it." Patriza added, "And what's with the pink bump on your head?"

Miranda had removed her visored cap. She ducked her head and spun to leave the laundry room. "Oh, nothing. Is that it? I'm going upstairs."

"Then take this load of folded clothes and towels with you."

The teen sucked her teeth in annoyance. With her arms stretched around a load of fragrant, fluffed towels she demonstrated her protest in loud stomps on the staircase. Patrizia took a deep breath and walked to the kitchen, watching Miranda leave. She sighed, "That went well."

Luis poked his head into the kitchen. "Mom? Can you help me take Gingerfoot to the water walk for the first time? I think today we'll walk her in and let her stand in the water for a few minutes. How 'bout it? She's so docile. I'm sure she'll be easy. I looked for Randa to help but couldn't find her. If you can't help now I'll get Kirk or Jose to help."

"Sit and eat. I'll help after lunch." Patrizia handed Luis a fat slab of Easter's ham and cheese on rye. Lunch was on and Tuxedo was back campaigning for a snack and got one. Patrizia joined with her own smaller sandwich and poured iced tea. They put to death the crumbs of a bag of chips as they chatted about Bumble B's first day, and confirmed that only Bud would manage Bumble's time in the water walk. They agreed to add Ginger to the already busy Dailys schedule. After ten minutes of preamble, Patrizia warmed up to the subject of Bud Coleman.

"Honey, I know you respect Mr. Coleman. He's a fabulous horseman, but I don't trust him."

Luis gulped, then mumbled through the ham, "That's a big change of heart since I talked to you at breakfast. What's up?"

"Yeah, well that was before I saw him descend on Miranda. Hell, he even called her 'Randa' as if he's one of us. I resent that, and he needs watching. I don't know how good you are about *not* losing Coleman's business, but he needs to be kept away from Miranda. Can you do that?"

"Should be easy enough." Luis wiped chip crumbs from his mouth. "Get Baxter over here, or send her over to Penny and Baxter's. Play up Baxt's maturity, his after school job, his new white Cadillac. Use the money angle."

Patrizia answered, "I never thought that Baxter would appeal to me as a solution to saving Miranda from her own hormones. Good thinking, Luis. That's why you get paid the big bucks around here." She snapped closed the dishwasher door and added, "Any update on you and the blond?"

Luis said, "I left a message for her to call back. This would be easier if we weren't on spring break from classes."

Patrizia tugged her shirt at the waist, "Okay, then. Good luck my son." She sighed. "Let's go introduce Gingerfoot to the famous Smitt's Farm Water Walk."

Chapter 4

THE WATER WALK

Luis dashed ahead of his mom to get Gingerfoot from her stall. He coaxed the affable young palomino to amble across the smooth concrete floor of the water walk area and tied her to the railing next to the bath. Patrizia joined and sang Gingerfoot's name repeatedly in a made-up tune. She stood next to the down ramp and gave the horse enough slack on the lead to walk down into the warm, still, water. Luis pulled a wide lamb's wool strap across the breadth of the water walk at Gingerfoot's chest level to prevent her from walking up the ramp and out of the water. Patrizia held onto the horse's lead where she sat on an old milking stool next to Ginger's head. "Luis, let's see how she tolerates the jets. She's so patient."

He turned on the jets. "Hey, look at the water. What are those dark flecks floating around? Wonder what that's all about. I changed the water yesterday for Bumble. No other horse was here so far, other than Bumble B early this morning. Maybe she dropped a soft stool in there. Shit! Sorry, but you know what I mean."

Luis noticed Mr. Heath's trailer carrying his stallion, Green Dragon, rumbling into the barn yard. "Better get Ginger out. Mr. Heath's here already."

Patrizia unclipped the lambswool strap and walked the cooperative filly from the water, up the ramp, to ground level. On terra firma once more, Ginger nickered and danced her feet in pretty little steps.

Luis said, "Why don't you hose her and squeegee her right here. I want her to watch Green Dragon's exercise." Luis ran back to Mr. Heath and took Dragon's lead.

Patrizia started to squeegee Ginger's coat. She called, "Hey, Luis, what's this? There's a dirty stripe around her body at the water line. Look, the dark specks are smeary."

Luis turned the lead back to Mr. Heath and hustled to Ginger's side. He ran his hands across the horse's back and was rewarded seeing his own, black, greasy fingers. He pressed on the dark fleck on the coat noting the pasty film between his fingers.

Patrizia ran her hands down the horse's belly leaving ten dark tracks. "I'll have to shampoo her. Luis, tell Mr. Heath that Green Dragon will have to wait half an hour while I change out the water."

Luiz wiped his hands across his pant legs. "Maybe some oil leaked through the jets. Never happened before. But I'll get the tub cleaned. If it happens again we'll have to cancel the Dailys until I can figure out what's up."

Luis's eyebrows pulled together. "I wonder if Bud knows anything about this." His volume and pitch were both elevating. "Dammit!" Luis kicked an empty shampoo bottle scudding across the concrete and landing in the bath. Good news was the bottle bobbed to the surface for easy retrieval. In too loud a voice he said, "This is what our business needs right now." His face pinked and he punched the air. "We have a Thoroughbred come all the way from Maryland specifically to use our water walk, and the stupid thing is broken or threatening to break down. I'm so mad I could orbit!"

Patrizia, pouring bottled shampoo on the horse, and lathering Ginger's back, turned to Luis and said between her teeth, "Retrieve that bottle from the water and bring that temper down a couple of notches, Mr. Smitt. Mr. Heath can see and hear your temper tantrum. Not cool."

Luis's radiating attitude was tempered but not cured. He drained the water walk, annoyed to note the dark flecks adhering to the stainless steel sides of the ditch, like a soap scum line around a tub. He grabbed a towel and rubbed away the streaks he'd created by pressing on the pasty flecks. He muttered at the extra work while Mr. Katz's horse and trailer pulled up, the appointment following Green Dragon.

Luis hustled from the ditch and watched the clean tepid water cover the treadmill's floor. Green Dragon was walked into his tropical aqua work out. The horse nickered neighborly to Gingerfoot, who was now sparkling clean and stayed to supervise Green Dragon's work out.

Green Dragon's chestnut colored head moved up and down with his smooth and steady pace on the treadmill. Ginger's bobbing head matched Green Dragon's head bouncing as she vocalized in her throat. Luis had to laugh. "Look at that Ginger. She almost speaks English." Luis drew in a few deep breaths, patching up an apology to his mother. He angled his shoulder away to avoid eye-to-eye contrition and changed the subject. "Sounds like Gingerfoot's purring. I think she liked it."

Patrizia nodded, recognizing the end of Luis's display of temper. She held Green Dragon's lead and supervised his exercise from the watcher's stool.

Luis changed gears when he saw the lateness of the hour. "Damn, we're running late. Where's Miranda when we need her? Ginger has to go back to her stall."

Patrizia answered, "I have Miranda on assignment. You finish up with Green Dragon. I'll take Ginger." Mother and son changed positions. She clicked her tongue. "Come on Ginger, we'll do this again tomorrow." Patriza led the palomino home, patted her white nose, and closed the stall's Dutch door behind the horse's hind end. Ginger turned to poke her head over the half door, raised her head and whinnied to Donkey Boy, in the next stall. Paley's Comet answered the young horse's bragging report.

Luis rinsed and squeegeed Green Dragon, finding no further evidence of black flecks in the water or on the horse. He returned the cleaned and exercised horse to Mr. Heath, who left with the parting words he'd return tomorrow.

Mr. Katz delivered his horse to the water exercise area, tied him up to the bar on the wall and waited for Luis. Mrs. Palmer pulled her horse trailer with Cody in tow, right behind Green Dragon's trailer. Patrizia walked down to greet her and to socialize, killing a little time while Luis did the Water Walk hustle.

Patrizia got the Best Mother Award that evening by announcing, "I'll do dishes. Number one daughter, I want to hear mandolin from your room. Although I give you credit for originality, I didn't fall for that trick of you playing a recording of you practicing last week. Good try." The kids shot looks at each other and laughed. "Number one son, I guess this is your chance for baseball cards. No need to put the Do Not Disturb sign on your door. I know you're busy.

"Hey, do either of you have any chocolates squirreled away? I thought I bought enough chocolates for Easter, but looks like I didn't and I'm beginning to decompensate." No answer. Miranda raised her eyebrows as she scooped a few marshmallow chicks from the Easter basket center-piece on her exit from the kitchen. Patrizia rinsed dishes and filled the dishwasher, flipped on the power, and turned off the kitchen lights. She sang an "aha," and pivoted right back into the kitchen, remembering where she'd stashed a bag of chocolate-covered raisins that never made it to the Easter baskets. "How fortuitous." She tossed back a healthy mouthful of chocolates, still chewing and smiling. She went to her office, applied rosin to her bow and worked on *1950s Country Favorites, Book II.*

Luis retreated to his desk to sort out the new baseball cards his mom delivered into his hands earlier that morning. He slumped over the cards on his desk. Shoulders up, head down. From the back, he looked as if he'd been beheaded. He pulled a tablet from his desk and started cataloging. He clicked on his rock station, drowning out both his sister's and mother's music, tapping his foot along with the righteous sizzling hot guitars and drums.

A memory of Luis's was watching his dad, bent over a clear plastic sleeve of baseball cards. "Luis if you like statistics, you'll never be out of opportunities to compile numbers on baseball. If you have an interest in the sport, the wonders are ongoing. If you have an interest in big business, or hilarious nicknames or like to match up with some other guy who has a fabulous memory for detail, like who was on third when so-and-so hit an in-the-park homer, then this game is for you. When I needed extra money to buy Paley's Comet, I sold some cards. It wasn't a million dollars but it was enough to buy Paley instead of the old nag they were showing." Luis laughed at the memory. His thoughts were louder than the music. I wondered if Dad would have liked the Tampa Bay Devils if he'd been alive to root for them. They were only an hour away, up in St. Petersburg. "Nah, he was the Mets and National League all the way." He pushed back on his chair and looked to the ceiling. "Dad, I sure miss you. We all do."

Chapter 5

BUMBLE'S RACE

Early on Tuesday morning, Luis chatted up Paley's Comet as he pulled her brown forelock through the front of her bridle. "Come on girl, we're gonna race today. Mom brought in some serious competition for you this week." He whispered, "I'm warning you though, she's a looker. But don't you worry, Comet, you're my main girl."

Paley's Comet pawed. "Settle down. Jealous, huh?" Luis laughed, patted her neck and swung to the saddle. "I loved you first. Come on. Let's see if this Bumble is more than just a pretty face."

They picked up the pace and found Bud, mounted on Bumble B, looking for irregularities on the track's surface, proof of where an armadillo burrowed up last night. When Bud saw Luis, he reined Bumble B around to face the oncoming rider. Luis called, "Hey, good morning, Mr. Coleman." Bumble's ears went back and her head dropped. She backed up and reared at Paley's Comet's entrance. Coleman muttered a reproach and brought Bumble B around with a stern rein.

Luis closed the distance to make the introductions. "My girl's name is Paley's Comet. Born in Kentucky. The ribbons in the tack room are hers, hers and Miranda's. Good looking *and* she's got some serious speed, which is why we're here. Guessed you'd want to work Bumble this morning. Did you finish walking the track?"

"Yeah, track looks clean."

Luis handed Mr. Coleman a helmet and a pair of goggles and pointed up to his own goggles attached to his helmet. He said over his shoulder as he paced Paley's Comet past Coleman, "Okay, give us a few minutes to warm up. Big Russ and Kirk are still getting the gate rolled onto the track." He pointed over his shoulder to the two pushing the gate into position at the straightaway.

As Luis put Comet through a short range of paces, he wondered if he'd smelled drink on Mr. Coleman. He knew he would not be able to tell if one's tainted breath was from consuming a fifth of hard liquor last night, or from a single shot for breakfast. He put the thought behind him and moved his horse down the track. Luis spoke to his horse, "Let's see how fast that newcomer is." Within ten minutes he turned back, clicked his tongue and paced to even up with Coleman and Bumble B.

Miranda showed up at the fence, brazenly wearing a lime green tee shirt, a short sleeved version of the shirt her mom wore yesterday. She tossed her pony tail which she'd tied off with a rope of matching lime yarn. If the excuse of buttering up the trainer worked for her mother, it was good enough for Miranda. She waved to Coleman and Luis, flashing the stopwatch in her hand. Big Russ stood by to pull the lever on the bell which would sound and spring open the starting gate. She sashayed to the starting position next to the fence.

The riders pulled their goggles to their eyes. Paley's Comet walked to the gate and settled inside while Bumble, the younger, reluctant, less practiced filly circled twice, ears down, swishing her tail, then backed away from the gate. Kirk ran over to grab Bumble's saliva slicked bridle and backing up, pulled her into the gate. He pedaled backwards and ducked out of the front, not wanting to engage with the horse's feet. Jose stood to the side and slapped the hind gate closed. All jumped from the scene. Paley's Comet stood still, in an obedient stance. Bumble B complained about the proximity of the other horse, but at last came to a temporary rest, caged and within ten feet of her competition.

Miranda hollered, "Okay, gentlemen, on THREE." The riders nodded. She counted, and shot her index finger at Big Russ on three. He pulled the lever. The bell jangled. The gates flashed open.

Both horses hung in animated stillness until the sound of the bell spurred their neurons into the race. Paley's Comet, no newcomer to racing, took off on her familiar track leaving a trail of dirt and dust. She stretched her legs in a wide smooth stride. Sun glinted off the eight hooves beating the track.

The farm workers quickly rolled the race gate off the racetrack to the side track.

Bumble B's speed did not come from Bud calling magical incantations into the horse's ear, but rather came when the Maryland horse saw Paley's Comet's rump in front of her. She put her heart and will and feet into action. Within seconds Bumble equaled Paley's Comet's lead and thundered next to her, matching stride for stride. Luis leaned forward, the seat of his jeans out of the saddle. He called encouragement to Paley's Comet. Despite Bud being taller and heavier, his horse pulled ahead at the turn in the track and stayed ahead by a full length for the remainder of the mile.

Luis's dirt spattered goggles were a testimony to his coming in second. He leaned in to his horse's neck and said, "Sorry Paley. That was beginner's luck." He rubbed Paley's neck. "She's a genuine racehorse who gets paid to win races, and she's quite a bit younger than you. But, I still can't believe she beat you. You're still my wonderful, best horse."

Standing high in his saddle, Bud Coleman slowed his horse after passing Miranda who was hopping in circles and yelling, "I could see the nails in her shoes! She flew."

Bud jumped from his saddle and slapped his horse's shoulder. "Nice ride." He leaned into Bumble B and spoke words through his teeth, unheard by the others.

Miranda dashed to Coleman, jumped up and threw herself into his arms with a high loud, "Yippee." He was the willing recipient of her electric charged congratulations, but replaced Miranda's feet to the ground, peeling her arms from his neck.

Luis ignored his sister's evident exuberance and leaned down to Coleman from Paley's saddle. "Hey, Mr. Coleman, Paley usually closes that piece of territory in two minutes, sixteen seconds. But you passed us! I couldn't believe my eyes. And I doubt if Paley's Comet believed her eyes either. I don't know if she ever saw the hind end of another horse."

He circled his horse. "What kind of numbers did you get, Randa?"

"I got two minutes, nine seconds. That's great, isn't it? Isn't anything under two and fifteen great, Luis?" Miranda was still air borne. "Boy, Mom's going to collapse when she hears about Bumble's time."

"Yeah, I'll say it's a great time. Coleman, you're going to win on Saturday." Luis leaned over and knocked his knuckles on Coleman's helmet. "I'll have the men lineup the starting gate on the side track so you can get in a little more gate training for the next few days."

Bud apologized, "She's had gate training. I guess she's particular about the new gate and the girl in the next slot." He wiped away a short gallows laugh.

Luis said, "In the meantime, shall I take her back to the stall to cool her down?"

Coleman said, "Yeah, rinse her then take her to her stall. I'll be right back to talk her up, and rub her down a bit. She's a woman, Luis. Gives her a chance to complain if something's on her mind. She can go to the pasture later."

Bud hustled off, recalling the scene of a training race, two weeks ago up north at Prescott Acres track.

Typesetter, a chestnut filly, Mr. Prescott's blue ribbon Thoroughbred-to-beat, with his young rider, trotted from the barn, appearing eager to show the two-year-old twins how a race was run. Typesetter was the horse by which all other racers were compared and measured.

Bud rode Bumble B., Ticky Bartholomew, the resident jockey was riding Prescott's Pride. A stable boy was perched high on Typesetter's back.

As the three horses paraded toward the racing gate, Ticky's filly circled and protested with complaining vocalizations. The rotund stableman, muttering at the inconvenience and danger, grabbed the horse's bridle and yelled, "Come on, Prescott's Pride. Come on! This damned skittish horse needs to learn how to get the hell into the gate." He tugged her willful head, and yanked her into her slot. He jumped backwards and clapped shut the hind gate, with the reward of her protesting swishing tail in his face. "One more bit of her showing off, and I would have backed that fool of a horse into the gate from the front." Prescott's Pride's dissatisfaction of her temporary confinement paid off in her explosion from the chute.

Within seconds, Mr. Prescott's three fastest horses thundered around the home, mile track observed by two stablemen, each holding a stop watch.

The farm's farrier and his trainee, distracted from setting up work on the packed dirt driveway to the barn, dropped their gloves and implements and hustled to the rail. Another stableman, still holding wire cutters, dropped a bale by his side and joined the spectators.

As Prescott's Pride shot past the finish line, Bumble B was less than a length behind, with Typesetter finishing a scant half-length behind the second place runner. Both of the timers came off their feet as if thrown from the ground by an earthquake. "Wahoos" filled the air. The men swung their stopwatches over their heads and slapped each other's backs in congratulation. Coleman yanked his goggles and helmet from his head and hollered to the timers standing by the rail, "Whatta race! What kind of time did you get?"

The older man continued to swing his stopwatch above his head, "Whooey, did you see that?"

"Let's see that time." Coleman dismounted his second place runner and strode up to the timer and grabbed the timepiece. "Do you think this thing could be wrong? Maybe this old watch is wrong." He shook the watch. "Can't be." The second timer held out his stopwatch to confirm that Bud was seeing the true time. Bud strafed his hand through his hair. "Did Mr. Prescott see us run this morning? Holy God, that's two minutes, three seconds!"

Ticky Bartholomew was still glowing from his first-place finish in the race. He called down to Coleman, now fanning his face with his cap, "Hey, Bud, did you enjoy that ride? Prescott's Pride showed me the smoothest gait, not like any other horse I've ever ridden before. Little Miss Bumble B is fast too, as she proved, but nothing like the syrup-smooth, sweet speed you get from that Prescott's Pride. What a dream horse!"

"I wouldn't give you a nickel for her," Coleman muttered and passed off Bumble B to a groom and walked away.

Today, in Florida's heat, Bud handed off his reins to Luis. He speed-walked to the bunkhouse with the promise to return to rub down and talk to Bumble B. Perhaps he was retreating to make calls, or to wet his whistle.

Luis dismounted. He rubbed Paley's Comet between her ears, then lifted her face and kissed her a little north of her wet velvety muzzle. "Don't mind that out-of-towner. You're my main girl."

Luis signaled for Miranda to take Paley's reins. The teens walked their sleek Thoroughbreds toward the stable. Miranda was still elated. "Luis, isn't this exciting? Do you think Bud will race Bumble B again tomorrow?"

"Let's see, the race is Saturday and today's Tuesday, so I guess he'll work her but not race again. She's still young, and he doesn't want to cause concussive foot injuries from pounding around the track, and he doesn't want to wear her out." Luis turned to Paley's Comet and said, "You did a fine job, Paley, my girl. I guess you surprised Bumble B. She didn't know she had a rocket to pass."

"Bumble's a beauty." Miranda put in her vote. "She's like the Yves Saint Laurent supermodel of horses. She rises above the dirt, somehow, always managing to have sparkling clean leg wraps."

Luis said, "Bud changes those wraps every morning before I get down to the barn. He's an early riser. He must have a top secret magic wrapping technique because he sure doesn't trust me to touch her special green-topped wraps."

"Hey Louie, did you know that Mom called a newspaper reporter to write up a story and to take some pictures here at the farm?"

"I hope not for today. Race is over."

"Nope, mainly to show off Bumble. She's a good advertisement for our water walk."

The Thoroughbred whinnied and pulled her head back from Luis's hold. She reared and backed. "Damn, this is an annoying horse. All beauty and no brains, but she's fast. Hey, she's a lot like you, Randa."

"Thanks, smart guy." She swung out her arm and landed a punch on her brother's arm. "What's Bumble's problem?"

"Oh, I guess Comet is walking too close to her. Anyway, let me pull ahead of you. Put Paley's Comet in the paddock until I finish rinsing and watering Bumble. Then I'll give my girl a good splashing. Okay, it's almost time for the Dailys to get here and it's your turn for the water walk."

Miranda pointed to Bumble's feet, "Her rear left sock is dragging off."

"Yeah, I'd better fix that. I'll rinse her first, then get her to the curry stall to re-wrap her leg. Won't take long." Luis led the regal horse to the hose by the water walk while Miranda led Paley's Comet to the paddock.

Luis clipped Bumble's bridle to both sides of the low ceilinged curry stall. He'd made a small pyramid of gauze wraps and tape within reaching distance of where he carefully approached Bumble's hind leg. Luis kept a patter of soothing conversation to Bumble as he started to wrap more gauze around the dangling material of the rear sock.

"What the hell do you think you're doing?" Bud's voice boomed a threat, startling Luis from his crouch. Losing his balance, Luis back pedaled and fell backwards into the sharp edge of the feed shelf. He pulled himself to his feet, rubbing his head. His mouth fell open at Coleman's angry chastising. "Who told you to mess around with my horse's feet?" Bud bolted forward and grabbed Luis's collar, pulling him to his full height. Luis ripped himself from Bud's hold and jumped behind the tall feed bucket.

Bumble provided a distraction to the scuffle by yanking her head at the bridle's restraints, failing in her attempt to rear up. She whinnied at Bud's excited hollering. Luis rubbed his head, feeling wetness on his fingers. He traced a thin trickle of blood to the top of his collar. His voice was almost a cry. "Miranda noticed that Bumble's sock came undone during the race. You'd gone to your cabin. I tried to help."

"I told you to give me privacy when I curry her," Bud growled.

Luis answered with more boldness than he felt. "What you said was you'd wrap her feet when there were no slamming doors and dogs barking and no other distractions. Again, I tried to help."

"Everything okay out here?" Patrizia stood at the door. "I heard a commotion."

Bud spun around and grabbed the bridle and said to the horse's face, "There, there, Prescott. Good girl. You're okay." The horse pawed and vocalized her discontent. "Calm down, Presco... uhh...Bumble B. Calm down, girl."

Luis's eyebrows went up and he bit away a laugh when Bud called the horse by his boss's name. He swiped his baseball cap's peak backwards to cover the blood on his neck. Patrizia turned to leave but looked back over her shoulder, questioning Luis's peculiar smirk.

"We're okay Mom," he said as he bent down, busy with the gauze and tape. Patrizia left the barn.

Bud said, "Sorry son. You can see she's mighty excitable. I'll finish up here."

Luis pressed some gauze into his hair and pushed past Bud. This time he was sure he smelled alcohol. Luis muttered to himself, "Okay, that was interesting. He's so drunk he forgets his horse's name. He did it twice. There's something wrong with that guy, not counting his drinking. He's always mad. What's the big deal about the horse's dumb leg wraps anyway? Oh well. It takes all kinds."

Chapter 6

MIRANDA'S DATE

Patrizia whispered sweet nothings to her VW, as some people do, as she washed the car and polished the hubcaps. At last she shined the windows. Job done of cleaning out the interior, she sighed as she carried the large plastic bag containing her extra sweater, CDs, box of tissues, flashlight, and jumper cables to the porch.

After changing into town clothes, she called to her daughter's closed bedroom door, "Randa, I'm going out. I'm taking the Beetle. There's a bowl of egg salad in the refrigerator if you're interested." Her voice trailed down the hall and stairs as she called back, "Peach pie's in the refrig. Help Luis if he asks."

Miranda answered a wan, "Yeah, bye." She stood at her open closet and clattered hangers aside, one after another, searching for her new leather vest. "Ahhh, here it is. Looking good, very twenty." She faced her reflection in the long mirror, sucked in her already flat teen stomach, and pushed out her hip in a posture known to gangly, pouting, magazine models. Miranda approved of her seasoned horsewoman look. "He'll think so," she told her mirror and pulled on her shined, brown show boots and swung her black braid over her shoulder. She scurried to the window, looking for the reward of seeing the VW's retreating cloud of dust. Seeing none, she concluded, Good. Mom's already gone.

Employing a new swing in her walk, Miranda moved on to stall seven where Luis and Bud were fussing with Bumble B. She ignored her brother and said to Bud. "Are you ready to go?" When Coleman saw Miranda in her dressed-up outfit, his face proved he understood she was inviting him to the circus horse compound.

"Okay, Luis. Bumble B's done for today. See ya later." He turned to Miranda and called, "One minute," and hustled to his bunkhouse.

Miranda admired Bud's back and his stride. She hopped into the truck's front seat to await her date. Suddenly, her mom, in her blue VW buzzed past the truck and barn, and peeled onto the lane. "Good God! I thought she was gone twenty minutes ago. Phew! Close call." She put her hand to her heart, pounding and rapid. She counted, one-one-thousand, two-one-thousand, then dared to poke her head above the dashboard at number seven-one-thousand, and squinting, scanned the barn yard. The single sign of life was Fleabag chasing Tuxedo onto the porch. Miranda settled herself into the driver's seat, pulled on a red baseball cap, leaving her braid to spill out above the open triangle at the back of the cap. She knew she looked best in red. She clipped the seat belt and hummed a happy made-up tune waiting for Bud. He arrived at the passenger door with a shined face and fresh shirt. Miranda's blink showed her admiration of his good looks. "Buckle up, Buckaroo." He did.

She pulled the truck from the barn, more quietly than a butterfly's wings, not causing a ripple in the air. She prayed her mother would not somehow witness this fall from grace. As the truck neared the end of the lane she reached over to tune the radio to the station she and Baxter listened to, then realized her choice was probably too immature for Bud. He had to be thirty. Well, thirty was a mere fourteen years older than she was and Grandmom was sixteen years younger than Granddad, and they had been fine as a couple, hadn't they? She snapped off the radio, covering the tactical error. "Oh, that Luis. Listens to such *noise.*" She pattered a little laugh and tossed her braid from her shoulder to her back.

At the end of the lane, she waited for three cars to pass, made a practiced left turn, passed a grapefruit and pecan candy stand, and three hundred yards later turned into a serpentine, dusty country road. Gigante's Specialty Stable had a circus poster on his property, facing the oncoming traffic, set back twenty feet from the road.

Driving up the dusty driveway, Miranda started with her lesson to Bud, "The Gigantes are a horse act for the circus. Their horses are gor-geous. You'll see. They claim to be famous direct descendants of gypsies, with stolen Arabian horses. That claim allows the men to wear Halloween type gypsy outfits with tight black pants and open tight shirts. Oh yeah, and bandanas around their heads. The women are striking. Dramatic. I don't know who is real family, or is part of the act. The women don't do much. Stand on the horse's back, you know, circus act stuff."

She avoided spinning up a rooster tail of dirt from the truck's tires. "And their 'stolen' horses are presented wearing a full face cover, with large decorative cut outs for the eyes. It's a takeoff on a bandit's mask across the eyes and nose. Ridiculous, stolen horses wearing face masks, as if they were the bandits, or maybe a disguise, but I guess the audience likes it."

She asked in a high excited voice as the thought occurred to her, "Hey, have you ever seen a circus horse act?" She looked at Bud with a wide smile and her eyebrows high.

"When I was a boy in Germany, our fifth grade class went to a circus, but it was a small affair, with their main act being bears, all big, brown, with huge paws. Also, a motorcycle in a cage. I guess there was more, like, clowns and trapeze acts, but all I remember is the motorcycles, because they were so loud and I loved the noise. Plus, the bears scared me, but I couldn't tell that to anyone."

Miranda bragged, "Not everybody knows this, but the circus doesn't own the horses. They are owned by the acts. Last time on tour, the circus had five separate horse acts. Three of those horse acts live pretty close to Sarasota. The others are in Georgia and in Delaware, of all places. But those are some good looking horses. If we're lucky, we'll see Hank, you know, the guy who's friends with Mom, who brought his horse and foal to our barn?"

Coleman nodded. At Gigante's, Hank was on duty but had to finish up some barn business before squiring Coleman around. Miranda needn't have worried about interrupting Hank because Bumble B coming to the neighborhood was the local big event to some of the horsey community. Both men ignored Miranda, the kid, as she busied herself with petting the horses who were interested enough to poke their heads from their stalls.

Hank showed Coleman around for an hour, then begged off the visit when the vet arrived to investigate a young colt's infected eye. As they returned to the truck, Coleman offered, "Well my little lady, would you like to go to lunch? Payment for bringing me to Gigante's? Where does a cowboy and his girl go for a hamburger around here?"

Miranda was breathless at the thought of being, "his girl," and on being on a date with Bud. She'd be too happy to demonstrate, in her casual way, her driving skills, at the narrow drive-through at nearby Sunny Burgers. However, given that Gigante's ranch was so close to home, she suggested an establishment a little farther afield. "Hey, let's go over to the restaurant with all the rocking chairs on the wide porch facing the highway." Coleman agreed.

Within fifteen minutes, which included a decent parking job, Miranda was confident and led Bud to the hostess's station. She held up two fingers. The smiling young woman, holding menus, made no visible judgment of a teen-aged girl bringing a man to lunch. The giveaway was Miranda's inability to hide her nervous, beaming victory smile. The two were seated. Miranda did a cursory glance around the establishment's wooden walled interior to look for friends, or others whose eyebrows might show either approval or disapproval of her lunch date. She sat back and theatrically ran her fingers through her hair, unbraiding her thick plait. She leaned forward on her elbows and smiled.

Coleman snapped his green Prescott Acres cap from his head the minute they were seated. He shoved the cap beneath the table, redirected his short blond hair with a few swipes, and smiled with teeth and eyes. Miranda was so flustered by his frank straight look that she dropped her gaze to the menu, then to the little wooden triangle holding golf tees on the table next to the mustard and ketchup bottles. She turned the game in her hand, showing Bud she was still on this date.

She relinquished the triangle block, and in touching his hands, felt she might faint. Stretching again for the appropriate bored expression, she propped her chin on both fists and watched the top of his beautiful head as he tackled the wooden golf tee game. "I haven't seen one of these things since Mom and me moved from Germany."

"When was that? Germany? That's interesting."

"Yeah, I was fifteen when my parents divorced. My older stepbrothers were working or married, so it was just us." He jumped a few golf tees in the triangle wood game in the tradition of checkers and laughed. "We moved to Ohio to be near Mom's cousin. Eventually Mom met, then married a good old country boy, Billy, a guy with horses. I learned everything from him. Old Pops. When I was a kid I used to follow him into our stable, me dragging the large barrel of feed. He'd talk to the horses, lined up at the half doors, talking to them like they were dignitaries. He'd say, 'Good morning, Ladies and Gentlemen. I trust you're well on this frosty morning. Yes, I'm well, thank you.' The horses sorta played along. They were glad to see him too."

Miranda tilted her head and asked, "How did you wind up in Maryland?"

"Short story ...," Bud showed an inch between his finger and thumb, "...after graduation, I followed a buddy to Prescott Acres, a Thoroughbred farm in Maryland. He quit after a time, but I liked the place and stayed because the pay was okay. Pops joined me after my mom died."

Miranda smiled and clinked the salt and pepper containers together in her own manual distraction. "What's your real name? I mean, Bud is a nickname, right?"

Without looking up, Bud exhaled. This was a first date question, no doubt about it. He held onto her question for another second. "Aw, my dad nicknamed me Bud from the start. No special reason I can think of. Maybe because I was the fourth son and they'd run out of boys' first, middle, and nicknames by the time they got to me. Mom called me B.C." He followed the ducked question with a, "Terrific, got down to only two tees in the triangle. Hey, I'm a genius— no, it says, *not* a genius." He looked up, then back to the triangle, he read, "Oh, 'genius' is when you have only one tee left." He re-read the instructions then declared, "I'm *pretty smart*. Good enough."

The waitress brought glasses of water and tapped her order tablet. She raised an eyebrow when she noticed Bud's boot slip against Miranda's foot. She watched Miranda's boot settle closer to Bud's. "You two ready?" She covered a smile with her order tablet.

Miranda figured a fish sandwich and iced coffee was a more adult choice than a hamburger and a childish soft drink. She ordered. Her heart pounded when Bud said, "Me too." The waitress scribbled the orders then scurried to the kitchen.

Thinking Bud was the sexiest thing in the world, Miranda scanned the restaurant for prying eyes, then propped her chin on her folded fists, resting her dreamy gaze upon Bud. She considered smoking in front of him later in the truck. No, Mom would find out.

After a few minutes, she was out of conversational start-ups. She rightly resisted the temptation to blow the straw wrapper at his head. As they sat back and waited for the lunch Bud asked, "How long has your mom run the ranch alone?"

Her eyes shot lightning at him. A question about Mom. "Dad died of cancer two years ago." There it was, The Story of Mom.

"So you were a pup when he died? Must have been hard."

"Well, it was a long time ago, and everybody dies sooner or later." She considered her last line was a little cruel, but did not want pity, nor to be treated like a little kid. "Believe me, we miss him." She took the wooden triangle game from his hand, and bent over the little pegs, humming. Bud conducted himself as a gentleman, denying the dining public any occasion for disdain.

Miranda tried to keep the conversation going. "So, did you have your own horse?" She leaned in and smiled broadly.

"We had a pony. I had no interest in riding the poor little thing. I wanted to teach it tricks. That pony was smart and cooperated. I taught him to bend his head to his front feet and fold his knees in a deep bow. But, it's work trying to teach tricks to a bone-headed horse."

"Bone-headed? That's not nice."

"I'd like to see somebody train Bumble B. Now there's a contrary filly. Hey, your brother said those ribbons in the tack room were yours. Good goin' Randa."

"Yeah, I was in Girl Scouts back then and going after the Equestrian badge. I went a little overboard with ribbons, but that's because Paley's Comet and I were an unbeatable team." She giggled. "And, there wasn't much competition."

Two adult lunches were delivered to the cowboy and his cowgirl as Miranda pushed back her shoulders and said, "I could teach Bumble. I know I could." Bud's answer was a muffled harrumph as he bit into his sandwich. She nibbled at her lunch with a glazed-over look, noticing nothing beyond her date's face.

The happy couple ate their sandwiches. Bud paid and peeled off a tip. Miranda drove back to the Water Walk Farm, strategizing on which trick to teach to Bumble B. She'd properly impress Bud.

Patrizia was back at her station on the porch, blowing steam from the top of her coffee mug when the truck returned. Miranda slowed next to the barn. Bud hopped out, pushed his cap back on his head and called into the barn to Luis, "Be right there to put my horse into the pasture. Just need to get out of these boots."

Patrizia marched straight to the truck and flung open the driver's door. She leaned over her daughter's knees and pulled the key from the ignition. "In the kitchen right now, Missy." Patrizia pivoted toward the porch. Without looking back she added a loud, "Now!" Court was in session.

Miranda's eyes widened. Her astonished expression faded and was replaced with anger, then embarrassment that perhaps Bud had seen her mom storm the truck. She composed herself to truculence. An automatic tic, she pushed hair behind her ear, and slid from the front seat to the black cinder driveway. She brushed past Barney without acknowledging his usual welcoming wet nose. The voluptuous scent of the orange orchard went unnoticed. She followed to the gallows, head down, swinging her red cap as she walked.

The mother, cooling down, stood at the kitchen sink keeping her full back to her daughter. Miranda plunked herself down at the table with a practiced teen challenge. Patrizia smacked a rubber spatula three smart cracks in her palm. "I'm so angry and disappointed with you right now I don't even know where to begin. I'll save you having to make things worse by lying, so I'll tell you what I already know. I know you waited until I left, then disobeying, you took the truck. And, against my most recent and I might say, vehement rules, you took a passenger with you."

Miranda kept her gaze on her fidgeting hands. She sighed and dropped her head down on her folded arms. Busted!

Patrizia continued. "I *think* you went to Gigante's. I don't know that for sure, but could find out. Then, I know where, and with whom you had lunch because I was there too." Patrizia slapped the spatula onto the sink and shoved both hands in her jeans pockets. Miranda's head came up to read her mother's expression. Her eyes widened.

"So, Miranda Martina Smitt, since you act like a little kid, I'll treat you like a little kid. This is not over. Mr. Coleman is off limits to you. Period! I'd kick him out but I have a contract with his boss which represents more money than I'd earn in a whole season. So, you are excused to go to your room until I'm ready to continue this. Right now I need time to think."

"Do I get a chance to talk?" Miranda whined, "Well, do I?"

Patrizia turned her tight lipped expression to her daughter, who forged through, without stopping for breath. "I had promised Bud, ahhh, Mr. Coleman to take him to Gigante's 'cause he misunderstood the circus sign on the end of the property, like a lot of people do, and thought Gigante's was the summer headquarters for the circus.

"So I took him, because he asked to go, and he didn't know I was grounded. As it turned out, Hank Gigante already knew about Bumble B coming because of your newspaper article. The men had a good time. After about an hour their vet showed up. That's when we went to lunch. That's all. I was going to drive through Sunny Burgers, but we decided to go to the rocking chair place because he wanted to repay me for taking him out, which I thought was nice of him. He told me about seeing his first circus when he was a kid in Germany. Isn't that interesting?" Miranda was going for her mom's interest in Bud to maybe make her forget how mad she was.

"Yes, that's all interesting. But, you said the *men* had a good time. That's right. Bud is a *man* and you are sixteen; too young to be out with him alone. That's the point."

Miranda broke in. "Only fourteen years."

Patrizia added, "I'd bet he's closer to forty. Should I ask him?"

"God, no!" Miranda's hands flew up to her face in the tradition of frightened women in silent movies.

"Okay, let's say fourteen years. That means he was in eighth or ninth grade, when you were born. I'm guessing he had a girlfriend and was already shaving by then, for heaven's sake. I watched you two, and you were on a date. I'm still so angry I don't know what to do other than to curtail your driving for a while. Go on up to your room."

Miranda looked at the floor, then changed the subject. "So where's your VW? I didn't see it parked next to the barn when we got home."

"Sold it. That's why I was in the restaurant. I had lunch with Jennie Brown from Johnson's Feed and Seed. She gave me the money and I handed over the car's title and repair records. Then she brought me home after lunch. Thank you for changing the subject." Her pointed hand came up. "To your room."

Miranda glared at her mother. "That's terrible. You loved that car."

The mother shifted her weight. "This interview is over."

The teen pouted as she turned to leave but summoned the nerve to say, "Well, you're hurting yourself without me driving. Now you'll have to do your own driving."

Patrizia laughed aloud. "Luis drives, and remember back to who did all the driving before you got your license two weeks ago? That was a good one, Miranda. I needed

70

a good laugh. Your room." She pointed again to the stairs. "See ya later, Toots."

In keeping with her already depressed mood, Patrizia sighed. She shuffled through the unpaid bills stacked on the windowsill, then reached for her pen and check book. Over an hour later, she called upstairs, awakening Miranda from the spontaneous nap that followed her crying into her pillow. "Randa, Baxter's on the phone for you." Miranda thought her mom didn't sound so angry although she hadn't called her, "honey" as usual.

"Okay, got it." The clock showed two p.m. She turned her attention to her pink phone. "Baxter, listen, I gotta run. Luis is waiting for me to help with the water walk. We've added Bumble B to the schedule, and you have no idea what a royal horse she is and how much extra effort she takes for everything." She rolled her eyes, "Only her trainer oversees her use of the water walk, curries her and wraps her feet so we have to coordinate the water therapy with him. Whatta pain." She rolled her eyes.

Her run-on speech was over. Before she took a breath Baxter suggested that perhaps she was breaking up with him. She groaned and flopped back onto her bed, looking at the ceiling. She took a deep breath and sallied on. "No, I'm not *not* seeing you Baxter. Don't be stupid. We're so, so busy, because of the fancy schmancy horse, that's all."

"Okay, okay, Randa. Hey, I'm speaking to you from my new cell phone. Mom got it for me because I'll need it when I go to Virginia Tech in September. I haven't told anyone about being accepted at Virgina Tech. Don't tell Luis yet though, because I still haven't signed the acceptance letter."

71

"Virginia Tech, huh? Wow, that's great, Bax. And a cell phone too. I'm envious."

Baxter changed the subject, trying again for a date. "Randa, it's spring break, for heaven's sake. Let's go out."

"Don't blame me. I'm not the one who broke the stupid water walk. I have to help Luis with the repair later today, that's all. Bumble B needs the hydrotherapy, and one of the jets isn't working right. Guess it's clogged, but that's what we have to figure out. She tapped Tuxedo's head and lied, "It might take all afternoon." After Miranda filled in the awkward silences with chatter and excuses, she moved to conclude the conversation.

Barney's barking interrupted the conversation. "Hold on a second." She jumped up from the bed to look down on the yard. "All I see is a brown delivery truck and the driver walking around looking for someone to sign for a package. There's mom, and ohhh," she swooned, but recovered her composure, "and the new trainer. Okay, Mom's carrying a huge box to the porch. Too early for Christmas. Wonder what's up. Okay, gotta go. We're all coddling our special horse. But you still owe me that ride around town in the new Cadillac."

Miranda had the sudden inspiration to show off the trainer rather than to hide him. Disguised as her interest in Baxter and Penny, she suggested, "Why don't you and Penny come over tomorrow morning about eight and watch Mr. Coleman, Bumble B's trainer, run his super horse? Mom has already arranged for someone from the newspaper to photograph the Thoroughbred's workout. We can visit a bit, but then I have to do my chores, like usual. But that'll be fun, huh?"

Baxter Blackerby was mollified. He'd gotten his date with Miranda, even if the date included the girl's brother, her mother, his own sister, the dude who rode the wonder horse, and a photographer from the newspaper.

Miranda pressed the receiver into the phone's base and shook the guilt from her hand.

The phone rang. Miranda, expecting the call was from Penny, answered with a silly "Hellloooo."

"Hello, Mrs. Smitt? This is Family First Radiologists in Palmetto." Randa explained she was not Mrs. Smitt, and called her mother to the phone.

Chapter 7

THE PAPERMAN

The tall, blond Blackerby kids arrived with the pinking sky and were met by Miranda. Luis was in his Mets cap and worn-out Mookie Wilson shirt. He was already atop Paley's Comet, checking the track. Bud, looking sharp in a fresh lime green shirt publicizing Prescott Acres, worked his horse, kicking up dirt and dust, in the paddock. When Luis saw Coleman turning his grand horse to the track, he felt second class in comparison to this polished, handsome man in a handsome, professional looking shirt. Maybe someday he'd look as good. He admitted to still having some growing and filling out to accomplish.

Miranda walked her friends to the rail, positioning Penny between herself and Baxter. Coleman's filly pranced to the track, shaking her head. She complained, Hnnnhnnn, hnnnhnnn.

Penny leaned in to Miranda and whispered, "That cowboy, trainer, whatsis, Mr. Coleman, looks positively edible doesn't he?" Miranda almost fainted at the words. Was she found out?

"Oh Penny, you're funny. I hadn't noticed."

Coleman rode to where the teens were standing, and was introduced all around. He growled about work ethic. "We're up, why can't the reporter be up? Is it too early in the morning for him to be on the job? Is he getting paid by the hour or by the story?" He reined Bumble B and turned to check the track, working around to Luis and Paley's Comet.

Luis finished his examination of the track about a hundred yards from where Miranda and her posse stood leaning on the racetrack's fence. As Bumble closed in and passed her competition, ambling toward her, she lifted her head, flipped her tail, and surprised Coleman by pivoting around and catching up with Paley's Comet. Paley's ears flicked backwards and a throaty vocalization rolled up her long neck like a distant thunder closing in. Luis said, "What's up gir...... ." Without an order from the riders, the two Thoroughbreds were in a spontaneous race. Both goggleless jockeys were along for the ride.

Luis shot a sideways glance at Bud to read his reaction. Bud squinted against the wind in his face. He called, "Hang on!" and erupted in a surprised and joyful laugh.

When Luis's Met's cap was whipped from his head, he yelled, "Yahoo!" He leaned forward to Paley's ear and hollered, "I wish you spoke better English."

With the distraction of the race, Baxter took the opportunity of both girls' excitement to walk to Miranda's other side. He pushed a slip of her dark brown hair behind her ear and inexpertly kissed her cheek. She pulled back and frowned at him. "Baxter, not here. We're working." He backed away and smiled at the chastisement. He placed a tentative hand on Miranda's shoulder. Both girls screamed and jumped in place as the horses rounded the bend, pounding the track. Baxter's hand fell to his side.

Pale rags of Spanish moss hanging from the distant trees blended into the morning's mist hugging the ground. The smudges of the chestnut and black Thoroughbreds, stretching their legs, ran neck and neck. The dark specks of the riders hunched forward, backsides above their saddles, creating an image as if from Degas's brush. The horses scorched the track.

The girls grasped each other's hands, jumping in a circle, squealing in excitement. Bumble and Paley's Comet surged past the audience, splattering all with churned up racetrack. Bumble B won by a neck.

The two riders called it a race and slowed their horses to a cool-down walk. As everyone laughed and congratulated Coleman and Bumble, a green truck pulled up and discharged a gangly, clean shaven, long-legged young man. He wore a pressed yellow business shirt open at the neck, and had a tan cowboy hat pushed back on his head. The fellow waved and joined the small crowd.

"I'm St. John Jones from the *Palmetto Palm Daily*." This introduction was confirmed by the black and white logo of the newspaper on the door of his truck. He spread a broad smile at the group of teens. "You can call me "Sin Jin" or St. John, or that handsome, intelligent Paperman." He pushed up his round wire-rimmed glasses on his nose. As the effect of delivering his name settled in, he removed his hat, smoothed back his curly hair, and replaced the hat.

Penny screwed up her mouth at the pronunciation of his first name. She raised a blond eyebrow to Miranda who returned the gesture with a surreptitious punch to her friend's arm.

St. John started, "I'm here to get pictures and a story on the best-odds-horse-to-win in Saturday's race." He directed his conversation to and smiled at Miranda, who had the air of authority. He looked up to see the horses and riders walking away from the track, "Or have they raced already?" he asked. On learning the unfortunate answer, he said, "Well, I missed the race, but I'm sure there's much more to be gotten here." He spread his arms to take in the entire farm, "After all, you have this wonderful spread, and high hopes in anticipation of a winning horse in a big race. I guess we can scrape up a story somehow, huh?" He smiled at the threesome. He took his pad from the front seat of his truck and the pen from the pocket protector in his shirt.

Miranda introduced herself and the Blackerbys to the reporter and included him in the walk to the paddock. St. John started, "Let me get the proper spelling of your names before I continue." After procuring the necessaries, he showed a toothy smile and looked up from his lined tablet. He pointed to Bumble B with the bottom of his pen, "So she's from Maryland, huh? Horse country," and nodded as he jotted notes to himself, then swept his gaze across the potential photo opportunities.

"Gosh, he's delicious, isn't he Randa?" Penny whispered, keeping her eyes on the reporter. "But what kind of name is Sin Jin?" Penny went vertical, hopping and giggling, resultant of the cute, lanky newspaper man.

Miranda whispered through the side of her mouth. "Penny, what's with you? First you think the trainer is 'positively edible' now you're ready to dine on the paperman. Did you miss breakfast?"

St. John heard the question about his name. He'd heard the same query all his life and expected to fill in the explanation within two beats of introducing himself. He leaned to Penny and said, "My parents didn't want me to get lost in the school system, my last name being Jones. I can assure you, being St. John banished those fears. I never got lost," he thought for a second and ended with a little laugh, "… on paper anyhow." All three teens nodded in congenial understanding.

Miranda was embarrassed by Penny's giddy behavior and was sure she didn't look quite as immature, foolish, and obvious when she was near Bud. She leaned to Penny and said, "He sure can talk. But I guess that's part of his job." She flashed a smile limited to her lips as she nodded to St. John. More lip gloss was quickly, expertly applied.

Luis jumped from Paley's Comet and was introduced to St. John. Coleman, still mounted, joined the throng, although Bumble backed out in protest of the gathering. Coleman grunted his hello to the reporter, winked at Miranda, dismounted and, handing his reins to Luis, stood back and watched the horses. He rubbed his chin, then nodded to Luis and peeled off from the teens. "Gotta make a call."

"Luis, I thought you weren't going to race her again before Saturday." Miranda smiled at St. John Jones, including him in the question directed to her brother.

"Well, that was the plan. Coleman and I agreed that we were out for a little run, but we didn't clear it with the horses first. Didn't expect a competition. That Bumble B shot past

Paley's Comet like a baseball smacked off Mookie's bat. Phew! Did you time us?"

Miranda was quick to answer, "Nah, there was no true beginning, then, Pow! All of a sudden, two horses came shooting around the track. At best, you did about three-quarters of the mile."

Luis said, "If nothing else, this competition is getting Paley's Comet to race faster than ever."

"But Bumble B spurted right past you." Miranda resisted her impulse to jump up and down.

Penny had the reporter's approving attention when she volunteered details Miranda had told her of Bumble's time yesterday. Miranda twisted a pinch of Penny's shirt to stop her talking. Penny pouted and pulled away. When St. John Jones asked if yesterday's time was accurate, Miranda gave a disclaimer, "… perhaps the stopwatch wasn't accurate. We didn't time today's race, but it sure *seemed* as if Bumble B was around the track in about two minutes. Not timed. Nothing official."

As St. John Jones wrote on his lined pad, Miranda gave Penny a steady glare. Penny rubbed her bruised arm and looked toward the orchard.

Patrizia joined the group to welcome and thank the young reporter for making the trip to the farm. St. John's face and neck reddened when he admitted to missing the morning's race, but compensated by bragging to the owner of Smitt's Water Walk Farm of his many recent photos published in the paper. He'd been the first on the scene, he wanted to remind Mrs. Smitt, of the small fire, limited to the feed barn, over at the circus grounds last month. Patrizia assured St. John that he was welcome to take candid photos and thanked him for coming to Smitt's Water Walk Farm. The article would be free advertisement for the farm. She returned to the house.

Coleman rejoined the group and rocked back on his boots as he asked the reporter, "When do you suppose these pictures will be published? Mr. Jones, I hope you don't intend to print any details on the horse's speed. Your article could ruin a big financial win for me. Although I don't see anything wrong mentioning she's an out-of-town horse."

St. John pressed his camera to his leg, listening as Coleman continued. "You can get some distant shots. She's high-strung and gets antsy with flashes going off in her face."

Not to appear intimidated by the visiting trainer, St. John Jones turned on the charm. "Well, doggone it, let's get a pix of this famous trainer and the farm owner's good looking, capable daughter. How about it? Come on folks, lean over here on the fence. Maybe get Bumble B's head between you. Won't need a flash in this bright sun." He posed Miranda and Bud, but Bumble, no surprise, would not cooperate to stand between the two.

Bud apologized, "I'll stand between the girl and this crazy horse. Bumble's a little wild, but that's what makes her a winner." He made big eyes at Miranda, who erupted in nervous laughter. She looked at Penny and theatrically blinked showing this was innocent fun, then took her place next to Bud. He stretched his arm around Miranda's shoulder. His thumb caressed the back of her neck, secreted by her long hair.

St. John snapped the picture. "Good. One more," and snapped again. "Okay folks. It's been a grand morning. Mr. Coleman, I wish you the best of luck in Saturday's race."

St. John Jones busied himself with snapping pictures of the horses, the picturesque curve of the rail at the track, the Smitt's Farm sign, the tack room with its ribbons, loops of rope, saddles, and bridles. And then, *Palmetto Palm*'s reporter was gone in his green truck. Coleman returned to his bunkhouse.

Penny turned to Miranda, "So when did you get a tattoo? I can't believe you got a tattoo without me knowing."

"What are you talking about? I don't have a tattoo." Miranda flicked her hand across the back of Penny's head. "Dork."

"I heard Luis say something to Mr. Coleman about 'her tattoo.'" She made quote signs in the air. "Who's he talking about?"

"Penny, you're a hoot. He was talking about Paley's Comet's lip tattoo that she got back when she ran her first race. I thought you knew this stuff."

Penny countered in a teasing, insulted tone, "Hey, I don't know nuttin' 'bout horses, racing or betting. Why would I? All we have at home is a beagle, and an aquarium. What do *you* know about betta fish? Huh, smart guy?"

Miranda continued the lesson. "Okay, okay, so the horse's tattoo's a safeguard against fraud, like racing a different horse than the one who is registered in the race. All race horses get their upper lip tattooed at the track before their first race. Then along comes some poor guy whose job it is to flip up the spitty lip to check the tattoo numbers against the list he has for all those jittery race horses lined up to get into their gates. Not a job I'd want."

Penny answered, "I'm disappointed that you didn't get a tattoo."

"Yeah, sorry, Penny, but you and I aren't old enough to get a tattoo. Besides, Mom would kill me. I can't even imagine how crazy she'd be."

Patrizia walked up behind the girls. "Yes, I would be verrry crazy. Come on in to breakfast. The chores can wait."

Miranda put her fingers to her lips to cover the smile that could give her away. She surreptitiously tapped her left buttocks cheek where a small red heart hid beneath her scanty panties. So far so good. Mom had not discovered the tattoo from the overnight, last winter, at her friend's house when the big sister gave a little tattoo to each of the girls who dared. Penny was unable to attend that party because of a sore throat. Miranda had dared.

Patrizia stood on the porch and called, "Breakfast!"

Chapter 8

SMITT'S SHIRTS

Before serving breakfast, Patrizia circled, appraising the Blackerbys' new white Cadillac SUV. She cooed, "It's gorgeous, Baxter. I didn't know Cadillacs came as SUVs."

"Yup, they do now." Penny beamed her heir's claim.

Luis said, "Hey Mom, this SUV could eat your VW." Both mother and daughter, eyebrows up, laughed. Patrizia called over her shoulder, "I don't think so," and hurried to the kitchen.

Baxter opened the back door of his Escalade to collect his gift for Luis. "Hey, Louie, I brought this bag of baseball cards for you. I was at the armory last Saturday and there was this new guy with a huge baseball card display. He was selling some old cards by the bag. He had some Becketts magazines, like you have, and some plastic covered packages of signed balls in his display, so I figured he was the real thing."

"Wow, that's great, Baxt. Come upstairs a minute. I'll have a quick look."

"The guy said he's from New Jersey and is traveling a circuit this spring. I took a fast look through the cards. I don't know if there are any valuable faces here, but you will. So here ya' go." Baxter handed over the bag, the size of a bag of Florida oranges, to his friend.

The boys banged up the stairs to Luis's room in a display of noise and testosterone. Baxter looked around his friend's room and said, "Wow, you have a third display case. You're moving up." He leaned in for a longer look. "I'll bet you have enough value here to pay for your first year of college, do you think? I guess the locked-up cards are worth more, huh? Which one's your most valuable?" Luis laughed but knew to disregard the question about value in the event word got around. He turned from where he'd pitched the bag to the bed and collected a five dollar bill from the jar on his desk and extended the limp bill to Baxter.

Baxter put up his hand, spreading his fingers, "Nah, Louie, it's a gift to you. It wasn't expensive. I saw the guy and bought it for you, that's all. Of course, I'll expect a piece of the action if you hit it big. Take it." He swatted the money away.

"Baxt, you know the rule. Money breaks up friendships. Take the darned fiver and shut up about it. But thanks a lot for the cards." Baxter pocketed the money.

"Hey Baxt. Guess who called me on Easter Day. Ashley Sousa."

"Yeah, Penny told me. Miranda told her. Ashley's cute with all that blond fluffy stuff."

Luis rubbed his hand across his brush cut, "That got around fast."

Baxter followed with his own head rub. "You know Lou, she used to go with Matthew Harrison. I didn't think he was out of the picture, but, what do I know? Good for you."

"Yeah, *she* called *me*. Seemed to be friendly. Sort of, 'into me.' My problem is, my time is really taken up with this Maryland horse right now. But we talked for a little while. I got the feeling she'd be willing to go out with me. I'd need to drive her around in Mom's Beetle, which is too small and inglorious. And the truck, well, the truck lacks class." Luis fumbled with the knot on the baseball card bag. "I can't compete with your Escalade to take a girl on a date."

Baxter laughed. "Are you kidding? This isn't Boston. Everybody in Florida has a truck. I'll bet Ashley drives a truck too. You're crazy, man."

"I'll call her later. Set up something for Friday night." Luis upturned the bag on the bedspread and swished through the hundred cards with the expertise of a seasoned jeweler searching the purple velvet cloth for the clearest diamond. He was distracted by Baxter's musings, but sorted with hums and blurted little sounds of approval. He lately remembered Baxter standing by.

"Huh? Oh yeah, Baxter. Those locked display cases. I have keys—somewhere." He laughed and said, "I can't find them right now. Embarrassing. Don't mention that little detail to Mom. She gets disgusted with me. Poor old girl has high hopes for me to be a lawyer, or some successful adult. I hope she's right, 'cause I can't even find those darned keys."

"Well, I guess that's what college is all about, Counselor." Baxter pointed to the U. of M. poster. "And you're going. You'll be great."

"You were right, Baxt. There's a lot of good stuff here." Luis smiled up from examining the heap of baseball cards. "This is fun. Here's an old Met, Kenny Singleton, and Phil Niekro when he was a Brave. These are old. Oh, here's Bucky Dent and Chipper Jones too. But there's lots of Chipper Jones cards out there. I'll have to check that signature. It's real ink, but I don't know if it's the real signature. I like the older cards, like from Dad's day. Thanks a ton, Baxt."

The mother on duty called all the teens to join the late morning Smitt's Farm family breakfast. The aroma of the warm apple cobbler and cinnamon filled the kitchen with a celebratory atmosphere. While the good-humored conversation bounced around the table like a child's game, Baxter announced his college acceptance.

Patrizia exclaimed, "Virginia Tech. Oh, Baxter that's great. And, a little closer than the other universities. Your mom must be thrilled. What'll be your major?"

"Math. Maybe slide into physics later. We'll see."

Penny shook her short blond flyaway hairdo, "Having a math genius in the family makes it hard on me. I'm no good at math, sorry to say."

Luis said, "But you're the one with an art portfolio, right? Baxter can't draw."

Penny jumped in, "True. He *still* can't color in the lines."

The friends regressed to their younger years when they'd gotten together; slapping, bumping, and hooting. They renewed their cheer and noise, and flipped one of Baxter's coins for who would get the last of the cobbler, the end result being four forks flying into the last of the pastry.

Patrizia interrupted, "Okay everybody. I have a surprise. Sit, sit. Don't move."

All sat still with quiet hands folded on the table top. Shoes kicking each other under the table persisted while Patrizia dashed to her back room. The sound of Mrs. Smitt's huffing and puffing preceded her as she struggled into the kitchen with her arms stretched to their limit around a large box.

"Oh, this is the box I saw delivered yesterday, huh, Mom?"

Patrizia pulled her chair from the table with her foot and with her widest smile, introduced in her best circus imitation, "Ladieees and gentlemen, I draw your attention to this taped-shut box which contains a big surprise. I thought this would show the new boarder that we are not a little backwater farm, but rather a nice successful business." She leaned over the carton with much grimacing and yanked at a flap of the cardboard. With a fair amount of grunting, she produced a loud victory rip of tape. She sang out a musical, "Tah-Dah."

She splashed white tissue paper to the floor and produced a red tee shirt with a wide black stripe running from the right shoulder, diagonally to the waist. Black block print on the left chest advertised, Smitt's Water Walk Farm. As the teens sat up straighter in their chairs and cheered, Patrizia called, "Wait, wait." She shifted from foot to foot as she dug into the box again and flourished a red baseball cap with black printed Water Walk above the black bill. She held the cap high and laughed aloud. Penny and Baxter hurrahed as the Smitt kids yanked on the new shirts and topped their heads with the new caps.

"Even before Bumble B arrived, I ordered the red and black personalized shirts with matching caps to give a good professional look for when the Maryland horse was here. And for all the Dailys to see, too. But the shirts were back ordered. Anyway, they're here now. The diagonal line makes them look like racing silks, don't you think?"

Miranda said, "At last we can get Luis out of his worn out Mookie baseball jersey and beat-up Mets cap." Patrizia and the Blackerby kids sent up a loud here-here.

Luis said, with his defending lawyer posture, gesturing his index finger into the air, "Hey, you know that Mookie Wilson was Dad's favorite. They even had the same birthday."

Miranda and Patrizia answered together, "February 9th. We know."

Little, quiet Penny, not one expected to have all the answers, said with unself-consciousness, "Yeah, Louie, but the Mets were your dad's favorite. Suppose your secret was that you liked the Yankees. Their spring training is right up the road in Naples." She pointed her thumb over her shoulder.

Luis responded with vigor. "The Yankees? Never. I'm a Florida Met for sure." He swung at Penny.

Patrizia said, "These shirts will make us look more like a business. Too bad the shipment was late, and to top it off, Coleman came resplendent in his own darned special shirt. Hell, even his truck and trailer are personalized. Oh well, lime green for Coleman and red and black for us."

Luis stood and leaned in to the table with a confidential stage whisper. "I'll bet Coleman wears pale green underwear."

All laughed except for Miranda who reddened up to her roots. She compensated by finding her voice. "Mom, I was wishing we had shirts too when Mr. Coleman showed up in his Prescott Acres shirt. These are terrific." She had a thrill in her speech.

Patrizia reached into the box. "Luis, take two shirts each and a cap apiece to the guys, would ya? Make sure Russ gets the extra-large. We can start looking like the successful business we are."

Luis, neat in his red and black shirt and cap, peeled off on a mission, ending the morning. As he disappeared to the porch he leaned toward his mother, apart from the Blackerby kids hearing, "This must have cost a lot, Mom, but it's worth it. They're great."

Penny said, "Let's get going, Baxt. I still have to get my pastels matted for the spring art show. Miranda will you be doing some mandolin thing for the concert?"

"Yeah, I'm working on a classical piece that everybody knows. It's a little long for a solo, so I'll make some cuts, but it'll do fine. Luis will probably show up with Bumble B, displaying the most beautiful horse in the world!" The girls laughed and hugged goodbye. Baxter took the hugging opportunity to get a public, legal, long hug with Miranda. He was sure no one was looking and closed his eyes, savoring the moment.

After seeing off their friends, Miranda started into the house. Luis came back to the porch after distributing the shirts and hats and grabbed her elbow, "Randa, help me at the water walk. I need to unclog one of the jets before the Dailys get here. And I still owe Paley's Comet a walk."

The Smitt kids in their matching shirts and caps admired their bright outfits, and ran off kicking through the straw to the horse's exercise area. At the water walk, Miranda drained the water from the treadmill to a foot below the level of the jets. Luis pulled off his work boots and emptied his pockets. He pulled on his tall rubber boots from under the side bench and waded into the half-filled, stainless steel-walled ditch where a short stout stick had inserted itself into an upper rear jet. He plucked the culprit stick from its lodging, redirected the jet spout, keeping the entire repair operation to under twenty minutes.

"Good thing I'm not paid by the hour around here. That little job would not have earned me lunch," he held up the renegade stick as he kicked off the rubber boots. "Miranda, you can refill the water now."

As Luis watched the water level rising in the ditch, he again noted a dark scum strip at the water line, and a fine dark patina on the stainless steel wall of the pool. He leaned into the ditch and rubbed at a section of the dirt. "What the hell? What *is* this? This is the second time the water has been speckled with these pasty dark flecks. As careful as I've been to have this bath be extra clean for Bumble's visit, the water seems to be dirtier than usual. Hey, Randa, turn off the water and help me clean the walls again."

She exhaled in a loud burst, not discriminating who was witness to her disgruntlement toward her brother's or her mother's request or direction. Luis softened. "You don't have to get in the water. I'll shine up the left side, you can swab the right side. That'll help a lot."

They worked for a few minutes until Miranda's withering expression of impatience caught Luis's attention. She said, "At least, fixing the water walk, I'm relieved to say, kept me from being stuck with Baxter."

Luis's head snapped up from his work, "Since when don't you want to be with Baxter?"

"Well, it's complicated." Her face showed she believed her adult words.

Job finished, Luis threw the black-stained towel to the bench and gave a philosophic shrug. As he watched the clean water level rise, he reloaded his pockets and said, "So, I'm done here, and you, m'lady, are free to be complicated. Go get your run in for today. Running is probably the best medicine for 'complicated.'"

Leaking small puddles behind, Luis said, "I need a quick shower." He picked up his boots and socks and headed to the house to clean up. "Will you get the feed ready for this afternoon Randa, so I can be ready for the eleven o'clock appointment?"

"How the hell do you expect me to run, as you said, *and* get the feed ready?" Luis turned the corner and was on the porch, past hearing her. She grumbled to herself and headed to the feed room to fill three baskets with afternoon feed. Maybe she would see Bud when he came in later to prepare Bumble's special meal.

"Well, hello Flea Bag." With her greeting she startled the cat who jerked backwards from her poised-to-pounce position. The cat gave Miranda a dirty look then belatedly poked her paw between the box of horses' shampoo bottles and the plastic bottles of bleach stacked on the floor. The moment was gone for the cat. "Oops. Sorry, cat." She leaned down to pull the heavy bags of shavings from under the feed shelf, and felt body weight against her legs and buttocks. Bud's hand slipped across her stomach. He pulled her against his legs and chest. She, like the cat, jolted upwards. She turned to him with her face flushed from being bent over, but more, from his touch. He kicked the door closed behind him and wrapped her in a tight hug and kissed her. Barney barked twice from the other side of the door. Coleman said, "He'll get over it."

Miranda caught her breath. She would have fallen backwards in a swoon, but Bud had her in a secure hug, lifting her heels from the floor. She responded with, "I, uh, I...uhhh ."

"Too much for you?" Bud smiled into her face, his mouth a breath away from hers. Before she could answer, he kissed her nose and forehead then landed a kiss on her mouth.

"Uhhh, no, not too much," she coughed and smiled. She gathered all her troop strength. Lying was becoming automatic, simple, even enjoyable with this little bit of practice she'd had since Bud Coleman and his horse arrived. She looked into his face, the single face she wanted to be this close to hers. Brown eyes open, she gave him a neat dry kiss at the corner of his smile, as she remembered her mom giving to her dad. They took a deep breath in unison. Bud dropped her to her feet, and both laughed.

"Well look at your pretty new red shirt." Her mouth gaped as she watched his tanned, wide hand trace across her breasts then follow the black stripe to her waist. "So miss honey doll, where does one go for a night out around here?" He stood back and hung his thumbs from his pocket tops.

"Well, I guess into Palmetto. There's the Dixie Star down on the highway a little past Humphries Truck and Tractor Sales." The barn phone rang. She looked to heaven and thanked the powers for the interruption when she was desperate to get away.

Miranda pushed the button connecting her to the fast-fading boyfriend. Before she started her lie to Baxter, Bud walked from the feed room and waved to her, mouthing the words, "You owe me," and went to his cabin.

Bud arrived in the bunkhouse to the metallic ringing of the old black phone on his table. "Mr. Prescott? Yes sir, everything here is going great. Her time on the track has been, well, you'd be mighty proud of her. She's settling in mighty nice.

"Who? You're sending Ticky Bartholomew? Yes sir, whatever you say, sir. No, the silks haven't arrived. Yup. I sure will call."

Coleman's tone changed. "Hey, Mr. Prescott, how's Pops Goff?" Bud tapped his foot waiting for the answer. Prescott delivered the worrisome and surprising information. Bud cried, "Signed out? What's AMA mean? Well, tell the old man I'm askin' about him. Okay sir, you be sure to watch the race on your closed circuit TV. You'll be pleased. I guarantee it."

Bud slammed the phone, swore and stepped onto the bunkhouse's porch. He sat on the top step to confide in Barney, always as close as his ankle. "Hey, there old boy, I got some boss problems." Barney leaned into the warm attention.

"The old guy hired the wrong jockey. I was expecting Cruz from Ocala. You see, Barney, Ticky has already ridden Prescott's Pride, and, his words, 'There's no other horse like her.' So he won't be fooled by the switch.

"But, even worse, that bastard made my Pops sign himself out of the hospital. Says the old man talks too much. What a sonofabitch that Prescott is."

Barney yawned. "Yeah, I guess that's the attitude I should adopt. This is the boss's horse, his race, his jockey, his money paying for this trip. His screw-up." His voice dropped. "But, Billy Goff is *my* good old stepdad." Barney's head was cocked up in a dedicated listening posture. More in a whisper than in audible words, Coleman added a philosophic, "Well, that's that. Ticky's comin'. And *he* might talk! There goes the retirement, for Pops and me, and Baja, the beach and the boat."

He pulled a cigarette from his shirt pocket, lighted it, caving in his cheeks in the deep drag. He squinted into the distance, past the orchard. He looked to the sky, muttered something about Pops and twisted out the cigarette's ash on the porch step. "I oughtta give him a call." Turning into the cabin, he stopped when he saw Luis walking toward him. "What's up, Kid?"

Luis slid both hands into his pockets. "Just wondering what time you expect to leave on Saturday morning, and do you want me to ride with you, or do you want to follow my truck up to Tampa Bay Downs?"

"You don't gotta go to the track. I'm pulling out real early. Checked the map. Like you said before, should be easy enough."

Luis squinted from under the new cap's bill, "You upset about something I can help you with, Mr. Coleman?"

Coleman, uncharacteristically looked into Luis's face to answer. "Albert Prescott sends his fastest horse all the hell the way to Tampa, across the damned continent for a race, then at the last minute hires the worst jockey in the whole damned world, Ticky Bartholomew. God, that's all we need."

Luis did not understand Bud's wrath over the choice of a jockey. "What's so wrong with this Ticky guy riding in Saturday's race?"

Bud bent forward, leaning his hands on his knees. He groaned a stream of expletives through his pretty teeth, and returned to the bunkhouse.

Luis stood alone. Without an answer, and no reason to linger in the vortex of Bud's toxic atmosphere, he turned back to the barn. He patted Donkey Boy's face and whispered, "This trainer is one angry guy. Wonder why."

Chapter 9

IN THE BAR

Bud Coleman leaned over his empty glass. His lids drooped over dull eyes. He leaned back and swung his arm over the chair back next to him and called, "Hey there, Bobby-boy-barkeep-p-p." He wagged his finger in the air. "Bring Suzy-Q, my little girlfrien' here, and me another a fosty, uhhh, frrrosty vodka." After placing the order, he blinked a long sleepy blink, fighting the gravity of his heavy lids. He smiled at his guest. He balled both hands and rapped his knuckles on the table in time with music. He sang along, "... and prop me up beside the juke box if I die ..."

Closing in on five o'clock, as two drinks were delivered, Luis Smitt poked his head into the bar and peered around for Bud. Bud spotted the kid in his red and black shirt and matching cap. Bud called to him, while pointing to the chair for Luis to join.

"Well, hey there, Louie, Luis, my man. Sit yerself down and keep me company. Miss Suzy-Q was already leaving." The lady in tight jeans, wearing a white cowgirl hat, and a white buckskin jacket with fringe dripping from the length of its arms, huffed at Bud's dismissing remark. She patted Bud's shoulder and leaned in for a farewell peck on his forehead. She swung out her fingers of many rings, and long

99

pink nails and plucked up her drink before moving to the bar.

Bud called, "Don't forget, Suz. Bumble B to win in the sixthhh race. Then you can be my guest in Baja. How 'bout it? We'll have some money to burn through." She turned and waved. Bud watched her denim rear pockets move up and down as she retreated, then he smiled up at Luis and said, "Suzy-Q. Quite the little filly." He winked with great effort.

Luis held his cap, fingering the brim and obediently turned to evaluate the perfect posterior moving away from Bud's table. He dropped his gaze and agreed with Bud with a polite, "Uh-huh."

Coleman cleared his vision with frowning blinks and squinting. "You chasing me down for anything in particular, Mr. Smitt?" He lifted his drink and sipped. "Don't ya love this song? God, I love this song. Ya know, in Maryland I play a little guitar and sing some with a little band. Don't ya love this song? God, I love this song."

As Luis nodded and pulled himself closer to the table, Suzy-Q stopped by with a bottle of Coke for him. "Here ya' go, young man. You must be important. I haven't been replaced by a tenderfoot in—well—never." She chucked Luis's chin. He held the bottle by its neck and examined the fork tine scars on the table top.

"Bud, mom sent me to find you. You had a call from Prescott Acres at two o'clock. Some emergency. Then, you got another call, but this time from *Mister* Prescott, himself, at three. He called again at four. That was when Mom sent me out to find you. Mr. Prescott said he needed to talk. I told him I'd try to find you and give you the message. Now he's expecting a call back from you before seven tonight. So, that's everything."

"Ohhh, so that's it. Old Prescott needs his Coleman, and ol' buddy boy Coleman isn't there to fix up and clean up for the old man. That's a gen-u-ine pity. Real pity. I'll call him tomorrow when I'm d-damn, darned good and ready, 'cause I'm *not* ready today. He hired that giant of a jockey, Ticky Bartholomew, and I'm not phoning. As a matter of fact, Ticky is why I'm drinking. For therapy. You might ought to try it." He "tsk-tsked" and shook his head. "Makes me so mad."

Luis checked his watch and pushed his chair back in a plan to make a run for the door. Bud's eyes were half-closed as he continued, "P-P-Prescott was pretty excited when he, when he, uhh, pardon me, Louie," Coleman burped loudly and clapped a hand to his mouth.

"That Prescott sat in his chair and ...," Bud suppressed a second burp, "was so excited about his horse's speed, he stuck his crooked finger up in the air," he broke his dialog to laugh into his almost emptied glass, "like some king in a portrait, 'That horse is the kind of horse who wins The Triple Crown. She'll bring photographers and newspaper reporters to my front door, mark my words,' he said. Then Misssster Albert Prescott agreed with himself and said, 'Damned right,' and pounded his fist on a pile of papers." Bud squinted at the tiny lights above the blinking beer sign, and got back to the phone call. "Oh, did Prescott say anything about Old Billy Goff?"

Luis shook his head. *Old billy goat?* "Mom would know. I'm here to give the message, that's all. Luis scanned the saloon's interior, with three others parked at the bar and pushed his noisy chair back to make his exit. Bud's hand clamped down on Luis's wrist. "What's the hurry Louie? Your ma, your mama knows you're here with me. Come on and settle back." He spoke into his drink. "It's the twin thing making the old man sweat."

Luis wrested his wrist from Coleman's fingers "Nah, Bud, I gotta go." He emptied his Coke, completing his mission.

"Oh, for Christ's sake, settle down, boy. You're all right here with me. You might learn something." He rubbed his nose with the back of his hand and frowned at Luis.

"Louie, old boy, I guess you know about Thoroughbreds and twins. You're a smart kid. You seem to know everything else about the ponies, but do you know how rare, I mean, really *rare* it is for a Thoroughbred mare to birth two perfect, healthy babies? Perfect twins? Two perfectly formed, perfectly healthy Thoroughbred babies? It's almost impossible, that's all."

Bud looked up from his hands holding the glass. His look required an answer. Luis rolled the bottom of his Coke bottle on the table top and said, "I never thought about it, Bud. Not all of mom's horses are Thoroughbreds, well except for Paley's Comet. We had a Shetland mare a long time ago who had twins. They all did okay. But I don't remember much about it other than they were cute, but not identical. Anyway, the ponies went to a family south of Naples. I doubt if they would have told me about it if one

102

of the ponies died later, because I was about six or seven." Luis hoped this little explanation would clear him from appearing as one in total ignorance, in fact, keeping him in the realm of the informed. He didn't want to lose face with Bud Coleman, the Big Guy with the Big Horse, bringing in Big Money from Maryland.

Bud picked up where he'd left off. "P-Per-perfect twin Thoroughbreds *never* happens, Louie. One of the two foals is too small to live, one might look good, but be born dead, or both born dead, both misshapen, well, you know how it is. It's against the nature of Thoroughbreds. It's their uteruses. Bears have twins all the time, and cats have litters, but with Thoroughbreds, it doesn't happen. But it *did*, Luis, my man, it did." He snorted a short laugh and continued to trip through his words.

Coleman tilted his chair on its back legs and patted his stomach. He took a long breath, then with a bang, dropped his chair's two front feet to the worn floor planks. The jolt seemed to waken him. He put his elbows on the table and leaned toward Luis, who leaned back, repelled by the alcohol breath.

The trainer took a deep breath and started with a renewed sobriety. "It happened two years ago in Caldemar Farms, in New York state, not that far from Saratoga. The vet who was to pinch off the second foal in the pregnancy was involved in a seri-serious SUV accident in a blizzard, then the vet was stuck in the hospital, then rehab." Bud's facial expression brightened as he continued, "Huh! Rehab, like a horse in the water walk. Old man Caldemar was unable to get another vet because of impassss-able snowy roads, and, well, several months later, the twins made it. The mare died, of course, but the foals were perfect.

"My boss, Prescott knew Caldemar since childhood, so when the foals needed a dedicated nursemaid, that's when Prescott got the, the, uh, you know, the call. Money changed hands and Prescott bought the fillies." Coleman burped and pounded his fist to his chest and blinked. Luis squirmed in his seat.

In his telling of the memory, Bud's voice softened and his words and sentences became clear and fluid. He squinted and smiled, looking over Luis's head. "Those twins were a sight to see. I drove Prescott's van up to New York to get them. It was like transporting two Great Danes. Caldemar's two teenaged granddaughters, each with a baby horse in her lap, rode down to Maryland overnight, and kept the baby bottles of milk going, and kept the foals still and safe. When I stopped for gas, I saw the girl, about your age, sleeping in the back of the van. Her hair hung over the foal's head, resting in her lap."

Coleman's eyes were almost shut, but his smile was beatific with his inebriated memory. He squinted up to the ceiling and said, "So beautiful. Her little sister was asleep with her head next to the other little horse's sleeping head on blankets on the floor. God, I'll never forget that."

Luis consulted his watch. He nodded to show his interest and engagement. Coleman took long pauses between his sentences, as if closing in on an unpremeditated nap. He did not notice Luis's momentary lack of attention. He continued, "I had two crates for the foals in the van." Bud looked up, "Did I tell you this already?" Luis averted his gaze and shook his head. "Okay. But the kids pretty much kept those foals on their laps, feeding and calming them all the way down to Maryland. Hell, I got in the left lane, and drove those pups to Maryland overnight. Flew the Caldemar girls back home to New York the next afternoon." He took a deep breath and slowed his story, wrapping up the events. "Those were some good kids. *Damned* good kids. Great kids." He wiped his mouth with the back of his hand.

Luis said softly, "Come on Bud, a storm's coming. It's going to be a real boomer. You'd better let me drive you home. Prescott's call will be coming in real soon." Luis pushed his chair back and stood behind Bud who kept looking into his glass. Luis hoisted him by the elbow.

Coleman staggered backwards a few steps. Luis steadied him. Bud went on, "The horse's facial stars were identical," here he stopped, looked up, amazement on his face, "and were perfectly centered on their foreheads." He shook his head in disbelief. "Amazing."

Bud kept talking into his own chest as he walked on unsteady feet. "Their color, identical, the single difference between the horses, Louie, is the height of the left rear sock. That left rear sock." Luis pulled back again at Bud's alcohol breath. Bud turned his head, closed his eyes and smiled dumbly, laying his forehead against Luis's. Bud repeated his last few words. Luis dismissed the impossible, slurred story.

Bud stumbled, but caught a chair back and steadied himself. "Hold it, hold it a sec... a second." He pulled his wallet from his pocket and dropped a twenty-dollar bill onto the table. "I hate to ask you this Louie-o, but my glasses are back at the cabin. This a twenty?"

"Yup, come on." Luis was reluctant to hold Bud's shoulders, but supported him. He was surprised that despite Coleman being too drunk to stand, he sure could spin a complicated story. As Luis held the door for Bud, he saw Suzy-Q watching them. He smiled, and quickly pulled a steadying hand from Bud's shoulder and waved.

After getting Bud back to his bunk house and after the family dinner, Luis sought refuge in his room. Patrizia and Miranda met in Patrizia's office for Wednesday night music practice. Miranda pulled the music stand closer to the floor lamp. "I'll sit here on the ottoman." She pulled her mandolin to her lap and settled herself, tucking a foot under her bottom. She leaned to the open instrument case, removed a small soft cloth and polished her instrument while her mom stroked her bow eight times across the small block of rosin. Miranda nudged Fleabag away from the music stand's unsturdy metal tripod. The cat stepped straight to the open mandolin case and settled, curling onto the velveteen cover for wrapping the instrument. Patrizia signaled she was ready to tune up.

To the sound of Patrizia's "e" and "a" strings being played in a double stop, Luis walked into the room carrying sheet music. "Here Randa, you dropped, 'The Old Rugged Cross' on the bottom step. Why a hymn? I thought you two were adding only classical music to the country stuff."

Patrizia answered. "We're expanding our repertoire. If we do a few standards, we'll be in good shape should someone want to hire us for parties, music at church dinners, funerals, you know. Besides, country music mostly requires fiddling and foot-tapping. I'd like to use some of my university music knowledge and technique. I yearn to do a long, down bow stroke and use vibrato for a change. Ahhh, I'm such a dreamer." Luis laughed and moved on.

Miranda said, "Mom, I thought you ordered Schubert's *Ave Maria*, so we could play weddings."

"Yep, it came in the mail yesterday, along with a few classics. First, let's start on Pachelbel's *Canon*. You have the intro. You'll recognize it."

Miranda bent to plucking and soft strumming, repeating measures of the familiar tune. She lifted her head and looking to her mother said, "Oh, I love this piece." Patrizia stopped her bow on her violin's string to look at her maturing young daughter's intelligent, concentrative expression.

Holding an after dinner muffin, Luis broke his mother's reverie when he passed the open door a second time. He poked his head into the musician's wake. "Pardon the intrusion Madame, but would you permit me use of your computer tonight when you've finished practicing?" Patrizia looked up without moving the violin from her chin and blinked "yes."

Luis stage whispered over the music, "Duet sounds good. Maybe I'll quit school and be your manager."

With his mom and sister occupied in his mom's office he scurried off to the kitchen to phone Ashley Sousa. Their conversation was congenial, but short. She said she'd be out of town on Friday night. Luis shrugged off the rejection, not knowing if a sad or cheerful rejoinder was the best practice. He knew he'd be rejected. Maybe Miranda was right. Maybe he wasn't Ashley's type. He took a deep breath, bringing with it a change of heart. But, maybe I *am* her type. Maybe she wants a Latin lover. Maybe she actually *is* busy on Friday night. Heck, everybody is busy sometimes. He ran upstairs. He harnessed his bouncing up and down feelings into steady work on his baseball cards until he got to that computer research later when he'd look up twin Thoroughbreds in New York.

Chapter 10

THE STORM

Brilliant lightning put an end to all sleeping. Florida thunder announced another threat. Flea Bag carried an early morning offering of a fat cricket into a hole of the barn. Barney, not in the guard dog union, slept fitfully inside the barn's double door, as his twitching feet followed the action of his dream.

Patrizia pulled a large pillow over her head to muffle the storm and dug in for more sleep. She neither consulted a clock nor had another thought before sinking back to deep, even breathing.

Luis pushed himself to his elbows in response to the lightning's sporadic illumination. Without being fully awake, he counted to calculate the closeness of the storm. He half dreamed. Luis yawned, rubbed his abdomen and yawned again. *Storm's coming. I'll give it that.* He sat up and squinted at the bright clock face. The room was especially dark for six a.m. "Six more weeks and high school is *over.* Cool!" He smiled and dropped back to his pillow.

Miranda heard the thunder and bolted to sitting straight up. Seeing no morning light and hearing the first of the rain, she whispered, "Ah, rain on the roof. How romantic." She curled down and gave her unsuspecting pillow a languorous kiss, then sighed, "Ohhh, Bud." Thunder and lightning provided the audio and visual effect to her chaste love scene.

A half smile tugged across Bud's cheek as he dreamily realized he'd be the one in the winner's circle at the Silver Bridle race, and best of all, the prize money! The win was almost guaranteed. Then, of course he'd return to train the horse for the Triple Crown races, next year when this speedy Thoroughbred would race in Kentucky, Maryland, and in New York, against other unsuspecting three-year-olds. His thoughts returned to Billy Goff lying in a hospital. As soon as the third race, the Belmont Stakes, was over, he'd grab up Pops, head for Baja, and a year-round tan, with sand in his beach shoes.

Now fully awaken by the storm, he plopped his feet to the floor boards and with his first deep breath sucked in the relief from his first cigarette. He ambled to the front porch to witness Luis's 'boomer' of a storm, then returned to the bunkhouse for the morning's necessities and shave. He rinsed his cheeks and chin then knocked his head into the spigot at the loud thunder clap. "Damn." He backed from the sink while consoling his head. "Damn again," he muttered as he kicked into the large paper bag from the drug store he'd earlier dropped at the foot of the bureau. Rolls of gauze and padding shot across the wooden floor. In an apparent attempt to escape, one of the two round, flat cans of black shoe polish wobbled itself under the bed. "Hell, looks like a day intent on going wrong." He captured the shoe polish cans and returned them to the bag to be carried to the barn. He squinted again at the downpour, pulled in a deep breath, and acknowledged that he was about to get

110

a soaking. He correctly surmised he would not be using the water walk today.

The view from his cabin window showed his reflection against a purple and gray streaked sky. The sunshine, high above an opaque lid of dark storm clouds, rushed west toward the Pacific and would not make a showing in Florida this morning. A few rain drops did a street beat on the cabin's tin roof, and within seconds escalated to a full, devoted snare buzz. Bud rubbed his forehead, muttered, combed his hair, gulped down his coffee, and stuffed a stiff, day old, jelly-filled donut in his mouth.

He reached for his brown rain jacket, which Luis encouraged him to bring in from his truck last night, after hearing the dire storm warnings for today. Before leaving the bunkhouse, Bud remembered to push into his jacket pocket the napkin-wrapped bones from the beef ribs he'd had last night. Barney would be ready for the treat. Bud pulled on his gray Stetson, stepped to the porch then sprinted through the downpour. He tipped his head to experience the southern Florida storm, and swore as a rivulet of cold water trickled into his collar. He stepped back as lightning bragged again, splitting the sky in a maple tree's root pattern. Bud counted. The thunder followed, loud and long.

Urgent rain slicked the barn, punished the ground and the tin roofs, beat against closed windows and shot right through the cracks between the lean-to's wall boards. Bud ran into the barn, pushing in through the door which was closed to the night. Barney was knocked from his slumber with Bud's sudden entrance. The basset yipped and stood,

111

confused at being on all fours while rain blew in. The barn trembled from the thunder.

Gingerfoot whinnied and pawed, repeatedly kicking her right hoof into the wall. Donkey Boy leaned his full side against the half wall that adjoined Paley's Comet's stall. He poked his head to his neighbor's apartment either for solace or supervision. Paley's Comet shifted her weight from the left to right, but kept all her feet on the floor.

Bud hurried to Bumble's stall to see his prize horse moving in narrow circles, complaining in low guttural sounds. Foamy spittle slung strings to her chest as she tossed her head. He ran to the saddle and tack room and pulled a few large blankets from a pole and ran back to Bumble's stall. He looked over his shoulder, wishing for help. Hearing the barn door slap open and shut he turned to see Luis heading in with a rain slicker held over his head.

Bud called over the rain, "I was about to call you. My girl is going crazy in there."

"How can I help you, Bud?" Luis threw down his slicker, patted Barney on his head, and hurried to Bumble's stall, passing Gingerfoot, still dedicated to pawing the floor. Both men halted in the middle of the barn in response to a loud thunder clap, as straw dust sifted down from the eaves. They both held their breath then laughed self-consciously at their fear and respect for the storm.

Coleman called, "Louie, one of us needs to hold Bumble while the other throws the long pasture blankets over her back. That'll calm her."

Luis said, "Let's move her to the curry stall. It's narrower and the ceiling is lower. She can't rear up. Gives her

112

less room to jitterbug. We can throw extra straw on the floor. What do you think?"

Bud agreed. Luis hollered over his shoulder, "I'll get all the overhead lights on so the lightning won't be such a contrast. Can't do anything about the noise of the thunder and pelting rain. This is a genuine-real-thing-Florida storm. We get some doozies here. Luckily it's not hurricane season yet. Dad was careful to not buy a farm in a flood zone."

The two managed to throw the blankets on Bumble's neck and back, weighting her down and calming her movements. Bud finessed a leather bridle onto his horse's swinging head. He held one strap as Luis handled her on the other side and walked the young race horse to the narrower curry stall. Bud called, "There you go, Bumble. Bring it down. Calm down."

Luis stood at Gingerfoot's stall and looked in. "I'll have to move this girl too. I see she's made a hole in the floor board. She'll calm down as the thunder gets farther away."

Luis grabbed up his slicker and ran out to slam shut the curry stall's window shutters. The rain continued although the last thunder was more distant.

Miranda, holding her raincoat over her head, dashed into the barn. "Oh, hi Bud." She looked past him searching for her brother. "I thought Luis was out here."

"He's outside securing the window covers. How are you today, pretty little Randa?" A slow smile stretched across his face. He leaned forward, inching in for a morning kiss. Miranda appreciated his intoxicating aftershave, smiled, closed her eyes and leaned into him.

As Bud considered his next dangerous move, Luis returned to the barn, slicked with rain, surprised and surprising. Miranda jumped back and ran to her brother's side. She blurted, "Do you two want to come in for bacon and eggs? Mom's still asleep, so I'll cook. Big Russ and the guys pulled up, so they'll take care of things out here."

Luis said, "Yeah, give me ten minutes." He turned to Bud, lifting his chin toward Bumble. "I think your girl is good. The storm's fading. We'll check on her again after breakfast. Thanks, Randa. We'll be right in."

After a satisfying Smitt's Farm breakfast, Miranda struck another Vogue pose making a little pretense of scrubbing the egg pan. Luis pushed his chair back and turned to Bud, "I've got to go to town for lumber for Gingerfoot's stall. I'll be back later. Sorry to leave you alone but the storm is moving away and Mom is around if you need help. The Dailys won't come in the rain and the track won't be any good for a couple of hours anyway. See you later though. Don't forget, Mom's a good help." Luis walked to the porch, opened his wallet to count his cash. Bud followed with a "see ya later" and sprinted to the barn.

Luis returned to the kitchen. "What the hell did I break up out there in the barn, Randa?"

"What? Nothing. I came in to invite you to breakfast, that's all."

Luis grunted, "Yeah, that's what it looked like, 'nothing.'"

"You don't need to worry. I'm allowed to have fun," she said to the suds in the frying pan.

"Yeah, well, quit it, if you know what's good for you. You know, Mom's going to kill you before this race is over. You'd better make yourself scarce to that guy. He's too old for you, Miranda Martina Smitt. I'm not kidding. Tell Mom I've gone for lumber to repair Gingerfoot's stall." He pounded from the kitchen and hopped into the truck. He punctuated his manly speech with a loud grinding of the truck's gears. His tires spun tall fans of brown water and crushed gravel. Miranda hid her smile behind a cleaned plate held to her face.

The cats and Barney ran from the barn and into the rain, only for the necessities. By ten in the morning, the late-rising, well-rested Patrizia laid out pet food bowls on the porch. In time she wandered to the barn to survey the rain damage.

"Oh, hi, Mr. Coleman. And good morning to you too, Barney." The dog thumped his tail in response to Patrizia but more in appreciation of yesterday's sticky rib bones Bud was serving the dog. Patrizia asked, "You moved Bumble?"

Bud wiped his fingers on the napkin, "Yes, Ma'am, she was going in circles in number seven stall. The curry stall was your boy's good idea." He spread straw on the curry stall's floor.

"Okay, come on in for coffee if you want. I'll have biscuits ready in twenty minutes. You can tell me about Bumble's running time on Tuesday. Luis said she really shot around the track."

"Yes, Ma'am. She flew all right. I'll turn her into the paddock as soon as the rain lets up. I'm sure to collect on that biscuit." He waved his wide-brimmed hat.

115

Miranda showed up in the kitchen as Patrizia covered the browned biscuits with a dry, checkered tea towel. "Oh, Randa. I hate to kick you out of breakfast in your own home, but a minute ago I invited Coleman in for coffee, so I'd like you to not be here. It's like I said, make yourself scarce to him. Please."

Miranda looked at the floor. "Well, I was up earlier, like we, well, like all the rest of the world, Mom, except for you. Anyway, Luis and Mr. Coleman and I already had breakfast." Patrizia showed a face of disapproval.

Miranda continued with a slight whine to her pitch. "Well, what was I supposed to say? 'You're not invited, Mr. Coleman. Only Luis and I are having bacon and eggs.'" Her remark delivered, she spun and retreated to her room with a ransom of two warm biscuits.

The morning rain that pounded the Tampa Bay area eased to a drizzle before noon. The sun picked up where it had left off yesterday, sucking up all droplets of water from the vegetation, and rolled the earth, barn, truck hoods, and roads dry by the afternoon.

After the coffee and biscuits with the tenant, Patrizia moved on to the chore of sweeping the porch clean of the storm's debris of leaves and small branches. Luis arrived with the truck bed carrying white lumber, nails, and a heavy duty extension cord. "Mom, I have the boards to repair Gingerfoot's floor. Here's your lumber yard bill." His tone was angry.

She reached for the bill, "Good. Luis, have a look at Gingerfoot's hooves. Her front coronets are a little swollen. I guess she was knocking her feet against the wall. I've moved her to number five. Maybe a little water walk for her when the storm is over, a little soaking with the jets, what do you think?"

"Don't know when I could get to it. Have to get Ginger's stall repaired. Jose can help me with the repair since we won't have much water walk business today. Maybe you can get Randa, or Kirk to water walk Gingerfoot?" He didn't wait for an answer but turned to the clearing afternoon.

Patrizia grabbed her son by the crook of his arm. "What are you so mad about?"

"Ohhh, only that the guy at the lumber yard wanted to know when you might be making a payment on the outstanding lumber bill, left over from when Dad was building the cabin."

Patrizia shifted her weight. "Luis, this is nothing to worry about."

"I happen to know that college is expensive."

"Honest to God, Luis, do I look worried about that piece of news? Help is on the way with Bumble B whether or not she wins. Prescott will owe us for the whole week. I already have the first payment, so, cool your jets, boy-o." She bent to the floor and swiped at some crumbs, ending the conversation. She started through the kitchen to her office, stopped and spun around to her son. "Hey, isn't April when the financial aid notice arrives from your college?"

Luis said, "Good luck with that." He held onto the back of the kitchen chair across the table from his mom and countered, "Oh, and for the record, I suppose your blue Beetle parked at the Feed and Seed was only an apparition? When did you sell the VW?" Patrizia's head tilted and her shoulders shrugged up in a "guilty" response. Not answering, she walked back to her office.

Luis unloaded the pickup and lugged the lumber to Gingerfoot's stall. He worked silently with a heaviness in his heart that dragged at every breath. The devil on his shoulder, bent on pushing him into adulthood, asked who would take care of the farm when he was at the university? Stupid Miranda's not any help around here. With or without money, the farm is never ending work. The devil was back, "And, Luis, if your mom was willing to sell her car she must need the money, don't you think?"

Luis had never thought about how much it costs to keep the farm going before. He muttered, "I guess it's pretty obvious."

He turned from the repair of the stall, ran into the house and up the steps to his room, slammed and locked his door. "I'll fix it. I can't find the key, but this will feel really good." He ran his hand down the length of the old baseball bat, held it up, balancing the wood, then stepped into a perfect, shoulder high swing. He connected with the unsuspecting baseball card display cabinets. The angry crash of wood on wood and glass was startling. Baseball cards fluttered quietly to the floor. His arms and hands stung from the blows. He heard his dad's voice saying, "Mookie Wilson and the Mets were *my* thing, Son, not yours. Love your own things, Luis."

Patrizia dashed upstairs. "Luis, what's going on?"

"Nothing, go away. I'm fixing something."

"Luis, you calm down. Stop this childish hot temper and open this door right now."

Luis sat on the floor reviewing the ruin at his feet. He sucked in deep breaths to calm his rebuttal to his mother. He couldn't let her hear the fear and anger in his voice. He spat angry words from his side of the sturdy, locked bedroom door, while his mother, standing in the hall, leaned over, sending calm words and reassurance through the keyhole. The exchange came to no resolution other than to have Patrizia leave in defeat after cajoling and reiterating that she did not need her son's money. The son was resolute, ending with a gutteral roar, "No. Go away. I'll get the money." He gave the cabinet another powerful whack sending one large and two small cabinets to the floor. "They're my cards to sell. Leave me alone."

Chapter 11

FLOOR REPAIR

Luis was spent. He slumped onto his bed and stared at the ceiling. After a minute of contemplation he exhaled and stood to pluck his valuable cards from the glass shards. Using a tablet's cardboard back, he swept the glass to the trash can, muttering he'd do a thorough job later. He sifted through the cards, wrapped them in tissues and carefully slipped them into a large brown envelope. "God, Whatta damned wimp I am." He propped his largest display cabinet against the desk's leg. The useless door dangled. "That's another lost cause," he rebuked himself. In kinder times when he had placed the cards into the cabinets, he unself-consciously and gently spoke to the faces on the cards, congratulating each hero's face. No stranger to talking aloud to himself as he worked or problem solved, today Luis offered his excuse to the universe. "Well, Dad, the baseball cards ARE my thing. I can sell the cards. Baseball cards are my own interest and they are mine to sell."

With his plan formulated and the baseball cards organized, he started back to the barn's floor repair. Luis slammed his bedroom door shut and pounded down the steps. "I look forward to using the buzz saw!" He clomped through the house, off the porch and into the barn.

Jose was in Gingerfoot's empty stall, sweeping the straw to the distant corner. Luis collected the electric saw, his retractable ruler, the hammer and nails and dropped the supplies next to the hole in Ginger's floor. He tested the floor boards by the outside wall by bouncing on his toes next to the wall. He announced, "A little spongy." To include Jose in the project he asked, "How do you think the Devil Rays will do this year? I guess it can't be worse than last year."

Jose answered, "You need to ask Big Russ. He's the baseball fan. But how good can a team be if they played together for one season? I think it's too early to tell."

Luis said, "I'm rooting for them. The good news is that the Devil Rays are in the American League, the Mets are National League, so I can root for both teams."

Luis and Jose, working shoulder to shoulder, wound up removing more floor than expected. Luis pulled off his cap and twisted sideways to fit between the absent floor boards as he said a reluctant, "Well, here goes." He took a deep breath and jumped into the crawl space as if jumping into a pool. He ducked under the barn's floor and fell to his knees. Jose handed him the flashlight. He scanned the light beam across the cool dirt floor.

"Well, Jose, the good news is, no rat's eyes are glinting back at me." The packed sandy black dirt was flat except for a few shards of broken brick and a broken Ball jar, abandoned years before. He called upwards, "The bad news is I don't see an old leather bag loaded with a treasure of gold. Oh! Wait. Here's a crusted nickel, 1957." He laughed

122

and smacked his elbow into the overhead floor board as he pocketed the coin. "Damn!"

Seeing he'd have to bolster the joist, he remembered that after building the trainer's bunkhouse, there were a few different lengths of leftover support beams stored in the shed. "Jose, I've gotta get some lumber. You've got time for a Mountain Dew if you want. I'll be right back." Putting his recent morning upper body workouts to a test, without effort, he pressed up from the cellar floor and landed squarely on his feet. "I wish I felt proud of my gymnastics, but I feel sick." He walked to the shed. The angel threatened, "Buck up, Luis, old man."

Luis walked to his dad's workshop, kicked at a shallow puddle sending a shower of sad, dark droplets into the air. He scanned the contents of the darkened building, filled with his dad's orphaned, spider-webbed, tools. The stacked boards provided shelves for a used tractor battery, a few boxes of square cans of motor oil, an old, empty oil can with its long-nosed spout, and loops of baling wire. Luis smiled at the smell of machine oil and rust mingled with the damp smell of the mud floor. "Smells like old times, Dad." Thin strips of dusty sunlight spread on the floor like bright ribbons. A strange quiet settled on Luis. Feeling his dad's presence as he had not felt before, he put his hands on his hips and said to the space, "Hey Dad. Don't worry. I'll fix it." He addressed himself, "Well come on, Luis, let's get going."

He walked from the shelter and called, "Hey, Jose, this is going to take me longer than I thought. You can go back to whatever else you were doing. I'll call you when I'm ready."

Jose called, "Aye, aye, Captain." He winked and saluted his fingers to the Smitt's Farm red cap, hitched up his suspenders over his red Smitt's Farm shirt, and left.

Luis returned to the lean-to, filled the decrepit wheelbarrow with thick posts, headed back to the barn, dropped the lumber to the floor and threw the posts into the crawl space. From his position in Ginger's stall, Luis could see a portion of Bud's arm and head as Bud talked on the phone. He paced back and forth, limited by the short telephone cord, taking three steps in each direction. Bud whipped his cap from his head, wiped his forehead with the back of his arm and called into the phone in a high voice, "He died yesterday? Poor old bugger. No, there's no way I could get there by then. Cheesus, that could change things." Coleman slammed the phone to its cradle. He wailed, "I should have killed the Rat myself."

Luis watched the trainer hustle into the bunkhouse and heard a sudden, distant crash of wood, maybe a kitchen chair transformed into splinters. Luis mumbled, "What was that? I guess this is a good day to wreck wood!" He hoped his mom hadn't heard Bud's tantrum. "Maybe I should check on him, but he'd probably beat me up if he caught me spying on him." Luis reconsidered that the damage to the bunkhouse property was on Coleman. "He'll have to even up with Mom. I don't envy him." Luis returned to the floor project, crouched next to the hole, ducked down and urged himself, "Back to work." As he wedged and hammered the four-by-four joists into position under the floor, he thought he heard Bud's voice again. He stopped his pounding, certain Bud was back on the barn phone in mid-fight.

Luis's head came up from the hole like a gopher's. Bud was sputtering into the phone, swearing and mentioning "the twins" and something about the old man, Prescott's pride, and yes, he kept the filly's pasterns covered, and what else could he be expected to do beyond the witch?

Luis sat back on the soil floor in his little cave and considered what he'd heard. Bud's talking about "twins" again and there, there, he made another reference to the rear pastern, as he had at the bar, and what the hell did he mean by the "witch"? Bud was almost always looped. Luis couldn't help but think Bud was doing something illegal and maybe dangerous. Otherwise, why all the sneaking around and the mystery? "It's hard knowing what he's up to other than to help his beautiful horse win the race, and I'm for that. Money for Mom. Prestige for our farm."

Later in the afternoon Luis stood again from his work and hopped up and out of the hole. He slipped his hands to his back pockets and smiled his satisfaction with the progress on the repair job. He pulled the floor planks into a line and measured, penciled the cut line, flipped the switch on the noisy saw and within half-an-hour had white, virgin planks nailed into place. He dusted the sawdust from his backside and returned Gingerfoot to her repaired stall. Coleman walked by the stall. "Shit man, how long have you been here?"

Luis said, "Bud, didn't you hear me hammering and sawing? I've been working on this floor for ...," he looked at his watch, "since two o'clock." Luis shook his head at Bud while rewinding the orange extension cord and hung it on the hook near the refrigerator.

The barn phone rang. Luis answered and heard, "Call me a genius. Good thing you're safe down in Florida." Luis wasn't sure if Baxt was playing with him, teasingly calling himself a genius. But the speaker's voice was wrong for Baxter. The voice went on to say, "The police were here. They want to know if Goff's family would be pressing charges against Prescott's Pride or if I intended to isolate the horse or…" Luis got his mouth to work and said, "Hold on a second, I think you want Mr. Coleman." Luis called, "Hey Bud, this call's from Maryland. If you want, I'll hang up and you can take it in the bunkhouse."

"Nah, phone's not working in the bunkhouse. Storm must have blown something loose or down. Have to take it here." The caller in Maryland continued talking to someone in the background and mentioned "euthanasia" when Bud snapped the phone from Luis's hand. Bud put the phone to one ear and pressed his other ear shut with a finger. He turned his back to better insulate himself to not miss a word.

Luis walked away pondering the words, "police were here," and "euthanasia" What's euthanasia got to do with anything? Why the police? Luis refilled the wheelbarrow with unused lumber and started back to the storage shed. As soon as he rounded the barn door, out of Bud's seeing him, he stopped and listened.

Coleman spoke loudly, accommodating Luis's unintentional eavesdropping. "Oh, hello Mr. Prescott. Fine, fine. Yes sir. About Mr. Goff? Yes, I heard. Very sorry, sir. Was a good ole boy. He'll be missed. Uh-huh, Ticky Bartholomew. Yes, the silks came yesterday, sir."

Bud stretched the phone's coiled wire to a straight line as he stepped from the barn. He carved his heel into the wet earth, creating a shallow ditch that immediately filled with water. "Uh-huh. Yeah, I got it. No sir, Mr. Prescott, no lip from me." Bud spat to the new puddle. "No sir. I'll see Ticky before the race on Saturday. Yes sir, Mr. Prescott. Yes sir. Goodbye, now."

Nothing more to hear, Luis pushed his wheelbarrow back to the lean-to and pulled an old wobbly piano stool without one of its rollers, from a dusty corner. He exhaled at the chance to rest, and paged through an old Farmers' Almanac. He sank into the relief of being alone and apart from Coleman's ongoing mystery and generally bad behavior.

Chapter 12

BILLY GOFF

With the phone conversation over, Bud sighed heavily and walked just as heavily, clipping his boot's heels out of the barn and straight to his afternoon slug and drag exercise with his pals, Tom and Winston. He entered his cabin, lit a cigarette, sucked in a mouthful of restorative smoke, coughed, then propped the pinched cigarette on the edge of the table. He rooted around under the sink to produce a bottle of something more substantial than the barn's offering of Mountain Dew. He smiled at the label of Wild Turkey, muttered a greeting to Tom, the turkey, and poured a half mug. He sat on the bottom bunk and pulled his feet to the bunk's thin striped bedspread. He held his cigarette in one hand and the mug of Wild Turkey in the other, alternating the drag, "Ahhh," then slug, "Ahhh." Before he'd smoked down to the filter, his eyes closed, his relaxed fingers reached the polished floor boards and allowed the last ash to burn itself out.

Bud had not witnessed the trampling, but arrived soon after, finding Billy Goff on the stable's floor. Two minutes preceding Billy's accident, the old man pulled the waist-high bucket of breakfast to Typesetter's feed basket. He sang a little ditty as he patted the four-year-old's forelock, then pushed on to the nine remaining stalls. Arriving at the last two Thoroughbreds, on the stable's east wall, he said, "Here's breakfast, you miraculous, beautiful, wonderful, super-duper jewels in Mr. Prescott's crown." Billy filled Bumble B's feed basket then moved to Prescott's Pride's stall where he looked up to see the wide dark web, complete with its formidable landlady, tending her territory between the window sill and a ceiling board.

Placing his hand on the filly's side to gentle her, he calmly advised, "Well looky here, girl, you have a no-count, uninvited, spider taking up valuable space. And, she's not paying you rent. Woo-wee, I've never seen a bigger, uglier spider. Oh she's a bad one."

The well-fed spider worked; spinning, closing, wrapping the most recently trapped delicacy in her web. Goff uttered a "Glory be," pushed his hat back on his gray curly hair, dropped the scoop and pushed the feed bucket aside with his foot. He shivered, shook his head and uttered an expletive as he unclipped Prescott's Pride's canvas mesh gate, jumped into the stall and re-clipped the lock. "Dammit, Prescott's Pride, I *hate* spiders!"

He flagged his handkerchief in three wide passes at the spider's web, swearing and swatting. With Goff's guttural yelling, "Git out o' here, damned hideous spider," the horse whinnied and reared, slamming the old stable manager into the rough wood of the wall, settling short splinters into his forehead and stubbly chin. His wire rimmed glasses flipped from his face and dangled from an ear. A thin trickle of blood slid from his nostril. Air was pushed from his lungs. He coughed, fighting to suck in breath.

The filly huffed and swung long steams of thick saliva into high arcs as she neighed and tossed her head. Goff slid to the swept clean concrete floor, curled to a protective ball and cupped his hands over his head. He sucked in a small painful breath. A tremble ran through him as he watched the fat spider crawl over his elbow, just three inches from his eye. He wanted to shake his arm wildly and yell, "Git off, git off," but he closed his eyes and whimpered. Feeling cloudiness in his head, he fought fading into unconsciousness and resisted the urge to sleep. He mumbled to himself, "You done it this time, Billy, you dunderheaded old-timer. You're a goner now."

As he concentrated on breathing and inching from the corner of the stall, the horse spun and struck her hoof on Billy's arm and shoulder. Exhaling with pain he was barely alert enough to respond, but quickly twisted to avoid being hit in his chest. A single pounding came to his adequately padded buttocks, missing his spine and ribcage.

"Cripes, Prescott," Billy whispered and watching the early morning light telescoping to a small dot, he blacked out. Peacefully unconscious, he was unaware of the nervous horse's last revenge. With a half-hearted turn, the rim of Prescott's sharp new shoe glanced Goff's cheek causing a grazing laceration without a direct hit to the bones of his face.

When sound returned like tide rushing in, Goff blinked open his eyes and saw the horse calmly nosing into her breakfast, standing between him and the mesh gate. The tantrum was over. Goff squirmed toward the exit, keeping his back to the wall, sweating with the effort. He fainted again before clearing his legs from the stall.

Later, from his hospital bed's telephone, Billy Goff and Bud traded the stories of their parts in the accident and Bud's fast work to save Pops from another trampling. Bud had sat back on his heels and brushed away bits of hay from the old man's gray curls. He'd bent to Goff's ear. "Don't you worry, Pops. We'll have our days in the sun in Baja, like we always planned. I love you, Pops." Coleman neglected to confess that he'd dropped to his knees and whispered, "God, help Pops. He's the finest man I ever met. Not like all those other sonsofbitches."

Bud recalled standing slope-shouldered next to his boss, Mr. Albert Prescott, who slumped in the padded seat of his mechanized scooter. Like two chastised, slack-jawed school boys, they watched Goff's ambulance diving off, wailing its warning for all other vehicles to clear a path.

Bud stormed to the horse's stall, stretched his wide hand around the horse's muzzle and roughly shook the filly's head. "You rat! If you were a man …," and he smacked his fist into the wall. The horse, unrepentant, blinked and turned back to her feed basket. Bud spat on the floor and wiped his mouth with the back of his throbbing hand. He pointed his index finger, like a cocked gun, to the horse's white blaze of a star, and threatened, "Nothing better happen to that old man."

Bud's anger wakened him, but only enough to roll to his side and pull his knees fully onto the bunk and to sink into a restless nap. He breathed deeply, and was back in Maryland again. He was out of his work boots, wearing his polished, tasseled loafers, standing on the thick Persian carpet of Albert Prescott's study. Coleman knew he was dreaming, but he couldn't break through to wakefulness. He watched himself and Mr. Prescott from above.

"Right on time, Coleman. I like that." Prescott's gnarled, arthritic hands wrapped around his scooter's control knob. The irascible man pulled his scooter close to his desk and, with curses, transferred himself to his captain's chair. He leaned forward in his chair, mumbling and swearing. He stretched his painful arms with difficulty, busying himself, opening drawers, closing them, and straightening papers on his desk. Coleman watched himself standing by, sober, at a version of parade rest, waiting for the next directive. Prescott leaned forward on his elbows and squinted at his trainer, "Sit down, Coleman, sit down." He waved a witch's crooked finger at Bud. "Coleman, you know Goff's situation could be a big problem." Bud rubbed at a rough thumbnail, but said nothing. "Gawd Almighty, Coleman! Today that young Thoroughbred broke some Triple Crown speed records! And Billy Goff would be only too happy to tell the world all about that horse walloping him."

Prescott ruffled through his papers. "The whole trampling episode could go away, or the newspapers could get a hold of the story and blow it out of proportion, public opinion and all. According to some computer research I did, my winning horse *could* be euthanized for a trampling. Maybe not, but there's always that chance. You know Old Man Goff is a talker. We need to prevent him from broadcasting who caused his 'accident.'"

Coleman coughed and sat up, now fully awake. He shivered and stared at the floor. He never told the boss that Goff was Bud's stepdad. No need. Not his business. "Ahhh, Pops, old man, why'd you go and die?" Bud shifted his position on his bunk and banged his elbow into the empty, tipped over mug. Angrily fully awake, he slung the cup to the bottom of his bed where it lay buried in the bedspread. "Pops, did Prescott do this to you because you talked a lot? You were being cheerful, making small of your pain. That's all. Ahhh, Pops. Nah, I won't go to Baja without you. I was just going 'cause you wanted to go." He jumped to pacing and muttering, his temper tantrum not yet over. He milled around, swinging his arms, shooting punches into the air, muttering, "Damn that Albert Prescott."

Coleman needed to get back to his anxious filly. Moving toward the barn, he was reminded of other irritating concerns; Ticky Bartholomew and Prescott's Pride.

Still slightly bleary-eyed, he looked around the barn and yelled, "Damned stinkin' horse." He picked up and threw the pitchfork, aiming straight into a bale of straw by the door. Barney, reposing in the shade of piled bales, felt the breeze over his back, yelped and jumped to his feet. The dog paced to the yard with his head down and tail between his legs. Coleman saw his mistake and called to the dog, "Ohhh, Barney, I'm so sorry. I didn't see you there. I could have hurt you. Here, boy. I'm sorry. Come back. Let me make it up to you." Despite the inviting intonation, the basset was not persuaded to return to Bud.

His mollifying efforts lost on Barney, Coleman returned to his tantrum, repeating expletives and the name, Ticky.

He took a deep breath and called, "Hey Louie. You around here?" Luis stepped from the tack room pouring back the last of his Dr Pepper. "Louie, put Bumble back into her stall. Storm's been over long enough for her to calm down. Damned excitable horse."

Luis ran to escort Bumble B from the curry stall back to number seven. The filly backed up and rolled her majestic head when she saw the teen. Luis pulled the blankets from her back, and marched her by the water station. He hosed then brushed straw from the horse's feet, legs and belly. As the horse licked at the stream of water, Luis laughed, "That's a good girl, Bumble. You're a regular old girl aren't you, huh? Looking for a little drink? Four feet on the ground, ol' girl, keep those four feet on the floor."

After tucking Bumble into her stall, Luis walked to the paddock. With both hands stuffed into his back pants pockets he reluctantly enjoyed the colorful early evening sky. He calculated he had time to give a little attention to Paley's Comet, so far ignored today due to the morning storm and floor repair. He returned to Paley's stall and saddled her. "Come on Girl. Let's have a little run. I need to talk." The track was now drained and dry from the Florida afternoon's hot sun. With the inspection complete, they moved to a brisk, all-out run. A quarter of a mile before the entrance to the paddock, the gallop flowed to a canter then eased to a brisk walk. Luis talked to his horse.

"Paley's Comet, my dear girl, I have a few problems, and I don't know how to fix any one of them. The trainer for our wonder horse is almost always drunk, or close to it. He's mean and he's dangerous. The only good thing about him is that his temper makes mine look tame. He talks about a witch and he doesn't like some jockey named Ticky, who, incidentally makes him mighty angry. I have no idea what's going on with him. He flirts with Miranda and is trying to get her alone, and, on top of that, Mom sold her VW to meet the last payment for building this track."

The polite horse's ears were turned back to catch Luis's words, although she made no remark. "I knew Mom had money problems, but I didn't know how tight the money was. And she still has some of Dad's old hospital bills..." Luis's therapy session ended abruptly when he noticed, on the far side of the track, visible above the bushes, a shiny blue roof of a car approaching the barn and house. He halted Paley's Comet and craned to see the unfamiliar car go out of view behind taller bushes and trees as it curved around the race track. "Guess we'll soon see who's coming to visit." Luis rubbed his horse's neck and continued toward the barn.

A blue Jeep pulled up next to the track. A tall man hopped from the driver's seat, leaving his vehicle running, with the driver's door left open. He walked to the track's fence and waved his brown Stetson cowboy hat toward Luis as a greeting. Luis nodded and made an imperceptible signal for his well-trained filly to go to the fence. When Luis was in easy speaking distance, the man smiled, showing square white teeth and deep suntanned smile lines at his mouth and eyes. "Hey, there young man, I was wondering if you could tell me a little bit about, uhhh, about ..." He consulted a small tablet pulled from his back pants pocket, then renewed his smile and read, "Five-year-old healthy mare. Good speed, Gentle, Must sell."

The man's gaze returned to Paley's Comet. His smiling eyes admired the horse. "My, she's tall for a mare, and a beauty. Is this the horse that's for sale?" He ended with another winning smile.

Luis was wearing his red Smitt's Farm shirt and supposed the man mistook him for a farm employee. However, the man was here with an interest in buying Paley's Comet. Luis had not yet answered the man. So, this was it. Had Mom written an ad? She needed the money and Paley's Comet would be sold.

The man rested a foot on the fence and started again. "How do? I'm Stan Horsham, large animal vet, from a little east of Sarasota. Looking for a nice fast horse to take home for my daughter's fourteenth birthday—but not today. I didn't bring a trailer with me." Luis removed his cap and sat back on his saddle. The man continued, "I've spoken to the owner on the phone, but I couldn't get here before today. Thought I'd have a look." Dr. Horsham took his foot from the rail. He held up a finger in the "wait a minute" sign, and took a few steps to his car, threw in his hat, turned off the ignition and slammed the door shut. He returned, appreciating Paley's Comet with a practiced buyer's eye.

Luis came off the horse's back not so much as in a dismount but rather slid from the saddle as if mortally wounded. He couldn't believe his ears. Luis extended his hand to return the vet's greeting, hoping the man was at the wrong farm. "Is there any possibility you have the wrong farm or the wrong horse?"

The doc scratched his head, pulled prescription glasses from his shirt pocket, put them on and read again, "Smitt's Water Walk Farm … Must sell."

Luis asked, "Could I see that paper please?" The vet handed over his scribbled tablet. "Everybody in Sarasota knows I've been horse shopping. A vet friend in Bradenton saw this ad and called me. Don't know if you can read my scribble. I copied the information from a phone call."

The doctor had done all the talking. Luis would soon have to say something intelligible. His head swam. Without a word he removed his helmet and scrubbed his hair. "I, uh, yes, this is, might be the horse for sale. How long ago did your friend see the ad, if you don't mind my asking?"

"He called about two weeks ago. Of course I was busy with the practice, but had to be in Palmetto today, so came over." The doctor waited, then snapped his fingers. "The horse's name was something like, 'Milkyway,' 'Nebula' or maybe something about the stars, you know?" He looked to Luis's face for a response. Luis had a silent, blank stare. The vet leaned in and touched Luis's arm. "Are you okay, young man?"

"Me? Oh, sure. The horse is 'Paley's Comet.' Sorta like Haley's Comet, my dad's joke." His voice sounded far away. His mouth was dry. His hands tingled.

The vet listened and nodded.

Luis was not contributing to the solution of this situation.

Dr. Horsham started again. "Perhaps I can talk to your boss, the person who put the ad in the paper?"

Luis turned to Paley's Comet. He swung up to the saddle" and pointed over the doctor's head, "You're almost there. Drive around the barn. You'll see the house. Go up on the porch and knock on the door. Call for Mrs. Smitt, or for Patrizia." Luis stammered, "She's there, in the house making dinner, but maybe in the barn, but prob ... probably in the house."

Luis was relieved to put space between himself and the man who would solve his mother's money problems. He spoke to his horse, "Paley, you're worth more than all of my baseball cards. Shit, I'm so dumb. I thought I could solve Mom's debts by selling my stupid cards." Tears blurred the racetrack. Luis repositioned his helmet and yelled, "Yee-Hah!" and ran Paley's Comet at top speed.

Chapter 13

PRE-RACE JITTERS

The sinking orange sun bragged its giant roundness and brilliant color. With the evening edging in, the big day was hours away. Bumble B, Paley's Comet, and Donkey Boy were in for the night. Luis left the barn and noticed Coleman moving about the Prescott Acres trailer, scrutinizing tires and the hook up. The two having little to say to one another, grumbled, "See you tomorrow," and went about their own projects. The next few hours stood like lined-up, tentative dominos facing their destruction, tilting toward tomorrow.

With dinner over, the Smitts prepared for Friday night. Patrizia was dressed in her best boots, a wide swinging denim skirt with a ruffled hem, an open necked plaid blouse and had her white cowgirl hat pushed back on her head. She walked from her bedroom past Luis's open door. "Hey, Luis, do you have a date with Miss Stars and Stripes tonight? I got busy with other things and forgot to ask if you need the truck. I'm riding with Betina, so I've left the keys for you on the kitchen table."

Luis looked up from his baseball card catalogue and groaned a reply. He hoped it sounded adult and maybe even philosophic and worldly. "Ashley said she'll be out of town tonight. But we left it open for another time."

"Oh, honey, I'm sorry. I know you must be disappointed."

He dropped his gaze to the desk to end the conversation. "Have fun tonight, Mom."

Patrizia threw a kiss to her son and answered, "Thanks, Dad." She walked to Miranda's room to say goodnight and to shake a mother's warning finger at her daughter.

Miranda erupted in a laugh. "Mom, you look like a scene from the Patsy Cline Story. Where did you get that skirt?"

"All of us musicians have the same skirt, blouse and cowgirl hats. We add our own boots and western kerchiefs. See what style and fun awaits you? We look like what we are, Betina's Country Cuties, ruffles, boots and country music. I'll be home late, but I'm counting on you to stay in. No tricks. No going out. And, needless to say, nobody here either.

"I'm sorry, but if you want to be trusted, you need to earn it. Okay." Patrizia took a deep breath and lightened her voice, "Betina's on her way to collect me. Goodnight. I love you. Be good." She blew a kiss to her daughter and twirled from the doorway. She stopped and backed up and whispered, "Miranda, Luis's date fell through. He feels terrible, so don't taunt him. Be nice. Okay, bye again."

The darkening horizon was sun striped and lit the porch posts with a pink glow. Patrizia stepped outside carrying her violin case and music satchel, and swung her string purse in rhythm with her walk to the picnic bench and sat. She caught Coleman's eye and nodded. Her first thought was that he was dressed up for a fellow killing time, hanging around the bunkhouse. He stood in the disc of light by the paddock fence leaning on an elbow, surreptitiously watching for Miranda and pretending he wasn't. He played with untangling a length of blue and white nylon rope. Barney sat by his feet. Patrizia took in the picture of man and dog. Maybe he's not all bad, creepy as he is, Barney likes him.

She pointed to her previously faithful dog and said, "That fickle basset is shameless about switching his allegiances." Both laughed a forced politeness. "Hey, Mr. Coleman, you're looking mighty fancy tonight. Could my friend and I drop you somewhere?" She lifted her hand toward the cloud of dust chasing Betina's red sporty car racing up Smitt's Lane.

Coleman said, "Nah, just out here admiring the Florida sky. But thanks. I have a friend coming to pick me up." He smiled with his eyes crinkled at the corners, comely deep creases at his smile lines. The devil in lizard skin boots checked his watch with some flare, looked up and convincingly lied. "She'll be here in a minute. Maybe you'll pass her as you drive out the lane." He put both hands on hips, demonstrating his authority. "You know how it is, Friday night pre-race jitters." Patrizia and Coleman watched Betina's incoming car make a Hollywood chase-scene stop. After the dust settled, all coughed, and laughed again.

Patrizia removed her cowgirl hat and stepped toward Betina's car while adding her cautionary remark. "Yeah, okay. Luis's here if you need anything." Coleman saluted the tip of his Stetson and watched her swing her adequate femaleness to Betina's car which backed, turned and sped away.

She ran her hand across her hair, leaned to the mirror on the visor and said, "Whooey, I let my dye in a little too long this time, huh? Mighty auburn."

Betina's eyebrows were up. "Do you require a remark from me, or should I say, "No, no, you look fine. You *do* look fine.""

Patrizia laughed and pushed her bangs to the side. "Just trying to look more like a Country Cutie." When buckled-in, she turned to Betina. "Let me borrow your dandy little cell phone, would you? I want to say one more word to my darling daughter. Want to check in."

Betina poked into her hand bag and served the phone across the front seat. "That is one handsome man, Patrizia. How do you not drool in front of him?"

"His handsomeness is the problem. Miranda thinks she's all grown up. He *is* good looking, I'll give you that. But, give me a break. She's sixteen! Other than that, she's a doll; practices her mandolin, runs every day, has good grades, she's help around the farm. What's the matter with that kid?"

Betina laughed. She shook her pedantic finger, unseen in the dark car. "The answer for you, my dear, is 'hormones.'"

After several rings Miranda answered. The call was short. Mother and daughter were feeling out the other. The mother lied some excuse for calling and the daughter lied an answer, pretending she intended to stay in. Satisfied, Patrizia returned the cell phone to Betina, "I'm relieved that that handsome trainer is going out tonight. I don't trust that Yankee."

Bud's wait paid off. In ten minutes Miranda blew through the screen door, singing under her breath and twirling the forbidden truck keys. She waved to Bud. He dropped the nylon cord he'd been twirling and took exaggerated long strides toward Miranda. He moved away from the dog at his ankles, "Sorry Barney. You've been replaced." He waved. "Hey there, honey doll. Think you could you drop me off at the Dixie Star if it's on your way?" He smiled his professional smile.

She melted. What didn't Mom like about this hunk, she wondered. She's jealous. His white shirt was brilliant against the rippled magenta sky. His hat was pushed back and framed his beautiful face. Whatta doll. She sighed.

One eyebrow up and a sly smile on his face, he asked, "Where's the man of the house tonight?"

"Luis? He's in the shower getting ready to go out with my b-... with Baxter. You met Baxter and his sister, Penny, the other day." She stepped into the truck and leaned out the open door. "Do you need him?"

"Nah, just askin'." Coleman reached out and petted Miranda's hair.

Her hair was straightened and hung longer and swung like a thick curtain. The smooth look took a lot of work, and was reserved for special occasions. She called, "Come on, get in. Where did you say you're headed," her head in a flirtatious tilt.

Bud stepped up into the passenger seat. He gave no direction but cooed, "My, my, don't you look all beautiful tonight? I love your hair. So thick. Gorgeous." He reached to pet her hair from her crown, down to her mid back.

145

Miranda beamed and blushed. She tipped her head back to elegantly shake the hair from her shoulders. She settled herself, clicked her seat belt and turned the key in the ignition. When she turned her head to the right to back the truck, her face brushed against Bud's. He moved his mouth to meet her lips. His kiss was soft and gentle, but the surprise and suddenness of a kiss caught her off guard. "Ooohhh!" she said, and jammed her foot on the brake. She licked her lips recognizing a taste of something sharper than mouthwash.

Coleman laughed and placed his fingers on her cheek and pulled her face to him and kissed her again. The kiss paled her practice kisses into her pillow. Her heart thumped blood and heat to her entire body, although her head felt light and heavy at the same time.

Bud slid closer to her, and in one motion took her hand from the steering wheel and placed it on his left shoulder. He turned off the ignition. Only the illumination of the interior lights remained. His right hand slid around Miranda's small waist. She noted the keys dangling wildly. Her heart beat as wildly. He kissed her again and tipped her teeth with his tongue. Her eyes popped open to see Bud's eyes squeezed closed. She decided she was in a serious situation, and should act the part. He still wore his wide brimmed hat which limited her caresses to the short hair on the back of his neck. She closed her eyes and ran her fingernail around the top of his collar, a technique learned from the innumerable TV kisses she'd studied. He pulled her closer and ran his hand against her skin, skimming over the elastic of her bra. Miranda's head was spinning. Her head fell back from his kiss.

"Wow." She laughed and covered her lips with her hand. She grabbed his fingers tracing around her waist line. She looked at Bud from under her lids and said, "Probably we shouldn't be doing this."

"Wow' is right. You're eighteen, right, Randa?" He looked into her eyes, willing her, *needing* her to be eighteen. She nodded. "Yes. Of course." The sky darkened around them. The outlines of his facial expressions were visible from the green light of the dash board. Friday night, Date Night had arrived.

"You've, uh, you know, you've done this before, haven't you? Like, you and Baxter, or some other guy? I thought Baxter because he hangs around here."

"No, not with Baxter, but yes," she lied into the darkness. The ghoulish green creases at Bud's smile lines stretched as he relaxed into her answer.

"Well, honey doll, should we go to somewhere we could get a little more comfortable? To the barn, or maybe, maybe my cabin, or your room?"

"I uh, don't know when Mom is coming home, and Luis's in the house." Miranda's resolve wavered. As she thought with her lips agape, Bud moved in to take advantage of the pouted lower lip and kissed her again. She hummed and leaned back. Bud jumped from the passenger seat and rounded the front of the truck breaking through the two spears of headlights. He opened her door and slid her across to the passenger seat and squeezed himself into the driver's seat. He quickly moved the bench seat back two notches to accommodate his longer legs. "I'd look for safety belts, but young lady, belts will *not* keep you safe tonight! He laughed aloud and swung his hand to rest on her thigh and playfully pinched her leg. Bud flicked off the headlights and slowly drove down the lane, minimally illuminated by the parking lights. "It's been a long time since I 'parked' but maybe we can find a nice little secluded spot. Should be fun." He turned on the radio and whistled. Miranda combed her fingers through her hair. She could think of nothing to say, she being distracted by her thumping heart. She dared to steal a look at Bud from her half closed eyes. Bud turned into a short turnoff, but Miranda said, "Oh no, not here." He pulled back to the road. A little farther down the road he nosed the truck to the right in a narrow lane. "No, not here."

"Yes, here should do all nice-like." He rocked the truck behind a stand of hedges. A ragged drapery of Spanish moss hung from a large old oak branch and hid the front windshield. He laughed under his breath. "This takes me back, but in those days we had Pop's old Nash where the seats went flat-back, but you wouldn't remember that." He smiled like a hungry wolf and slid the seat back to the rear wall. He tossed his Stetson to the dashboard and unbuckled his silver buckle. "Ahhh, that's more comfortable. Now come over here, my little dolly."

Before Miranda could answer he pulled her to his lap. He kissed her neck and nuzzled his nose under her collar. His prickly cheek made her squeal and pull her chin to her shoulder. He laughed with her and with a low, playful growling, he kissed her. She lay still, an obedient dog following unspoken orders.

He caressed her from her neck down to her crotch. His hand pressed her pubic bone, then traveled up to her jeans zipper and popped open the snap. His mouth covered hers. She whimpered. His tongue pushed against hers, pressing her toward womanhood. He forced his tongue against hers which she resisted, her own firmly pressed to the roof of her mouth. He, the expert, slid his hand against, and into her panties, she could not protest as he moved his fingers into the folds of her vulva. Her breath was pressed into his cheek.

She tried to pull back, but he held her to him, with his one long leg swung over her protesting legs. Miranda yelped and popped straight up from his lap. She protested, pulling backwards, her opened blouse exposing her baby blue, lacy bra. She did not think this is how being kissed by Bud would go. Miranda cried, "Stop Bud! You have to stop. I can't do this. Really, I'm sixteen and I never did this before." Her tears flowed.

Bud stopped. He sat back hard on his seat and banged his head against the head rest. He exhaled a long and loud burst of breath. He turned and scowled. "You're not eighteen, like you said?"

His words were more like a threat than a question. She sniffed and shook her head, seeking privacy behind her loosened hair. Tears flowed over her bitten lips. Through uneven sobs, she made busying motions of straightening and closing her blouse, wiggling out of his lap, and re-snapping her jeans.

Bud clucked his teeth as he re-buckled his belt in exaggerated, dramatic movements. He pushed Miranda to the passenger seat, and whispered in measured words, "Miranda, I'll drive to the Dixie Star, and you can drive home. I'll catch a ride back later. Thanks for the ride, you sweet thing. No hard feelings?" She recognized that the tone of his voice was not as friendly as his words. She looked down at her shaking hands and pushed her full weight into the passenger door to be as small and far from the man in the driver's seat as possible.

Bud squinted at the dark road split by headlights. He ruminated. "She's under eighteen and the daughter of where I'm sleeping at. Shit. It's me all over again! How can I clean this up?" He frowned and drove in silence. Miranda was silent except to indicate his destination dead ahead on the left. He pulled into the roadhouse's lit-up parking lot where groups of girlfriends and stags were calling greetings, pressing out smokes, and entering the Dixie Star, singly and in couples. Country music poured from the dark interior each time the doors opened. Small, sparkling lights lit the dark interior. Bud drawled, "You okay, Darlin'?" Not waiting for an answer, he opened his door and stepped out of the truck. He pressed against the lump in his jeans, re-tucked his shirt then straightened. He clapped his Stetson on his head, cocked it down over his eyebrows, and started into Dixie Star's night life. He crossed the lot behind the tail lights, stopped and spun back to the truck, calling to get her attention before she drove away. "Randa? Randa?" he called, waving and chasing her for six loping paces. She heard her name, blinked back burning tears and stopped the truck. Bud arrived at the already open passenger window, leaned both arms on the door, half inside the car, and smiled his best cheek-pleating smile. "Randa, when you go home, I wonder if you'd do me a big, big favor. Go into Bumble's stall and make sure she isn't wearing any bridle tonight. I wouldn't want the leather to rub her face. Would you do that for me? Be sure she doesn't have any hot or tender spots to make her uncomfortable before the big race. Maybe you can pet her and talk to her a little. Maybe teach her a little trick, huh? Spend some time with her to keep her calm. Tomorrow's the big day. Thank you, Sweet Thing. Get home safe, now."

Bud did not wait to see her agree. Maybe now he'd be rid of her, the little bitch. After delivering his request, he burned a path into the Dixie Star.

Chapter 14

MIRANDA'S TASK

Luis tapped on Miranda's door. He leaned into the triangle of yellow light from the hall lighting up the acorn-
topped posters of her bed. He was surprised to see his sister's sleeping form under blankets, although he couldn't
make out her head among her clutter of assorted sizes,
shapes and colors of pillows. "Hey Randa, why are you in
bed already? It's not even nine thirty." The tone of his voice
showed concern. He stepped into her room. "Are you sick
or something?"

She lifted her head to peer through teary eyes at Luis's
silhouette. "What? I thought you went out hours ago." She
flipped around for a full-on look at her brother.

"Nah, I had to do some baseball card organizing.
Business stuff. Baxt is coming to get me in about twenty
minutes."

She sniffed, "What's so important that couldn't wait 'til
tomorrow? Or are you doing a bed check for Mom?"

"Randa, we have to talk. This is nothing about Mom."
Luis watched the floor, stepping between articles of her
peeled off underwear strewn on her carpet. "You're a real
mess for a girl, you know. No wonder Mom bawls you out."
He sat on the foot of her bed as she sat up, pushed at a tear
and pulled her knees to her chin.

"Shit, Luis, if you came in here to yell at me, then you can go to hell." She scrubbed at her tangled hair. She leaned past her brother to grab a tissue from the bedside box. She dabbed at her nose and swiped her sleeve across her cheek.

"I came by your room at eight, but you were gone—with the truck. Randa, you know Mom grounded you."

"I guess she's not doing a good job, huh?" Miranda sniffed. She grabbed a ruffled pillow and whacked her brother. She kicked against Luis's bottom. "Move. Get off my bed. Get out of here, Luis."

He stood to go, but leaned in for a better look at his sister. "Have you been crying?" He leaned back a bit, knowing that crying girls were trouble.

"No, smart guy. I'm allergic to you and you make my eyes water. Now get out of here."

"I'm sorry Randa, but seriously, I have, we all have a huge problem. It's about Bumble. Did Coleman tell you about Bumble being a twin? About her hind white sock?"

"No, we have better things to talk about." She snickered, and rubbed her tissue under her nose.

Luis ignored her response, busy in his own head. "I'm suspicious of Coleman, beyond his drinking, which I don't think Mom knows about. I've been putting his wild ravings together and I think Bumble B is a twin. And the single difference between her and the sister is the height of the left rear sock, which Coleman told me, but I didn't know he was talking about this horse. Who do you know who is crazy nuts about keeping his horse's hind pasterns covered? Huh?" Tapping Miranda's head he called, "Hello in there?" She looked up as Luis sat back on his heels. "Bumble's hind

154

legs are always wrapped. Who knew? I wondered if twin Thoroughbreds are as rare as ol' drunk Coleman says they are, so I figured I'd look for information on Mom's computer. Come on, get up, I want to show you."

"Now?"

"Yes, now." Luis led the way downstairs to Patrizia's office, sat at the computer and kicked it up. He turned on the overhead light and pointed for Miranda, who padded behind him, barefooted, to drag the side chair next to the computer screen. "Scoot closer so you can see better. Look. Sure enough, among a whole bunch of veterinary medical articles on twin Thoroughbreds, there's a little story. Look here." He pointed to the screen. A photo with the sign of Prescott Acres hung on a white fence. The second photo was of a laughing old man in sunglasses, sitting in a wheelchair with an arm around the neck of each twin foal as one little horse nibbled his ear. "Here, Randa, look at this, 'Live, perfect, twin foals were born in Elmont, New York, with the solitary difference between them being their hind socks.'" Luis's elbows on his knees, he dropped his head to his hands and spoke to the floor. "Born in 1997 would mean those little foals would now be ready for all the races for two-year-olds. To be precise, the Sterling Bridle Sweepstakes. I wonder if that's a race limited to maidens. If so, Bumble hasn't raced yet, and doesn't have a tattoo."

"Oh, Look! There's Bud in the background." Miranda giggled and pointed to the screen. "He's a little blurry, but that's him alright." Her heart thrilled with the discovery of the handsome brute, but instantly morphed to cold stone with the recall of his recent behavior. She followed with,

"Never mind." After a moment of somber introspection she watched Luis scrolling through articles about Prescott Acres. She sat straight, focusing her puffy red eyes. "Okay, Stupid, you've got my attention. What are you talking about? What do twins from New York have to do with this Maryland horse?" Miranda swiped a rubber band from her mom's desktop tray of paperclips and rubber bands, and pulled her hair back to a low ponytail. She hugged a throw pillow from her mom's chair. "Start talking. What's this about a rear sock?" She noticed Luis's expression and said, "Boy, I can see this is going to be good. Let's hear it."

"Miranda? Didn't Coleman say anything to you about the twin horses and their rear socks?" She spoke her 'no' with her mouth in an exaggerated silent pronunciation. Luis flopped back into the chair and addressed the office ceiling. He described the drunken lecture he'd received from Bud in the bar. "Coleman and Prescott are hiding something. Why else would there be all the mystery and anger? I don't know why they'd switch horses. I wonder what the other twin's name is."

Luis bolted straight up. He hit the desk top with his fist. "That's it! Bud wasn't saying something about a 'witch.' Boy, am I ever stupid! He said 'switch.' Hey! And I'll bet those damned black flecks in the water walk are whatever he uses to cover the white sock of that horse. What could it be? Paint? Something black and waxy—sort of pasty. Shoe polish? Black shoe polish! That would explain why the flecks were always there after Bumble's early morning exercise and never there after I changed out the water. I saw a can of black polish in his back pocket, but never thought about it. I mean, like why would I? Other than he doesn't wear black shoes or boots."

Miranda shrugged, showing her palms to the ceiling. "What does shoe polish have to do with anything?" She tucked her heels under her hips on the seat cushion, waiting for an explanation.

"I'll bet that's why Bud insists on privacy when he used the water walk." His eyes widened. "That's why he was so nuts when I tried to fix up Bumble's sock wrap that day he slammed me around. He uses black polish, or something like it to cover Bumble B's taller left rear sock so she'd pass for the other twin—or whatever the hell he's up to. Coleman about confessed everything, but he was drunk and doesn't remember it, and how was I supposed to know he was talking about Bumble B as a twin?"

Miranda asked, "Why wouldn't he use hair dye on the leg? Easier, and you have to do it once."

Hell, I don't know. Maybe dye stays on too long and he needs to keep part of the white sock covered for this one week, then the race." Luis rubbed his head. "I'll tell you one thing. I'd hate to be the one with my head down by Bumble B's feet, applying dye OR shoe polish. You'd get brained." Luis flopped back on the chair. He turned off the computer. The only sound in that moment was the sound of the scales falling from his eyes.

"That explains why Bud's so fired up about the change in jockeys. You should have heard him on the phone." Luis looked at Miranda's face, "Bud told the guy on the other end of the phone that this Ticky Bartholomew, has ridden the *real* Prescott's Pride. Hell, I thought "pride" was another word for what Mr. Prescott felt for his favorite horse. How're you supposed to know? How can I find out the name of the other horse?"

Miranda answered, "It sounds like the other horse's name *is* Prescott's Pride. Maybe there's a registry in Maryland for Thoroughbred's names."

"Yeah, I'll look it up when I get back from being out with Baxt, later tonight." Luis jumped up from his seat. "Damn. I need to figure this out. You've got to admit that 'Prescott's Pride' is kind of a dumb name, but, hell, anything goes for a Thoroughbred's name. I also don't get why all the hocus-pocus about switching horses. If that's what happened."

Randa rallied with adult knowledge. "Well, Mom says when you can't understand something, you know, like when things don't add up, then the reason is always love or money."

Luis leaned his elbows on his knees and looked up to Miranda's face. "Love or money, huh? Okay, what are we talking about here? How about prestige and power? Like the Kentucky Derby next year and the Triple Crown for three-year-olds? Coleman wouldn't be able to switch the horses if they'd already gotten their tattoos. Unless of course, if their numbers are consecutive and the checker isn't careful. Why would he be? Who would look past the first four numbers in a spitty upper lip of a horse who is tossing her head?"

Luis looked to Miranda. She shrugged and asked, "Have you looked for a tattoo?"

"Holy crap. Can you see me getting caught poking around in Bumble's mouth? Coleman would kill me. I mean, he scares me. I don't know who's worse; the horse or the trainer." Bewilderment left his voice as it leapt to accusation, "I don't know how you can be so cozy with him. Something about him stinks, Randa. And I don't mean his alcohol breath. Mom's right."

Baxter knocked on the kitchen door and called, "Luis, you ready?"

"Yeah, come on in. I'm in Mom's office."

Miranda straightened as if hit by a bolt of electricity. "God! Luis! I don't want Baxter to see me like this." Her hands flew to her hair then pulled the low neck of her circus nightshirt to her throat as if she were a modest Victorian woman covering her nakedness. She ran to the back stairs, hissing insults to Luis as she exited.

Luis followed her, watching her bare feet flash pink soles as they carried her upstairs. He laughed at the sight of her, then called to her back, "If Bud has switched horses, he's defrauding the race and running the wrong horse." She disappeared into the dark at the top of the stairs. He continued to himself, "Defrauding would disqualify the horse. Maybe old man Prescott would try to cheat Mom out of her boarding money too. Oh, God. Could he do that? We'd go out of business. Mom's already spent some of the Prescott money, like on Dad's radiology bills and for our shirts and caps. This would kill her."

Baxter walked into the office. Luis snapped his lips shut to not divulge any money problem with the family business. "Hey Baxt, I'll be out in two minutes. Take a cupcake from the table. I'm right behind you." Baxter exited through the kitchen, scooping a cupcake, while Luis dashed upstairs to finish his thought.

Miranda sat on her bedside, tangling her fingers through her hair. She looked up. "So, Luis, what do you want me to do? Am I supposed to cozy up to big, mean Coleman and get information? Then what? You gonna report the switch? Mom loses the money? Perfect, Luis." She let two beats go by. "You know about Mom selling her Beetle?"

"Yeah, but she's sick about selling that car of hers, so don't say anything to her about it," he answered and kicked Miranda's flopped-over boot.

Miranda frowned at her boot landing across the room. "Yeah, you're right. She has no idea about Thoroughbred twins or any problem. How could she?"

Luis heaved his shoulders. "Anyway, I'm going out with your boyfriend. I've got pre-race jitters. If Mom asks, we'll be down at Gringo's Bar & Grill, girl watching. Don't worry about Baxter. He's already hen-pecked. I'll be home by midnight. Sorry you're crying. Goodnight."

Miranda called after him, "Don't you dare tell Baxt anything about me crying or why I'm grounded. Luis? I mean it." She slid off the bottom of her bed hollering a threat, "I'm warning you. Don't you dare tell Baxter I've been crying."

Miranda listened for the slam of the kitchen door and the hum of Baxter's Escalade, then flopped back on her bed considering the story she'd been told. "It's too fantastic." She popped up to finish her plan and kicked her feet to the floor. "Guess I should have a look at somebody's rear sock. Mom should be in on this. Oh shit! I almost forgot to obey his highness's order to go in to the stall to remove Bumble's bridle and to teach his pony a trick." She bent and sifted through the heap of worn and flung clothing at the foot of her bed. She tugged on her running shorts. "That horse and I need to have a little talk. Maybe I should take a pot of tea and two tea cups so we two girls can have a nice sophisticated little chat. Heck, I could read her tea leaves. Aaare yooouuu a twinnn?" She pulled the sleeveless top over her head, and pulled on her boots."

Miranda knocked on her mother's bedroom door to no response. Peeking into the orderly room she remarked aloud, "Oh, I forgot, she's a Country Cutie tonight. I'll bring her up to date on Luis's story tomorrow." Thunder obscured her words spoken to her mom's empty bedroom.

Miranda ran downstairs and into the kitchen seeking an apple for her horse-new-best-friend. "Damn, a whole horse farm and I can't find an apple when I need one," and slammed the refrigerator door. She noticed large peaches and pears in a bowl on the table, and plucked a pear from the still life. "Let's see if the mystery horse likes pears." She took a cupcake for herself and dashed to the barn as a new storm lit up the sky and rumbled long and with authority. "Good grief. Another storm."

Barney met her at the barn door, wagging his tail, glad for the company. She flipped on the overhead lights and tapped the dog's head. "Hiya Barney, yeah, I know, more rain and lots of noise. Here, finish this cupcake." The dog was accommodating.

"Hiya, Gingerfoot, sorry girlfriend. Noisy and scary, huh? Hiya, Donkey Boy, Paley's Comet, how's business?" The two ignored Miranda's unusual nighttime trip to the barn. She banged her heels into the floor, and clumped quickly to Bumble's stall. The young horse was pacing in her large, square stall.

She greeted the Thoroughbred. "There you are, my Black Beauty. Look what I have for you." She spoke to the horse and held the pear on the flat of her hand over the top of the stall's Dutch door. The velvety upper lip rolled the pear from the proffered palm. Miranda inhaled the horse's warm body heat and smiled at her beauty. Thunder rumbled the barn as Bumble stood at the gate and chewed.

Miranda's attention was directed to the overhead loft as straw and dust fell, not drifting, but urgently, as snows falls in a blizzard. Bumble backed, shaking her head, where straw had dropped to her face, mane and neck. The rain pounded. Wind whipped, ripping at a corner of the barn's metal roof with a shrill whistling sound.

"Yikes, what was that?" She looked up to the loft where a tumbled bale lay catty-corner across the slatted floor. Above the bale was a wet wall, dark with rain. "Oh boy, Mom's going to flip when she sees this new problem." She opened the bottom Dutch door and entered Bumble's stall, and keeping a distance from the horse, made a visor of her hand to shield her eyes from the falling straw. "Why is all this straw raining down all of a sudden? I wonder if I should move you to another stall."

162

Bumble B vocalized as straw slid from the loft and on to her rump and her back. Lightning cracked, followed by closer, louder thunder.

To make the best of her time in the stall Miranda cooed, "Okay, you-horse-with-a-secret, as long as I'm right here, let's see who you are." The horse tracked backwards, turned her head, warily watching from one eye.

"How can I find a lip tattoo if you walk away and hide your head?" Miranda brushed straw from the horse's head. She cooed and slipped her fingers under the brown leather bridle and started to unhook the buckle when the horse put her ears back and jerked her head upwards. "Yeeeow!" The sudden momentum of the horse pulled Miranda from her feet. The bridle's old leather ripped apart in her hand. She staggered forward, landing on her knees. Her heart pounded when she saw her proximity to the flighty horse. She bounced up to her feet. Still holding to the shredded leather of the bridle she nervously looked up and said a sardonic, "Oh, good. That was easy." Feeling defeated, she jumped from the stall, emphasis paid to securely closing the door behind her. She scurried to the desk, dropped the torn bridle and waited for the storm to calm. Another clap of thunder shook the barn. She ducked her head. "Oooh, that was close. I wonder if we're hit. Nah, I guess not. Thanks Dad for having the rods installed."

Within ten minutes, spent talking to and petting Barney, the storm calmed. The pear gone, the horse faced Miranda again. Straw no longer fell from the loft. "Bumble, my dear, I won't need to move you if this storm stays gone. So, let's have a look at your upper lip." Not knowing her

163

words were prophetic she said, "It's now or never, old girl." Miranda returned to the stall, opened the low door and moved toward the horse. She slipped her arm under the horse's neck and reached up to hold her face in the crook of her arm. Miranda rubbed the black flat cheek, her nose and mouth, working up to the moment she would roll up the horse's lip to look for the tattoo. She laid her cheek next to the horse's face and spoke sweet, soothing sounds to her. Bumble pulled away, complaining at being held. The black beauty whinnied and reared up, curling her front feet high. The sharp hooves came down on Miranda.

Chapter 15

IN THE BARN

After piled-high hamburgers and Gringo's famous fried onion rings, Luis tried to appear cheerful. He was on vacation from money problems at home. Staring into the brown foam of his thick milk shake, he hoped his gallant effort to sell off his most expensive baseball cards would put a dent in his mom's financial worries. The packaged baseball cards, ready for sale, were wrapped and set atop his dresser. He'd miss all those young athletes' smiling faces looking out from the display case in his room.

He laughed aloud and cheered for the karaoke singers when he saw a blur of blond hair across the dark room. At the same moment Baxter saw the yellow cloud and started to call Luis's attention to Ashley draped over Matthew Harrison, but put on his brakes. Luis said, "Yeah, she's out of town all right. I'm such a loser for believing her. Baxt, too bad I'm not a real drinker, because this situation is like a sad sack country song."

Baxter slapped Luis's back and sang a made-up tune covered by the karaoke's loud speakers, but effective in Luis's ear, "My frizzy headed girl, With egg-yolk-colored curl, Done gone off and out the door, Cause she don't love me any morrrre." Both looked down to their plates and chuckled at Baxt's spontaneous rhymes.

Luis felt the vibe, swung his arm around Baxter's shoulder in the manner of a drunk, and continued the sad ballad. The rotating glittering globe stood in for a full moon as Luis howled, "It's more than ah can take. Ohhh, barkeep, send another chocolate shake … Mah woman is flying on her broom … She's up there on that moon!" As they laughed at their own wit, Luis's left shoulder was bumped from the rear. He turned to see Matthew Harrison escorting the stumbling Ashley from the bar.

She was well past needing to be taken home, but recognizing Luis, Ashley gushed, "Oh hiii, Louie." Her nose was two inches from his. Luis looked up in surprise at Matthew standing over him, holding onto Ashley's arm, preventing her fall into Luis's lap.

Both boys, with mouths hanging open, watched the young couple exit Gringo's. Baxter spoke first. "Somebody must be sporting a fake ID."

Luis said, "No lie. I'm pretty shocked. They sat back and laughed. Luis took a deep breath, laid his hand across his heart and sang along to the ending of "My Maria" now being sung by three girls up on the stage, arms around each other's waists, all rocking side to side, "Oh Ashleee, … like a ship sailing on the sea, … Oh Ashleee, my mom will be *so* disappointed in me …

The song ended, the singers laughed, handed the mic back to the cheery disc jockey and left the stage. The beer-bellied man announced the next song would be the much sung old standby, "Bohemian Rhapsody." The boys looked up to the stage to see St. John singing with a tall, thin waitress, with much enthusiasm, swaying, cheek to cheek, hip to hip, sharing one mic, their lips a mere kiss apart. His round lenses were opaque with blue and gold reflecting the lights of the twirling ceiling ball. St. John laughed when he recognized Luis and Baxter. After his song he grabbed the neck of his beer bottle by two fingers and joined the fellows.

"Hey, how goes it, Smitt's Water Walk Farm?" St. John straddled a backwards chair.

Luis teased, "Well, aren't you full of surprises? And you sing too?"

"Yep, it's a good way to meet the girls." St. John indicated by lifting his bottle toward the singing partner waitress. He winked at her and took a gulp of his beer.

Luis repeated, "A good way to meet girls, Baxter," and both laughed again.

St. John spoke. "Say Luis, tomorrow's the big race, huh? How about I come by in the morning to get a few pictures of loading the horse in her truck for her trip up to Tampa Bay? I'll get a Before picture at the farm and the After photo of her in the winner's circle."

"Yeah, sure, why not." Luis and Baxt looked into their empty milkshake glasses and decided to get going. They'd stretched their disposable income keeping them in their seats, listening and joining in with the karaoke until almost midnight. Luis called over his shoulder to St. John, "Hey Jonesie, make sure you're plenty early."

St. John now stood with his arm around the slender waitress's shoulder. She giggled and pulled her shoulder to her ear as he leaned in to whisper. "'Early' tomorrow will be too early."

Luis and Baxter reviewed their requirements for their ideal girlfriends as they drove back to Smitt's farm. Luis coaxed Baxter to come to the barn to see the new repair job he'd done on Gingerfoot's floor. As the friends stepped from Baxter's SUV, rain hit heavy, straight and noisy. The sudden storm puddled the tire ruts in the soil and shot into the collected rain in the upturned feed bucket left by the barn door. The boys dashed for cover. Hearing Bumble's complaint through the barn doors, Luis said, "Oh, there goes our problem child. Guess the storm upset her again."

His aggressive push against the barn door met resistance. "What the H … ? We're getting soaked in the pounding rain and the barn door won't open." He gave the door a second hard shove and slapped into the rear of Bumble B. "Shit! What's this horse doing out of her stall? Who turned on the lights?" He looked at the horse and asked, "How did you get out of your bridle?"

"Quick, Baxt hand me that blue nylon bridle on the wall right next to you." Baxter followed instructions. Both cats ran from the boys' path. Bumble whinnied and backed away from the boys, stopping by the bench and wall phone where Luis was able to slip a bridle onto her head.

Luis turned to Baxter. "At least I know what to do this time. Grab a pasture blanket to throw on her back from the posts over there. That trick calmed her during the last storm."

Luis threw the blanket onto the horse's back and walked her to stall number seven. He stopped at the door where Miranda lay in a heap, her head partially covered by kicked-up straw. Her hair was spread, covering her face. Luis was stricken with shock.

He called in a high, panicky voice, "Miranda, what the hell are you doing here?" She did not respond. "Baxter, come quick! It's Randa. She's, she's been trampled. Be careful. The damned horse is still out of her stall." A rebellious whinny proved Luis's words.

A second horse blanket fell to the floor from Baxter's loosened grasp. He stood with his limp arms and useless hands hanging by his side. "Luis? Is she, is she dead?"

Luis croaked, "I don't know if she's knocked out or ... I can't get this stupid horse to settle down. She's too wild for me to get close. I'll try to get her backed into the straw storage area across from her stall. Baxter, pull Miranda out of Bumble's stall by her boots. Call as soon as she's clear."

Lightning lit the stall. Thunder followed within seconds. Luis windmilled his arms at the horse, hollering her back into the corner, where she was surrounded by stacked bales of straw. Simultaneously, Baxter bent down and pulled Miranda free of the stall. "She's out!"

Luis threatened, both fists in the air, "Damned horse, get back, get back." The filly backed into the bales but clipped Luis's flailing arm, shoulder and chest the second his head was turned to see if Baxter had Miranda pulled from the stall. The force of the hit sent Luis backpedaling. He landed on his backside with such force his hat flew from his head. He pulled his knees to his chest and squeezed his eyes shut in anticipation of a further beating. Bumble, ears forward and tail high, nonchalantly, passed Luis and trotted into her own stall. She nosed into her feed basket. Baxter jumped up and slammed the stall's half door. The horse whinnied her discontent at the storm and at being corralled.

"Good. Thanks Baxter." Luis rested his forehead on the wall. He pulled in a painful breath. "Baxt, Bumble got me too." He lay still for a moment, then rolled to regard his sister. Randa had purple bruises and dried sprays of blood on her disfigured face, and her shirt. She appeared to be sleeping, although there was no air left in her. Blood no longer pumped through her broken body.

Blood trickled from under Luis's cuff and puddled in his open hand. He leaned over Miranda's face feeling for her exhaled breath. He kneeled and looked up with a sick expression. His hands dropped to his lap. "Oh God! How could things have gotten worse? She's gone, Baxt. She's dead." Both young men sat on their heels in silence and stared at Miranda. Her eyes stared, unfocused. Luis placed his fingers on her eye lids to close them, but the lids refused to close.

Luis bent over his sister, too devastated to cry. Without looking away from his sister, he called, "Baxter, let's wrap her in the pasture blanket. I have to think, I have to think." He squeezed his eyes shut and kissed her face.

"Baxt, lead Gingerfoot out of her stall and into stall five. She's gentle. I need to get back into her stall." Baxter followed the instruction and returned to Luis. Pull Miranda over here. Help me for God's sake." Luis squeezed the cuff of his blood- soaked left shirt sleeve to stem the new evidence of his injury. He said, surprised at his conclusion, "Christ, Baxter, I can't stop the bleeding."

"Lou, I gotta get going."

"You can't go. I need your help, Baxter. And this has to be a secret."

"How can you keep this a secret? Luis? Are you crazy?"

"Yes, Baxter. Yes, I'm crazy now, but I have to do this. Come back, Baxt. How can I do this by myself? I need you to help me hide her. Nobody would ever look under the new floor. I replaced the floor boards yesterday, after the storm. The hammer and box of nails are still in the feed room on the refrigerator. Come on Baxt, I'm bleedin' to death. Please, give me a hand."

Baxter stifled a sob. His hand covered his face and his shoulders shook. He returned with the hammer and nails. He stage-whispered, "Christ, Luis, I can't stay here. She's dead. What are you going to do?" Not waiting for an answer, Baxter collapsed into sobs. He fell to his knees leaning over Miranda's body. "Miranda, ohhh, Miranda." He stroked a swath of her thick, dark hair pulled through his fingers.

"Baxt, what are you worried about? You didn't do anything wrong. The damned friggin' horse ... the horse did it." Luis crumbled forward with his hands grasping his knees. "Oh God I can't even say it. The damned horse killed her. You're not in any trouble. You helped me. You got her out of the stall when I was getting a pounding. You're a hero for God's sake. You saved my life by being here." He grunted as he wrenched three pale new boards from the floor.

Baxter said no more. He saw the orange extension cord with the attached light bulb hanging from a hook inside the barn door. He grabbed the cord and flung it to Luis. "Here, Louie, this will help."

The firm rubberized cage surrounding the light bulb caught the back of Luis's head. Luis rubbed his head, "Ya' jerk, are ya trying to kill me?" Luis jumped up, with his left arm hanging loose. His other hand reached and grabbed Baxter by his collar. He squeezed and shook. Luis's nose was two inches from Baxter's as Baxt pulled back as far as he could from the choking clutch.

Baxter called, "Louie, Luis. Quit it! You're killing me too." Baxt stumbled backwards and landed against the rough boards of a stall. He consoled his neck and warily regarded his best friend, now a stranger, from a safe distance.

Luis saw himself through the eyes of a horrified observer. He whispered, "Look at me. I'm trying to kill my best friend." Ashamed to face Baxter, he turned his back, shook himself and eased to sit on a bale of straw. He struggled to extend his hand for a forgiving hand shake, but winced and dropped the arm to his lap. "Baxt. I'm sorry. I'm so, so sorry. I'm a mad man. Forgive me." He soberly said, "You've always been my best friend, since, since, well, forever. Please forgive me. I almost hurt you, my best friend."

"Dammit, Lou. Let me get your mother."

"No, not tonight. You wouldn't understand because you don't know the story about Coleman and this devil horse. I couldn't tell you before. Mom'll freak. I can tell her tomorrow after the race but not tonight." Lightning lit the grisly scene on the barn floor. Thunder sounded. "Baxt, I need your help." Luis's voice cracked as he gasped to catch his breath. He rubbed his head where the light bulb's cage had hit him, and with his geriatric shuffle moved to the space where he'd removed floor boards. In agony, leg by leg, angled himself to drop four feet to the barn's crawl space. He swung his arms wide, like the crucified Christ, his hands sweeping across the floor to prevent himself from crumbling onto the dirt. "Help me slide her into this space. I'll have to back up to fit her in."

Luis gasped his instructions. "I'll need you to get a bucket of water and soap. We've got to clean up that blood on Bumble's floor." Luis wiped his forehead with the back of his sleeve. More to himself he mumbled, "What am I going to do about Bumble's blood stained feet and the wraps?"

"I should go for your mom," Baxter said, wringing his hands.

"We can't. We just can't. Maybe they'd bar the horse from the race if they find out she trampled someone. Mom is depending on Prescott's money. Besides, Mom gets a fat bonus when that horse wins, and you know she'll win.

"I'll tell Mom that Randa has gone to your sister's for an overnight for some dumb girl thing. Mom will be relieved she's away from Coleman. Believe me, I know. Of course, she'll be mad that Miranda disobeyed, but that's nothing new. We can't let any reason to prevent Bumble from running, but it puts off me telling her the truth." He sucked in a deep sob, but recovered his demeanor of control, instruction and work to be done. He touched his injured rib cage. Slumping in the hole, he dropped his head on his arms folded on the floor. He fought blood loss and was too weary to lift his head.

"Hiding Miranda here is until the race is over. A few hours. Only a few hours. I swear I don't know what else to do." Luis cried, "I'm so goddam scared and hurting so much

I can't think straight. He stood, half out of the hole, wiped his face leaving a smear of mud and blood across his forehead, nose and cheek. He looked back at his sister's form in the green blanket. Luis ducked back into the hole to prepare an even, flat place for his sister. His voice was weak. "Baxt, you grab that end of the blanket, and I got this side. Pull." The two heaved and pulled. Luis groaned from pain and exhaustion. He blubbered, "I'm cooked. I'll never get away with this. But, what am I supposed to do?" He tightened the cuff at the new trickle of blood and gave over to outright crying. Bumble was silent except for some nervous tip-tapping of her front hooves on the bloody straw-strewn floor.

"Okay, Baxt, help me pull her over here." The two tugged at Miranda's dead weight. "Oh God, I'm too done in to lift her down. Oh my God, Baxter. This is impossible. Roll her over to me. I'll pull her feet in first."

They struggled. Randa's feet and legs took up the space of the removed floor. Luis crawled backwards under the floor and tugged her body onto the soil. Baxter stood above looking down, slack expression, slack arms by his side.

Luis rolled Miranda to her side and straightened her legs. He touched her broken face and smoothed back her hair. He tucked the blanket lovingly around her head and over her face. He started to leave her, then turned back to her and whispered, "I'm so sorry, Randa. What were you doing in the stall?" His words came between sobs. "I'll come back for you. Soon." He put his head on his sister's shoulder and cried. "Don't be afraid. This is just for tonight, Miranda. I won't leave you here, I promise."

"Luis, for God's sake what's taking so long? Do you want to get caught?" Baxt called, pressing his rolled knuckles into his eyes like a crying child.

"Help me out, Baxt." Baxter, also weakened from fear, struggled to get Luis above the floor.

Luis slumped to his knees on the barn floor. "Baxter, can you hammer those nails in the same holes I made before? I'm too unsteady to hammer. I'll clean up the bloody straw." Luis limped to Bumble's stall. He grabbed the bridle on her elegant head, and swearing oaths to the horse of what was in store for her, he led her to the curry stall where he secured her in place.

Luis noticed the rear leg wraps were falling off Bumble's hind legs and lay in a small soiled heap, in the curry stall, out of his reach. "Poor, stupid horse is so nervous she's been chewing at her wraps." Using the handle of the straw rake, wincing with the difficulty, he was able to retrieve the blackened bandage from the floor. He brought the gauze, stained with greasy black smears to his nose to see if the stain was blood. "It's the same stuff that was smeared in the tub and was speckled on Gingerfoot's back and haunches during her first water walk." He frowned, then brought the material to his nose again. "Yup, that's it. Shoe polish!"

He pulled two large black plastic bags to lucky-number-seven stall and raked the stained straw from the wide aisle between the stalls into the garbage bags as Baxter hammered. Baxter straightened, after pounding the nails back into the fresh planks. He interrupted Luis's rumination. "Okay Louie, what else?"

"Come here a second, Baxt, and tell me, what's this black smeary stuff on the leg wrap?"

Baxter examined the black streaks on the soiled gauze. "It's familiar, but I can't place it. Where'd you get it?"

"I think it's shoe polish, and part of the horse's leg wrap."

"You're right. It is shoe polish." Baxter handed the bandage back to Luis, who stuffed the material into his back pocket. "Why shoe polish on a leg wrap?"

Luis spoke in a hoarse whisper, "Don't know. I still have some figuring out to do. In the meantime, take these bags in your trunk and dump them where no one will find them and ask about bloody straw, and where no animals will drag the stuff out of the bag. Can you think of a safe dumping place?"

"Yeah, I'll do it," he mumbled without looking up. "Mom'll kill me if there's even one dust particle of straw in the Escalade, but I'll manage it."

"Hey, Baxter, Go home. Go straight home. Check to see if you have any blood on you." Baxter stopped mid-step. The thought that he might have blood on him hadn't occurred to him. He examined both arms, turning them over. He checked his chest and swiped dust from his dungaree knees, and shoes.

"No, I don't see any blood. Do you?" He turned around for Luis to inspect his back, but Luis dropped his head, too weary to look up.

"Baxter, go home before the storm comes up again. And shut up." If anyone asks, say you were with me, that you dropped me off at the barn, like you did, because I had

176

to check up on Bumble, because of the storm. Don't mention Miranda, unless you say the truth: that she didn't go out with us tonight. Baxt, tell the truth, like how we went in your car to Gringo's Grill, like we did. Plenty of people saw us. You don't have to lie. Go ahead, Baxter. Thanks, man, you saved my life. I'm so sorry. I'm so, so sorry." Luis broke down and cried again. Baxter could not understand his words, but understood the dismissing wave of Luis's arm. "Go ahead. I'll talk to you tomorrow. Go. Thanks, Baxt. It'll be over tomorrow."

Miranda's true blue eighteen-year-old boyfriend sniffed back tears and scuffed from the barn. Luis watched Baxter head for the double door, dragging the garbage bags behind him. Luis leaned against the feed room door. "Partners in crime," he whispered to himself as Baxter slammed the SUV's back door, closing in the garbage bags, and obediently drove from Smitt's Water Walk Farm. The light visible from his vehicle were random glints from the fading shots of lightning sparkling off the chrome grille.

Luis looked at his watch. After midnight—the perfect time for a crime. No new line of blood trickled from his arm. He said aloud, "Okay, Luis, old man, get this place cleaned up." He reached for the empty feed bucket and pulled himself to his feet to start work on the small pools of blood and the remaining blood-stained straw, overlooked by Baxter. He exhaled at his effort of standing, and replaced the hammer and nails to the shelf. He limped through his work, sniffing and sobbing. The thunder sounded distant and the less frequent lightning showed a pale, sad sky.

Chapter 16

MIDNIGHT

Gingerfoot, Donkey Boy, and Paley's Comet watched the events of the night without comment. Donkey Boy hee-hawed an answer to Bumble's complaint, as if to reproach the uppity Maryland horse.

After sending Baxter out with the soiled straw, Luis dumped the water bucket and made an anemic attempt to spread fresh straw. He slumped on the bench beneath the wall phone. I've gotta sit. For a minute. Sit for one minute, he thought. He dropped his head to his hands and fell into a combination of sleep and unconsciousness.

He saw Miranda unrolling the wraps from Bumble B's legs. She was singing and whistling. She was wearing her high school track shirt, her wild hair poking out of her braid. Luis watched the horse's feet kick and he heard her cry. She was five years old and sitting at the dinner table holding a balloon and pointing at her slice of birthday cake, which, she cried, was too small. Daddy was leaning over her saying, "There, there, honey."

"Luis, honey, Luis!" His head shot up. His eyes focused on his mother standing in the door way. "Luis, what the hell has happened here?"

Patrizia reached for him and laughed, "Did my eighteen-year-old son imbibe tonight? Hummm?" She interrupted his sputtering apology when she saw blood on his face and shirt. Patrizia's wide eyes saw her son's shirt covered in dry blood. As if to further her concern, a fresh thin line of blood slid from under Luis's stiff cuff into his mother's view.

Luis struggled to stand and staggered. "Mom!" He opened his eyes.

Patrizia glowered. She stood back to peruse her young son and parentally propped her hands on her hips. He remembered. His heart squeezed in pain. His mouth was dry. "Mom, oh Mom, it's Bumble B. She uh, she cut her front fetlock somehow, and I couldn't steady her in the storm. She's too wild and I couldn't examine her. I don't know. She's the jumpiest damnedest horse. Bumble and I both look worse than we are. Bud isn't answering his phone."

Patrizia put her hand on her son's head. "What is this? Cobwebs in your hair?"

"Cobwebs? Oh, I guess from when I was in Bumble's stall. I guess."

Patrizia ran to Bumble's stall, turned and came back to find the Thoroughbred in the curry stall. "There's blood on Bumble's floor and both of her front feet are blood spattered." Luis grunted and staggered backwards again.

Ohhh, God, I missed some of the blood on Bumble's floor. Shit. Oh, I'm such a jerk, how could I miss blood? I guess the filled trash bags covered it. His eyes quickly searched the floor for other evidence of the crime that had happened a mere ninety minutes earlier. He felt faint.

"Good God, Luis. You're hurt! We have to get you to the hospital. Get one of the horse's towels around your arm and get into the truck." Luis did not move. "Go ahead, Luis. Look at your shirt. Are you hurt anywhere else?"

Luis shook his head. "Mom, you don't want to do anything that would interfere with the race tomorrow. If you report this maybe Bumble would be disqualified." He hollered, "Mom, THINK! Think about it, Mom."

Luis was relieved that his mother thought the blood on the floor was his.

"What's going on here?" Both Patrizia and Luis jumped at Bud Coleman's booming voice. He stood in the light of an overhead bulb and whipped his Stetson from his head.

Luis started, "Because of the new storm tonight, I came in to check on Bumble, and, and, …. she'd cut her fetlock. I think with a hind shoe. So I rushed in to see her. It was dumb I know, but I had to see she was safe." Luis straightened and gave a wide, used car salesman smile, still grasping his shirt cuff. He frowned, but soldiered on in his story. "She gets so spooked, well everyone knows. It was the thunder again and the flashes of lightning. I grabbed her bridle but it snapped when she pulled backwards. Anyway, I couldn't do anything for her because she gave me a few good punches before I could tie her down. That's all."

Bud ran to stall seven with Luis and Patrizia right behind him. "Holy Christ, look at all this blood. Is this your blood Luis? Where the hell is my horse? Luis, where's my horse?" His shoulders rolled forward in a threat as his fingers curled into fists.

Luis backed up. "You passed her. She's in the curry stall. I put her in to calm her down. So far the narrow curry stall is all that works to calm her."

Bud swore and angrily banged his heels as he walked down the aisle of the barn. He gave a practiced instantaneous scan of the horse and yelled, "The wrap from her left foot is gone. Where's that wrap?" Bud scowled and took a step toward Luis. Luis was too weak and too tired to think. He shrugged.

Bud said aloud, more to himself than to the others, "Oh, my God. Prescott's going to kill me if this filly doesn't win tomorrow. Let me get her settled."

Patrizia noticed Ginger wasn't in her stall. "Luis, why's Gingerfoot in number five?" The question stabbed at his heart. Baxter had to move Gingerfoot and neither of them thought to return her to her own stall.

Luis bent over to think of another plausible lie. "Oh, I took her out because she wasn't used to the new floor boards. I didn't want her banging her sore feet against the wall again with tonight's storm." Was that enough of a lie to satisfy his mom and Bud? "Here, let me move Gingerfoot back. Storm's over, she'll be okay in her own stall tonight." Luis's mind raced as he forced his feet to walk to stall five. Would Ginger know Miranda's body was under the boards? Would she react?

Patrizia watched Bud examine Bumble B. He straightened and wrung his Stetson's brim in his hands. "Mrs. Smitt, is there any way I can convince you to not go to the hospital tonight? I mean, all bad press. She'd still run, because nobody got killed, after all, but I'd like to save her

182

reputation. Like all good cowboys, I keep an emergency box in the van, you know, with a few suture kits, rolls of tape, slings and Velcro splints. Would you let me have a look at your son after I get this filly put to bed?"

Luis's mouth was dry from his face-to-face with Coleman. He stood and nodded agreement to Bud's plan. "We'll go inside. I'll wash up. All the animals are settled again. Storm's over."

Patrizia supported Luis, helping him walk to the back porch and into the kitchen. "Luis if the injuries are serious, you *will* go to the hospital. I don't care about Coleman's horse or his money." She gingerly touched her son's ribs. He twisted away. "Honey, can you breathe alright, 'cause if you can't we'll go to the hospital right now."

"I can breathe, only real sore. Bleeding stopped. I'll get showered."

"Honey, be quiet so you don't wake Randa."

"Randa?" His heart shot into overdrive. "Uh-huh." He limped from the kitchen and looked over his shoulder to his mother who had turned away and was walking from him. Her heart will break. Poor Mom. She'll never get over this.

Chapter 17

RACE DAY

The sun was doing its best to bake Florida's earth dry. Luis's eyes popped open at six a.m. After a scintilla of consciousness he remembered that his sister was wrapped in a blanket under the floor of the barn. Images flitted through his throbbing head, too painful and too heavy to lift from his pillow. He groaned and unfolded his aching body. He was unable to straighten his left side. He swallowed his involuntarily whispered, "ooo's" of pain as he hobbled to the bathroom, past his mother's bedroom. Her door was still closed. Thank God, she must be still sleeping. He closed the bathroom door with his foot, and twisted the handle of the cold water spigot to cover the sound of his vomiting.

Limping back to his room, he glanced into his sister's room to see if the cluttered and messed-up bed might appear that she was still in bed. Last night was a gruesome dream. She'd be wrapped in a blanket with her arm thrown over her messy hair and her sleeping eyes. Her foot would be poking from under her coverlet. Yes, her bed was a lumpy form top to bottom, but there were no coral painted toes showing from beneath her blanket. He closed her door.

Last night after Bud closed Luis's bleeding lacerations with a variety of butterfly bandages from the first aid kit in the truck's cab, he snapped open a blue canvas sling and adjusted the white straps behind Luis's neck. This morning, with great effort Luis examined his contusions, lacerations and bruises. He hollered a loud gasp of pain as he fit his left arm through the sleeve of his red and black Smitt's tee shirt. He quieted to listen for his mother's response to his painful wail. Hearing nothing, he resettled his injured arm in the sling.

He considered his descent down the steps. He crouched to sitting on the top step and inched forward, moving his backside down, step by step, all the way to the kitchen. This had been a game when he was a child, but today there was not a shred of childhood left in him. He crept to the back porch and stood in the splendid sunshine which had now broken through the dissipating cloud cover. He cringed, working his arms, bent his knees and stretched his posture in slow increments. His head felt light, and he was not yet past the nausea.

Luis found nothing of Bud remaining in the bunk-house. One of the two kitchen chairs was a collection of sticks, a flat seat and rungs, now propped beside the kitchen counter. Folded newspapers tipped the trash basket to the floor. Dishes showed over the lip of the sink. The new bed-spread was pitched to the floor. Luis limped from the cabin to start the painful work of readying Bumble for the trip to Tampa Bay. The Prescott Acres trailer was backed up to the barn's entrance. Luis squeezed past the truck.

Bud threw the tack into the back of the cab. In his haste, the toe of his boot accidentally kicked a half empty bottle of Wild Turkey which had been set by the barn door, last to be loaded. The spinning bottle created a hollow sound, as if this were a child's kissing game. They both stood dumbfounded, and watched until Bud bent and grabbed the bottle. "The whiskey bottle never happened, right?" Bud looked around for Patrizia. "Where's your mother?"

Luis answered, "I guess she's still in bed. She's not one to be up before nine. You've cleared out of your cabin. Were you coming back after the race to even up with Mom, or are you hitting the trail right away?"

Bumble was already trailered, although the back ramp was down. She swished her tail and tapped her feet in the trailer's small space. Her hooves were cleaned of blood and her clean bright leg wraps with lime green borders showed above the padded travel wraps. She looked like a winner. Luis remembered his first view of her as he helped her from the rear of the trailer. Was that only six days ago? His exclamation when he first saw Bumble B was that she was a magnificent piece of horseflesh. She looked like the horse from the movie. Her sleek black coat glistened, her mane and tail were full, brushed, smooth and shining. Last week felt like a year ago. So much had happened. Luis's bruised heart moaned in his ribs.

"Even up, huh?" Bud sneered. He stepped up to the boy. His closeness threw a shadow across Luis's face. "Your mom is paid from Mr. Prescott. Not me." He looked around to be sure Patrizia was not in the wings. Bud turned back to Luis and grabbed him by the collar and aggressively walked him backwards shoving him up against the side of the trailer. Luis almost fainted from the rough handling.

"What the hell were you doing with Bumble B? Why were her rear wraps off? Huh? Why? Am I gonna have to tell Prescott that your mom did not provide the care she was signed to provide? Maybe she ..."

Luis was on his toes from Bud hauling him up and pinching him between the trailer and Bud's chest. Tears came to Luis' eyes. His ineffectual fists came up to Bud's face, "Look Coleman, like the last time you accused me of messing with her wraps, the damned things came off while she was busy trampling my sister. Miranda is lying dead, trampled to death by your horse. My sixteen-year-old sister is dead. Dead, because of you." He shook a trembling, damning finger at Coleman's chest. Coleman stood wordless, his jaw slack. "That's whose blood you saw. You were right. It was too much blood to be from one person."

Bud dropped Luis from his hold. His hands fell to his side. He looked at Luis's twisted expression, purple with anger. "She's dead, your sister? Randa, trampled?" He took a significant step backward and rubbed his hand across his face.

Luis touched his injured ribs and turned from Coleman. His head swam. Coleman's face drained of blood. Luis pushed for a voice of power but felt inadequate, ineffectual. Taking advantage of Coleman's surprise, he continued his tirade. "Don't get tough with me, because I doubt the Tampa Bay sheriff will lose any money if today's winning horse is euthanized." Luis's voice broke. "So, my mom will be paid the full amount. You might even brag about us when you get back to Maryland."

"Kid, I don't know what to say." He backed away, pushed his hat back on his head, and looked at the ground.

Luis jumped in, "Good, because I have plenty to say, and you'd better listen. Mom still doesn't know. I hid Miranda's body last night so you can go and win your race, pay my mom, and get the hell out of here." Luis scuttled to the barn's open door, supported himself against the outside wall with his right arm and bent forward and wretched. He wiped at his mouth and spat. "I don't know how I'm going to tell her."

Coleman stammered "Hey kid, I–I–I'm so sorry. How did this happen?" He tripped over his words, "Why was she in the … Ohhh!" He ripped his Stetson from his head. Did Miranda take him seriously when he told her to go into the stall? Did he make her go in?" He blinked, perhaps recalling his last words to her. "Oh, my God. She really went into the stall!"

Luis straightened, "What's that supposed to mean, 'she really went into the stall?'" He pulled his painful shoulders back, poked out his chest, rubbed his injured arm in the sling. He said, "Well, I'm pretty sure the authorities will know exactly what to make of this." Luis was used up by yesterday's tragedy and today's confrontation. He limped back to the porch and into the house, composing another lie to tell his mother if she were to ask about Miranda's whereabouts this morning.

Absent from Coleman's routine was the slow, patient cajoling conversation earlier exchanged in the trailering of his filly. Barney pressed into Coleman's leg. With a rude push with his foot against Barney's side, Bud growled, "Get outta here, Barney. Go." Barney moved slowly from Coleman's side.

Coleman's parting words to Bumble's hind quarters as he slammed the trailer's doors were, "You are a rat! I should have had an 'accident' with you after you busted up old Billy. You'd better win today." Bud pulled himself into the cab of the lime green truck and loudly shifted gears. He automatically lit a cigarette drawn from the pack. He sucked in a deep drag. Wasting not a word, not a minute, not a wasted movement, his immediate goal was to put Smitt's Water Walk Farm into his rear view mirror. Bud's mind was galloping, also breaking speed records.

With urgency, he left the farm in a haze of black dust. Coleman consulted himself with mumbled questions through dry lips. "Why did I tell her to go into Bumble's stall? Because she toyed with me. God, I was ready to burst and she cries in her little girl voice, 'Stop. I'm sixteen.' The little prick. All girls lie about their age. Did I think she'd really go into the stall?" He checked the rear view mirror for the answer from the man in the reflection. "Did I think the horse would give her a good pounding?" He took a deep breath then shouted to the cab, "She deserved to get pounded. I hoped she'd get pounded." His voice changed to a sarcastic falsetto, "I can't. I'm sixteen and I've never done this before." He turned onto the highway, straight north to Tampa Bay Downs. "She had it coming, the little bitch." He thought no more about Miranda.

Luis returned to the yard and watched the devil drive from his family's life. He stared into the shallow ruts left by the trailer hauling Prescott Acres' murderer and accomplice. He settled on the top porch step, and breathed with

190

practiced effort, reviewing the scene of the Prescott Acres trailer shrinking in size to a dot, like the closing scene in a movie. He was heartsick and dry-mouthed. He pulled off his red and black cap. Luis was whipped, outmaneuvered, and outclassed, and his sister lay dead. He leaned back against the porch support and squinted toward the orchard, absent-mindedly stroking his left arm propped on his knees, then drifted to a short nap.

"Hey, Luis. Today's the day."

Luis straightened, waking to see a blurry St. John, who was as he said he would be, back for another chance to photograph Bumble B. Luis was speechless. He replaced his cap, bill backwards and looked away from the wide-awake, eager face of St. John.

St. John smacked his fist into his hand, "Don't tell me I'm too late for that darned horse again. Geeze." He looked at his watch, "Hell, it's a few minutes after six. Damn." St. John Jones's immediate expression changed to a questioning gape. He stepped from his truck with his hand out to Luis. "What in the world happened to you? You were fine when you and Baxter left Gringo's last night. Did you have an accident on the way home?"

"Oh, no. Oh, Jonesie. You can't be here. I'm okay but you can't be here."

"What are you talking about? I told you I'd be here to get some early morning pictures of loading the horse for the race. It's six a.m. What changed?" He kicked at a small stone, continuing his soliloquy. "I got up at five, no time for breakfast. I got some tasteless, tepid coffee on the run from the waffle joint, and I'm still late. I can't believe I missed her again. She is the fastest horse!"

"Jonesie, the horse has to be at the track hours before the race. She needs to be examined by the vet, get washed, tattooed, saddled, viewed by bettors, on and on."

"What time is the sixth race?"

"Between two and three p.m. I'm not sure."

"Good, I have plenty of time to get there. Let's talk about what the hell happened to you. Is Baxter okay?"

Luis nodded. His head would not clear. Would talking to the reporter be a good thing, or the worst thing? He was reluctant to share his information. He prayed he wouldn't break down and cry in front of this young reporter.

Last night amidst all the blood and pain, hiding his sister from his mother seemed like the right idea. But, now in the cool clean morning, facing this young man looking for a story, Luis couldn't be sure he had done the right thing with Miranda last night, in fact he was becoming sure he'd done the most wrong thing. Luis stood with feet wide apart for balance, his shoulders slumped, and his face was slack and expressionless.

"Hey, Luis, you alright? You look like you might faint." St. John stepped forward to grab Luis as his friend's eyes closed and his knees crumpled in a collapse. The bill of Luis's cap hit the ground and flipped from his head.

"Christ, kid, don't faint on me." St. John looked around for help as he knelt at Luis's side. He reached for the boy's shoulder, but pulled his hand back, as if stung, to not touch the sling.

St. John jumped up and ran to the house and pounded on the kitchen door. "Mrs. Smitt, Mrs. Smitt." Patrizia's head was well tucked under her pillow, upstairs, in the most distant bedroom from the porch, shielding her from unwanted noise.

Hearing St. John's panicky voice, Luis began to rouse from his faint. "Hey, Jonesie. Help me up, would ya?" Luis rolled to his knees. His voice caught with pain as St. John cupped his good elbow to pull him to his feet. Luis staggered and slipped to sit on the running board of St. John's truck. He replaced his cap to hide his betraying face behind the cap's bill, and caught himself in a sob which deteriorated to undignified boo-hooing.

St. John was speechless. His first impression was to back away from Luis, but the sobs touched him. He was inclined to comfort the kid, but was a stranger to patting and reassuring. He blurted, "What is it? Is this about the horse? Or the race? Or your sling? Or …" St. John's voice drifted off.

Luis answered in a whisper, "I can't tell you."

"Do you mean you can't tell me because you don't know what to say, or because it's a big secret, or because I'm a newspaper man?"

Luis nodded. "Newspapers."

"Oh, then I guess I'm obliged to keep your secret, old man." St. John said this to Luis, who, yesterday was proud and secure, and was in control of his enviable life. Today he was beaten down. Luis worked his fingers and consoled his arm inside the sling.

St. John bossed, "Get into the truck. We'll go get some coffee. We can talk."

Luis looked up to St. John's face. "No, I have to stay here to protect ... Well, in case Mom gets up."

"Louie, isn't your mom the lady who sleeps late? Come on. You need to get away for a few minutes. For coffee, maybe a donut. I'm paying. We'll be right back. It's not even ten after six. Your mom won't be up for hours. Right?" He opened the passenger door of the green truck and grabbing Luis's waistband, hoisted him into the cab.

Chapter 18

CONFESSION

Patrizia rolled over and squinted at the sun slicing through the gap between her heavy maroon curtains. The clock showed six fifteen. She was sure she'd heard someone calling her name. Wasn't Luis's or Randa's voice. She must have been dreaming. She sighed and rolled to her stomach, securing the pillow over her head with her flung arm. After a moment of conscious consideration, she arched up to better listen. But, her kids didn't call her Mrs. Smitt. Huh! Patrizia reached the front porch, wrapped in her chenille robe and hugged her arms as the newspaper reporter's green truck disappeared in the black dust of the lane. She wondered why Luis and the reporter were off already, but guessed they were following Coleman's trailer up to Tampa Bay. She turned to go into the house, glad to see the last of Prescott Acres' horse and trainer. She'd have Miranda back under her wing again, away from that sleaze. She could not know her life had been dashed into irrevocable sadness and that she was not yet finished with the horse being trailered away from her farm. She would not have Miranda back under her wing.

Luis and St. John sat in the parking lot of Sunny Burgers' drive-thru, taking their morning caffeine in tall plastic cups filled with cherry flavored, icy cola. Luis stared straight ahead.

St. John started. "Hey, Luis, like I was saying before, after I left you the other day, I went back to do some research on your famous Maryland horse. You know she's a twin and her sister's in trouble up in Maryland for trampling an old stable worker?"

Luis sat straight. "Her twin? Somebody got trampled? You found that out on the computer?" He leaned on his knees and swallowed a sob.

"Hell, yeah, that was on the computer, and a whole lot more." St. John flipped pages in his note book, eager to divulge the rest of his information. "I've been dying to tell you about it."

Luis squinted at St. John, "When did that happen? The trampling?" He ran his hand to his face, covering his mouth and chin.

"About the same time your horse would have been decamping from Maryland. And probably under cover of darkness. Well, the old guy didn't die at the time of the incident, but died a few days later, so I don't know if that qualifies as a trampling death. Manslaughter, maybe. I don't know the laws in Maryland."

Luis snapped to attention. Puzzle pieces were falling into their grooves. He echoed, "The old man died a few days ago? Was his name something like Billy Goat or Gross or Graft?"

"William Goff."

"Yeah, that's right. 'Billy Goff!' I heard Bud on the barn phone, but I didn't know who he was talking about.

I'll tell you what. When he found out the old man had died, he hung up and stomped into the bunkhouse and had a real temper tantrum. He smashed one of the kitchen chairs to smithereens. He called the old man 'Pops.' Do you think he was Coleman's father? But they had different last names. Maybe he's a grandfather."

St. John shrugged. "Maybe, but lots of old men are called, 'Pops.'" Both shook their heads.

Luis said, "Coleman was always drunk. He told me a long story about twin Thoroughbreds as foals, but never mentioned the horses' names. Nothing he rambled about made sense to me until yesterday when some of the story's pieces came together."

St. John consulted his notes. "Right, Bumble B is a twin to Prescott's Pride. They were born in 1997 in—uhhh, I have the notes right here."

Luis laughed a gallows laugh. "So, the other horse *is* named Prescott's Pride?' That's a hot one, but it explains a lot. When Coleman kept saying, 'Prescott's pride,' I thought he was talking about the owner's favorite horse. Like that."

St. John looked back to his notes. "The twins haven't been tattooed yet. Still not in any big races. Records show, and this is local papers reporting, that both fillies were fast as bullets, and owned by a Mr. Albert Prescott in Maryland, in a funny sounding town name."

"Prescott Acres in Long Green, Maryland." Luis pulled his visor over his eyes and petted his left arm.

The reporter answered, "Yeah, darned straight, but get this." He consulted his tablet. "On April third, there was a small piece of news, that a trainer, no name provided, from a Long Green farm was trampled and taken to a hospital. I called some Maryland hospitals. Tried to get some info but everything these days is privacy, privacy, privacy." He shook his head. "The lady who answered the phone at the hospital was distracted, but mumbled to herself away from the mouth piece of the phone, something like, 'Oh, a Mr. Goff. Signed out AMA'. Then she came back to me and said she had no information to share with me. I love this job. Then, Luis my man, a further thread on the name Goff took me to an obit for a Mr. William Goff, 76 years old, died on April 9th, 1999. Private funeral at family request. A few days ago."

St. John clapped his hands and continued, "But, was I satisfied? No indeedy, my friend. I called around to a few Maryland funeral homes, gave my sob story…" in an aside, "really, reporters can be ruthless. I finally found the right funeral home, and tricked, uhhh, *finessed* them into giving me the family home phone number. I dialed. The phone was answered by a man, not saying, 'Hello,' but he said, 'Albert Prescott.' I slammed the phone down. Prescott owned Mr. Goff. And Goff died. I'll bet ya anything the boss wouldn't let the old man stay in the hospital in case the old trainer blabbed the name of the horse that trampled him. Hell, I don't know Maryland's rules, but maybe the state, or county, or some official would euthanize Prescott's fastest horse. Yipes, ya know?"

Luis mumbled. "You understand, I'm making up this scenario, but that would explain why Prescott might be pretending this horse is Bumble B. He's hiding the murderer horse, the faster of the twins, here and keeping her camouflaged with the black shoe polish and tall leg wraps until the race is over. If the Maryland authorities want to euthanize a killer horse, they'll take the slower horse from the stall marked with her sister's name, up in Maryland. Shitty, huh? I think Mr. Prescott sent the real Prescott's Pride here to prevent her from being euthanized. Because she's a money maker, for sure." He looked up. "If you allow that hiding a tall white sock with wraps is an intentional disguise. Wow." He shook his head. "Am I right, Jonesie?"

St. John answered, "And you say that the trainer intentionally kept his horse's identity hidden by keeping his horse's pasterns wrapped, and put her in the water walk when everybody else was sleeping, or generally not around, right?" Luis nodded. "But, Louie, I don't see we have any true evidence that the guy switched horses. Given that he's already gone to the racetrack and can't tell us anything."

Luis said, "Oh, I think I have proof. He worked the folded wrap stained with black shoe polish from his jeans pocket. "Here ya go. This is from Bumble's leg. Found it in her stall last night." Luis sat up taller at his contribution to solving his mystery.

St. John fingered the material and said, "Luis, this proves that Coleman may have polished a shoe or boot with black polish." Both flopped back in their seats to reconsider their angle.

Luis jolted upright. "The water walk! Hey, there'll be shoe polish residue in the water walk right now from him cleaning up Bumble B this morning. Come on. Let's get back to the farm. An average horse would allow the trainer to hose off last night's blood from her feet, but not Bumble.

Or whoever she is. The evil twin. The water walk is the one reason he came to our farm in the first place."

The young men jumped up as if on cue, Luis the slower of the two, and dunked their empty cups into the trash. St. John kicked the old green pickup into gear and the cowboys were headed back to the farm. After a period of silence Luis said, "You know, Jonesie, this is hard to say. I don't care a thing about the swap of the horses. The story gets much worse. Much worse." Luis put his head down, the bill of his cap shading his face. "The reason I was so upset when you came this morning was, well, I'll tell you when you're not driving."

They looked straight ahead without speaking. Turning into Smitt's lane, Luis pointed to the flat ground underneath a large oak made private by tall yellow, weedy grasses on three sides. "Pull up here, Jonesie."

St. John stopped the truck, turned off the ignition and turned to face the somber young man. Luis breathed, "I gotta say it." Having blurted the facts to Coleman an hour before made it easier to tell St. John. "Jonesie, that devil twin Thoroughbred trampled my sister. Trampled her to death last night." He stopped to compose himself as his voice broke on the short sentence. St. John's head snapped forward and his mouth dropped open.

St. John stared. Time stood still for the young men. The eloquent reporter searched for words. He coughed out, "You're kidding!" He frowned, looking through the windshield. He turned to Luis, "Trampled to death? Your sister's dead?"

Luis leaned his head against the passenger window. His tired voice dropped. His breath fogged the glass as he told his truth. "I don't know why she was in Bumble's stall. It's my fault because I went to Randa's room last night to tell her I thought there was something fishy going on. I still hadn't figured what or why. I didn't know about the old stable manager getting trampled and dying in Maryland. Miranda and I talked. We didn't know if Bumble had a lip tattoo yet, which would positively identify which horse was which. Oh, Jonesie, I can't talk about it."

"Yes, you've got to. Go on Luis, go on."

"I never thought Randa'd go to the stall alone. She *knew* better than to be alone with that horse. I left her in her bed last night." Luis rubbed his sling. He twisted the visor to the back of his head. "She, uh, she was grounded, but that's another story, and I went out with Baxter. Well, you know, to Gringo's Grill, where we saw you." Luis squeezed his eyes shut and stopped to catch his breath. He tripped through telling the details of finding his sister, dead in Bumble's stall.

St. John reached his hand to shake Luis's shoulder and again, pulled back his hand. "Is that how you got pounded too?" Luis nodded. St. John asked. "So where is your sister now, you know, her body?"

"That's the worst part. Today it seems so lame and gruesome, but last night I was trying to protect Mom." He cried through his confession, explaining his rationale, and his worries. His mom's heart will be broken. She'll never be the same. Nothing will ever be the same. Luis leaned his head on the truck's dashboard, and rubbed the left arm.

St. John, speechless, fanned his face with his hat. He sat back and stared straight ahead. "So, where's Miranda now?" With Luis's confession, St. John gasped. "In your barn?" He plucked off his glasses. He faced Luis for his answer. Luis nodded.

"Louie, you have to tell your mom. She deserves to know. I'll go with you, but your mom needs to know."

Luis said, "No, I can't. Not yet. She'll freak. She'll die if she sees Miranda where she is now. Oh, it gets worse by the minute. I'll have to get her out and maybe put her into her own bed." Luis looked up for some solidarity from his new confidant.

St. John jumped from the front seat, took a few steps, flattening the tall grass, then turned and came back to lean into the open window. "Lou, if you move her, maybe that could be considered, by law, to be a criminal act. I don't know the legalities, except you can't move a body. Maybe it's different if *you* move her from where you originally put her. God, I don't know." He paced. "Could we put her somewhere in the barn, not up to her bedroom, but on a bed of straw, under some blankets, and never say she was ever under the floor? I know you panicked last night, but putting her under the floor sounds like, well, a little crazy, you know? I mean you can see how someone might think that you hid her for some other reason? I don't know what reason, Louie, but nothing good. Think about it. I mean, under the floor?"

"Baxter helped me because I was too busted up to do the thing by myself. Christ, he'll never lie." Luis licked his lips and bit away a sob. He opened his truck door and slid to his feet. He grimaced and rocked back and forth for the comfort of the rocking motion.

St. John said, "Actually, Baxter needs to know the story has changed. You'd better hurry up and get a hold of him as soon as possible to let him know how the story has changed. Do it now. Before your mom wakes up."

Both young men consulted their watches. "Yeah, it's almost seven-thirty. Mom will be up soon and so will Miran … " Luis stopped.

St. John swore, "Shit! Rigor will have set in. Lord, lord, I hope we can get her out from under the floor without injuring her body even more. Louie, we need to hurry and get Miranda 'placed' before your mom is out of bed." St. John kept talking as he moved in a five-foot circle.

Luis floated the idea, "Yeah, Baxter's probably frantic this morning. I'll bet he didn't sleep much either. Miranda is, no, she *was* his girlfriend. I'll tell him that I had a change of heart after he went home last night. I'll say I couldn't leave Miranda alone under the floor, and made a little bed of blankets for her in the back of the barn, and covered her. Baxter's soft. He's a sweet guy and he'll believe me. He was broken up last night, but I was dying too."

St. John spoke in a low voice, looking at Luis over the tops of his glasses. "You're sure he'll go for it, because if he starts talking, you and I will be in big trouble. No joke. Shit, I'd lose my job, maybe go to prison for lying. Hell, you're right. This is some deep stuff. Well, I don't know if we're committing a crime, and I don't want to find out."

The young men went right to work. They shuffled loose straw into a soft bier among the stacked bales in the corner of the barn. St. John fashioned a small wall of stacked bales to hide Miranda from being accidentally discovered. Luis undid every move he'd made last night. Once her body was pulled from under Gingerfoot's stall, Luis tucked the edges of the blanket around her face, allowing her to 'breathe.' He made an awkward attempt at straightening his sister's wild hair. Her jaw and temple had purple bruises and torn skin on her raised irregular cheek bone which no longer bled. Her brother petted her cool, waxy forehead and told her in a soft, confidential voice, "Everything will be okay." He flicked away the dirt from the blanket wrapped around her like a baby's bunting. He rocked back on his heels. He stood and looked down in disbelief. The glint of Miranda's teeth were visible between her parted lips. St. John went on to re-nail Gingerfoot's floor. He scattered the hay in her stall, covering the new boards.

St. John stood behind Luis and carefully slipped his hand to the teen's uninjured shoulder. "Louie, you know that Coleman might be held for murder, or at least an accomplice. From what you tell me, he knew that old Mr. Goff was trampled by one of the twins. Then the old guy died. Coleman made no attempt to remove his horse from the race, nor told anybody here about it. I think if a person dies within twenty-four hours of the crime, then the perpetrator can be held for murder." The two sat on the bench by the barn's wall phone. "Of course, the old man died several days later, so I don't know if Miranda's death will count as a second death. I mean, incident." St. John looked to Luis who returned a blank expression. "I think there's some legal term about 'reckless indifference.' In Florida, anyhow."

Luis said, "But Coleman's actions were no accident. His crime was intentional. He drove all the way down here with a loaded gun. I mean that's like giving your ex-girlfriend an expensive jewelry box with a poisonous snake in it. He knew the horse was dangerous and didn't do anything to prevent anyone else from getting hurt or ki... You know what I mean. Coleman's in deep if you ask me." Luis stared straight ahead. "He'll blame his employer, Mr. Prescott."

St. John helped Luis to his feet. "Maybe, but Coleman's the one who drove the horse every damned mile down here and let your family board her. I'm not saying that Prescott isn't guilty of murder, or manslaughter at the very least. Coleman had to know all about switching the horses. He's the trainer for heaven's sake. I've met Coleman once, but I don't get the feeling he thought this up by himself. And of course, I'm sure Prescott bankrolled the trip down here." St. John leaned back against a wall then sat on a bale of hay. "Maybe they'll call it third degree, because they didn't send the horse here to specifically kill. You know, intent and all." He looked up to Luis's flat expression. "I haven't covered any murder trials so far, but I follow them, and I know a little. Maybe the laws are different in Maryland. Don't know about charges between states and extradition. Beats me. But I'll find out, guaranteed. Hey Louie, maybe after you've gone to law school you can tell me all about it."

Luis rubbed his upper arm. "Damned horse. I should have shot her last night. The first time I saw that monster was on Sunday, six days ago. I thought she was the image of perfection with her symmetrical white star. The sunlight shining on her black silky hide, her noble high head, ears perked forward, high-stepping hooves, tail thick. Oh, she was a beauty. Now I'm sick with hate at the thought of her. I should have known she was wild when Bud had a handkerchief over her eyes to get her out of the trailer. I mean, walking down a ramp is simple enough for a race-horse. And I remember his excuse for covering her eyes. He said, 'She can really dance.' No shit." Luis plucked off his cap, wiped his head with his good arm, took a staggered breath, and returned the Smitt's cap to his head. "Let's get my poor mother out of bed." He sobbed, looked away and continued a slow walk to the house. "This will kill her."

Chapter 19

TRAVAIL

The cats, settled in the hay loft, licked each other's heads and ears, then curled and looked down onto the silent scene of the broken crèche below them. Huddled on their knees and bent over the mother's wrapped child, the family was surrounded by the beasts of the barn. Pale morning sun lit up dust from the hay and straw, giving a soft haloed focus to the sad scene. Humid air, heavy after last night's rain weighed down the atmosphere in the barn. The heady fragrance from the new bales of hay was lost to the awareness of the mourners.

Patrizia collapsed over her lifeless daughter, Miranda, recently so full of potential, talent, humor, love and beauty. Luis stood in stupid silence. His arms hung like empty sleeves as he watched with unbelieving eyes. Silence was broken with the mother's wail. Luis watched and waited for his mother to pull in a new breath. Her shoulders shook over her child who was impossibly, unthinkably dead, wrapped in a horse blanket. His darling mother petted and rocked Randa, speaking and crying into her lifeless daughter's ear. Barney trotted to his mother's side from his post at the door. He whined and leaned heavily against Patrizia's shoulder where she knelt on the straw. Luis felt as ineffectual as a scarecrow missing most of its stuffing. He had nothing left to say.

Patrizia lifted her head. She whimpered to her son, "How could this happen? Yesterday we were a busy little family, helping and joking with each other. I was a parent, doling out discipline and love, cajoling, and mentally spending the money for our future. Our biggest problems yesterday were if, if Miranda would actually obey, and stay in, and if you would be home before midnight." Her sentences were greatly unintelligible, lost in inhaled wet breath and broken words. "And, and Luis, I don't know what Bud Coleman has to do with this, but *I know* he's to blame." She collapsed into her son's arms and bawled. Luis patted his mother's heaving back. She broke away and leaned forward with renewed whimpering, and rocking. She rested her wet cheek against Miranda's cool hands.

Today, Race Day, their farm was a crime scene. More than a crime scene, the barn held the irrevocably crushed lives of a previously young and healthy family.

A dust storm followed Dr. Henreddy's old black car as it closed in on the farm house. Jose, Russ and Kirk arrived for work and were turned back to their homes. Kirk insisted on staying to manage the needs of the horses and the barn. Big Russ pulled the barn refrigerator from the wall to close a mouse hole in the wall. Jose went to the barn phone to cancel Saturday's and Sunday's water walk clients.

The doctor escorted Patrizia to her living room. The Palmetto police arrived ten minutes after the medical examiner, who gathered his supplies and notebook, joking with the officers about weekend crimes being job security. They laughingly swapped familiar exchanges in poor taste for the occasion.

Mr. St. John Jones of the *Palmetto Palm Daily* newspaper stayed on after his morning session with Luis, and busied himself making notes of the revelations and suspicions for the police report. He re-tucked his shirt and stood tall to approach the police with his best authority. "Gentlemen, you need to lose that jocular attitude. This is not a scene of two bad guys shooting it out, but of a family who lost their father two years ago to cancer, and now have lost their only daughter to a senseless killing by a wild horse. A family member is within earshot, so please temper your comments and be aware of the grieving all around you." St. John put his head down and retreated.

St. John went on to photograph Bumble's empty, crime scene stall. He documented the officer leaning half in the water walk as he obtained evidence of pasty, black flecks floating in the water and adhered to the treadmill walls. He snapped several frames of the forensic officer obtaining blood smeared straw, which was overlooked by the two boys last night. The samples would be matched to the victim, to Luis, and the horse.

Luis remarked to a policeman collecting the water samples, "Those black flecks, which, by the way, are black boot polish, will prove the trainer tried to hide the true identity of his horse." The officer grumbled his response.

As a new thought came to him, the policeman turned to Luis, "Young man, did I overhear you saying this horse killed another person up in Maryland? How long ago was that?"

Luis answered, "I overheard Bud Coleman, the trainer, talking on the phone to his boss up in Maryland two days ago. He said a man named Goff, G-o-f-f, was trampled by a horse and died a couple days later. Do they euthanize horses for trampling deaths?"

The officer drawled, "Well, at this time we don't have proof this horse is the same one that trampled the Maryland man, although we have a trampled victim here in Florida. About euthanasia for a wild horse, I think it's the owner's responsibility to isolate the horse. Perhaps the victim's family forces the owner into court for a decree to euthanize. Might depend on how deep the horse owner's pockets are. The owner could get a good lawyer to save his horse. He'd say the 'accident' was the girl's fault. You know, rich people, they get their way. I've never seen this before, but *if* the horse is responsible for two deaths, well…" He rubbed his chin and said no more.

Without family witness, Miranda's wrapped body was moved to the medical examiner's vehicle with decorum, and was delivered to the Palmetto morgue.

Baxter received his early morning call from Luis. On hearing the incredible news, Counselor Jeanette Blackerby insisted that her son drive her to be with Patrizia. Luis was worried about seeing Baxter, not knowing if he'd have to fine tune the lie, hoping the police wouldn't separate them for questioning. Or maybe that technique was done only in TV stories.

Tears filled Luis's eyes as Baxter's mom parked next to the porch. Her expression of pain and quiet efficiency showed Luis she'd be a comfort to Patrizia. She carried a cellophane covered cake into the kitchen. Mrs. Blackerby turned to Luis and placed her hands on his shoulders and at straight arm's length, gave him a searching, sober look. Luis feared she would hug or kiss him, but he was too exhausted to think of a kind, appropriate exit from her strong grip. She closed her eyes and shook her head. Her hands dropped to her side. "Oh Luis, I'm so, so sorry. I don't have words to describe what's in my heart. Our family is so stunned. What a tragedy." She turned to Patrizia's kitchen and started the kettle for tea. She gathered tea cups.

"Mom's in the living room," Luis said indicating with a nod. "I think she's calling our minister." Jeanette Blackerby pulled a tissue from her slacks pocket and dabbed at her eyes, then started into the living room to find her grieving friend. Patrizia was no longer on the phone but meandered to the kitchen. The women met and melted together in a tight, rocking, whimpering hug.

Baxter slid out to the porch. Randa's death was unbelievable, inconceivable. Yesterday she was his steady girlfriend who would call him, write to him, and visit him in her last year in high school as he went off to the university. Today she was gone. Cruelly gone. He shared Patrizia's and Luis's shock and deep physical pain, painted over by numbness. Baxter stood on the porch and waited for Luis, looking at, but not seeing the orchard. Nature tried in vain to compensate in a small way by sending the sweet fragrance of the orange blossoms through the bright day.

Luis looked in to see the women, their arms laced around each other, returning Patrizia to the couch. He turned to join Baxter on the porch. The young men faced one another without speaking. Luis looked to his shoes.

211

Baxter gazed up to the eaves of the porch ceiling and said, "Oh look, a spring nest."

Luis nodded. "Pigeons." He swung his arm out to include his friend in a walk to the barn. "Come on, Baxt."

Baxter pointed to Luis's sling as the two walked toward the barn. Luis nodded. "I'll tell you about it later."

They avoided proximity to the few officers who were speaking, moving around the barn. Luis and Baxter kept their voices low while their eyes scanned the floor for smears of blood, of overlooked evidence. "You know everything except after you left I sat down to catch my breath and fell to sleep. Mom found me and five minutes later Coleman showed up, drunk as usual."

Baxter whispered, "God, Louie, I'm so relieved that you moved Miranda. Where did you put her?" Luis swung his good arm around Baxter's shoulder and walked him to the little rise of straw he and St. John had fashioned in the morning.

Luis mushed some dry straw in a small circle with his foot as he considered embellishing the story. He lied. "After you left, I got to bed but couldn't sleep knowing poor Randa was under the ... well, you know. So I sneaked back out here and this is where I hid her. Better than under ... I was so upset last night I couldn't think straight."

The forensic team had tossed the bales of straw to the side, landing scattered and tilted, no longer the short wall of privacy for Miranda. Luis was relieved the medical examiner's workers had taken Miranda's body before Baxter had a chance to observe her. Baxter's head was bowed. He rolled his lips into his teeth and nodded. "Lou, I didn't say we

212

buried her. I said we wrapped her in the horse blanket and moved her to the back of the barn like you said on the phone this morning. It's a good thing you told me." Baxter did not question how Luis, with an arm in a sling, managed to stack bales into a short wall, and how by a miracle managed to get Miranda lifted and pulled from under the floor to the fresh bier.

Luis's arm throbbed. "Yeah, hey, look Baxter, I have to go take something for pain. My ribs and this arm and shoulder are all throbbing like the devil. Damn, the pain is killing me."

The young men walked without conversation to the house. Luis and Baxt stood behind the kitchen door frame watching their mothers in the living room. Mrs. Blackerby poured hot tea for Dr. Henreddy. Patrizia sat up straight, making an attempt at normalcy but covered her face with a tissue and tipped over to the arm of the couch and keened a heart wrenching sound which backed the boys onto the porch. Luis was reluctant to run across the living room to go upstairs to the medicine cabinet. As he waited for the opportunity to dash to the stairs, St. John walked across the yard and called to the boys' backs.

"Hey, Luis. I'm done here. Gotta get going." St. John consulted his watch and jumped to action. "Damn, I'm late again. I'm covering Bumble's race and have to leave, like, ten minutes ago."

St. John pushed past Luis's side in a slow, respectful walk towards Patrizia and Mrs. Blackerby. "Mrs. Smitt, I'll be back right after the race." St. John, a talker, was handicapped at having to keep the information succinct and private. "You know." He resorted to communication with his eyes and eyebrows as he took Luis's good arm and pulled him to the porch.

"Look, Louie, I'll call you as soon as I hear what's going on with Bud's arrest."

"No, Jonesie, I've got to go with you. Suppose Coleman gets away? I've got to get him."

"You can't go. Look at you. If someone blows on you, you'll fall over. You're weak, heartsick, and bruised, and you lost blood." He tapped Luis's sling, "You're actually taped together, and your mom needs you here. Baxter will be with you. But I've gotta get going. It's my job. I'll call you." St. John tapped Luis's head as if in a parting benediction and dashed to his green truck and peeled off to Tampa Bay.

Luis slumped against the kitchen doorpost. Baxter folded into a kitchen chair at the table where a few days ago all the teens laughed as they kicked each others' feet under the table.

Dr. Henreddy entered the kitchen from the living room. "Hang on a minute, son. Let me have a look at you." Luis winced and inhaled his sobs with the doctor's prodding examination. The physician said, "You'll need some x-rays. Then you can pick up some pain medication." The doctor's head was bowed, showing his pink bald spot as he initialed the prescription pad while giving instructions to Luis. He looked over the silver rims of his glasses, "You allergic to any medicines?" Luis shook his head. "Good. The ER will call me after they've reviewed your films in case we have to do anything else with your injuries. Ribs heal slowly, with a lot of pain, but they heal on their own. Right now I think you may come out of this with a cast on that arm, but let's be sure." The doctor looked at Baxter. "My man, can you take this fine fellow to the emergency room for x-rays?" Baxter appeared to be relieved to have a role other than standing around, being in the way, his hands jammed into his jeans, looking worried and feeling sick.

Dr. Henreddy walked to Patrizia who stared ahead, focusing on nothing as she leaned back into the overstuffed pillows of the couch. Barney padded up to the pillow next to his mistress and laid his chin in her lap. Jeanette Blackerby relinquished her seat to the dog, a beloved family member, and returned to the relative cheeriness of the bright kitchen to manage the few dishes in the sink.

The teens headed for Baxter's SUV. As soon as Baxter rolled the Escalade into reverse, a police lieutenant interrupted talking into his walkie-talkie, held up both hands to stop the boys' escape. He waved to Luis who was sure he would die if one more thing went wrong, so terribly wrong. The lieutenant instructed Luis to report to the Palmetto police department after his x-rays. "For questioning, young man." Luis put his right hand to his chest, certain his heart was about to fail. "We have questions about the horse and his trainer. You're eighteen, right? Your mom's in no shape to be questioned right now. Shouldn't take long. We'll be out to the racetrack to question the trainer directly." Luis nodded a sober yes to the officer's instructions.

Dr. Henreddy left a few pills and a prescription for Patrizia, talked to Mrs. Blackerby about contacting the extended family, then proceeded to his day's work, including a trip to the morgue.

Chapter 20

ST. JOHN'S RACE

As soon as Baxter received the police lieutenant's instructions and rolled up his window, Luis twisted in his seat and with his good hand grabbed Baxter's knee and squeezed. Baxt slapped at Luis's punishing grip. "OW! What are you doing?"

"Baxter we have to go to the race. What's Jonesie gonna do? He's seen Coleman only once. He can't do anything. I've got to get there."

"What about going to the hospital and police station?"

"Shit, man, we can do that anytime. Nothing is faster than your new car. Believe me, we'll make it."

Baxter moaned, "All right, but quit killing my leg. You're strong for some shot-up guy. Let go of me for God's sake. Mom'll kill me if anything happens to this damned Caddy." Baxter turned to the entrance to US Interstate 75. The two sped on.

St. John, ahead of Luis and Baxter by twenty minutes, clicked on the truck's radio as he sped toward Tampa Bay Downs, muttering and damning himself for being late again. Race two at the track was in full rumble while three lanes of northbound traffic slowed, being slimmed to two, then to one lane. The traffic throbbed in impatience. The accident was being cleared. St. John's fleeting thought was to look for a *Palmetto Palm Daily* news vehicle on duty to cover the automobile accident. Seeing no crony on duty and no activity other than the cleanup crew sweeping and hosing away pulverized glass and plastic, he knew his twin horse story would be even bigger. His head pounded. His mind returned to the what-ifs and possible consequences of the events of Luis's story of last night. He snapped off the radio to have silence and succumbed to the reality that he would be late for the sixth race. He pressed the accelerator.

Luis and Baxter, now a few miles behind St. John, sat in stopped traffic from the accident farther up the road. "Baxt, get off at the next exit and we'll cut over to 41. More traffic lights but it's an inside track, shorter distance than the interstate. God only knows how long we'll sit here."

"Yup, okay." Baxter had taken on the affect of the bank getaway driver and pulled the new vehicle onto the apron of cinders, flipped on his blinkers, leaned on the horn, and raced to the exit two hundred yards dead ahead. They were moving again, full speed ahead to Tampa.

Afraid he'd miss some important racetrack news, St. John tuned back to the radio and shook his head at a funeral home's announcement, which segued to a tire sale in Tampa. He growled aloud and thrummed his fingers on the steering wheel. The racetrack's announcer returned and reported the bettors had had their chance to check out the horses at the paddock and the post parade.

St. John drove faster as he listened to commentary on the silks and which horse was looking hopeful today, to the description of the two-year-olds being guided into the starting gate. He unwrapped a stick of orange flavored gum to prepare for war and, taking advantage of the newspaper logo on his truck doors, he pulled the truck to the breakdown lane and jammed the gas pedal to the floor.

"Bumble B, the filly from Maryland, the favored horse in this race, has drawn gate four." St. John leaned forward in his cab and chewed loudly and aggressively. He was jerked from worry about his lateness when he heard Bumble B's name mentioned in that last announcement. "Oh God, that's Bumble B. They're starting the sixth race. Shit-shit-shit, I'll get fired for sure."

The announcer broke from naming other hopefuls in line to succeed to next year's big stakes races and the Triple Crown. St. John said aloud to the radio, "Hey, you heard it from me first, Mr. St. John Jones of the *Palmetto Palm Daily*, Bumble B will not be going to the Triple Crown. Heck, man, this is her last race. She's doomed, brother. Doomed."

The announcer continued in a magnanimous manner, "Bumble B, the Maryland filly is protesting the escort pony's nearness and is shying away from the gate. "Oh, she's turning in circles like a circus horse. Her jockey has his work cut out for him." He laughed a good-humored chuckle. "Okay folks, help is on the way and she's being led into the gate."

St. John was less than a mile from the track's back gate.

A clanging bell and the sixth race, the Sterling Bridle Stakes with a purse of $200,000 was on. The radio blared at its top volume. In his own race, St. John swept his hand across the inside windshield, knocking papers and gum wrappers to the floor, clearing his view. "Ahhh, I'm so close. This trip has been a punishment."

A heaven sent stream of steady green traffic lights sped Luis and Baxter forward. "Baxt, we should be listening to the race." Baxter agreed and found the station on his new dashboard. Both leaned forward listening for news of the sixth race.

Luis said, "I don't envy the tattoo-identifier. I'd hate to be the guy who has to look into that wild horse's face and flip up her lip. Can you imagine? Cheeze." He gave a short wry laugh. Luis was swept into the charging adrenaline rush of the race but hated this horse, post number four, a murderer. "Die you bastard," he muttered through his teeth. "But win first."

The radio transmitted a static jangling starting bell, lurching eleven two-year-olds from their gates. They, and all the radio listening public heard that Ticky Bartholomew brought Bumble to an immediate wide lead. Luis rocked back and forth in his seat, seemingly forcing the new SUV forward.

Bumble's starting lead was a nice insurance against a horse in the rear who might decide to make his owner rich with a last minute run for the gold. The grandstand crowd was on their feet. Bumble seemed to be encouraged by the thunder of hooves behind her. The announcer was scream-ing into the microphone, "…a margin of distance I've never seen before so early in a race. Ladies and gentlemen, this Maryland horse isn't racing, she's out for a pleasant run. A closer has no chance in this race." He hollered that, at the first turn, a red horse named Apple Shine, number nine, pulled from the gang to eye Bumble's shoulder. Number five, a filly as black as Bumble, wearing a mask of blue and yellow, gamboled on, catching up, and by the third turn passed Apple Shine. Ticky and Bumble saw the interloper but pulled ahead without effort. The finish line was in easy reach.

A string of damnable static interrupted the announcer's words. "This Maryl... orse ... Maiden ra ... will b ... moving up ... tucky Derby," followed by clattering commotion in the announcer's booth. A moment of dead air stretched out. Baxter punched the air, "Well, that's typical. Radio conks out before the winner is announced."

The radio returned with excellent reception for an advertisement for motor oil, followed by a reminder to attend the Line Street Baptist Church, then went on to station identification. Luis yelled to the dashboard. "Why are you stalling? What the hell happened?"

The announcer's voice returned to the airwaves in the middle of his remarks about the variety of states represented at the Sterling Bridle Stakes race. He broke from the informative chatter to report a problem. "Ladies and gentlemen, although Bumble B, number four from Maryland handily won the sixth race by two lengths, she is struggling to make her way to the winner's circle. We are still awaiting her official time, but I can tell you, it was a beauty. Her jockey, Ticky Bartholomew has jumped from his limping filly to lead her to the field inside the track. She is being met by her trainer and the crew from the horse vanbulance. She's bypassing the winner's circle. The veterinarian is making her way to the horse now. Ladies and gentlemen, Bumble B, number four from Maryland is limping, not using her left hind foot. The veterinarian is standing next to the trainer now. I cannot give you any more news at this time other than to tell you the winner in the sixth race was Bumble B, number four, owned by Albert Prescott out of Long Green, Maryland, in two minutes and six point eleven seconds, What a FAB-ulous time!"

"Holy heavens above, what's going on?" St. John hollered to his windshield. The newspaper's green truck, not a looker, was good for speed and maneuverability. He was flagged through the service gates of the Tampa Bay Downs Racetrack and parked his truck in the designated Press space. He grabbed his camera, all the while muttering in anxious fragments and sentences. He scooped the shoulder bag with his photographic equipment and took off. The bag pounded against his back as he ran.

The overhead announcement crackled, "Ladies and gentlemen, race number seven will be postponed for fifteen minutes. Please visit our refreshment bar. Bear with us in this emergency, a sad time for all of us horse lovers."

St. John stopped in his run to grab a security officer. Showing his identification card and swinging up his camera, he called, "How can I get to the horse vanbulance?"

The officer pointed ahead to a crowd around the van in the infield. "Damned shame," he told St. John, "the stakes winner is limping. Can't even get to the winner's circle. Probably broke her leg." St. John pivoted and sped off at his best speed. The officer hollered after him, "Maybe euthanizing her. Don't know." Hearing the word euthanizing," St. John poured more effort into the dash.

His mind shouted, "Euthanizing? They can't do that without the owner's permission. He won't go for it. Let's see." He made faster, longer strides.

Bud Coleman's immediate and automatic response on seeing the familiar face of St. John was to wave. As soon as his hand shot up he pulled his hand back, considering that the young reporter might know about the young girl, lying dead in the Smitt's barn. He jumped through the side door into the vanbulance. St. John pounded on the van's door. A vet tech cracked the door wide enough to reveal Bumble, lathered at her withers and haunches. She was on her feet with the wraps removed from both hind legs. White shone against her black, left hind fetlock. St. John didn't know if he glimpsed bone or if lather had slipped to her foot. Coleman had her eyes covered again.

Coleman yelled, "Keep him outta here. He's crazy. Let's get the van rolling."

St. John hollered with lying bravado, "Coleman, the police are right behind me. You and your horse can't leave Florida." He was so close to getting that photo.

Coleman answered, "Not my horse. Contact the owner for any problems." St. John snapped a photo of Coleman's palm, fingers splayed wide to block the photo. Coleman's body obscured the horse's rear before he slammed the door to St. John's view. St. John circled the vanbulance taking photos as he went.

As St. John pounded on the door a second time the van shook as the whinnying horse attempted to rear and fell. The door flew open and the vet and tech flew out as Bumble's sharp hooves flailed in an attempt to right herself.

The van's floor, slippery with her slobber, lather and sweat kept her from regaining her footing. Alone with the injured horse Coleman yelled, "You damned horse. You deserve this for killing Pops."

The van's door flew open with the rocking of the van. Coleman leaned out, gesticulated and hollered to the van techs, "You two sons of bitches get in here and help. She's a champion for God's sake. Help her!" The horse's feet flailed. The tech stood outside the door, looked in and called back to Coleman in a high, shrill voice, "Sir, there's no place to stand until she calms down. We'd get kicked to death!" Bumble's side heaved where she lay. Her head came off the floor then sank with a sickening thud. Her whinny tailed off with her heaving breaths.

Standing at the open door and witnessing the great horse's thrashing, St. John gaped, and by reflex brought up his camera to flash the scene. He documented the vet and tech as they reentered the van near the horse's head, and covered her. They padded and steadied her head.

Coleman's head snapped up from his inspection of his horse when he heard police sirens closing in. He slammed the door, mouthing silent oaths. The vanbulance stilled. With the seeming resolution of the tantrum, the Thoroughbred remained on her side, eyes still covered, heaving her breaths. Coleman grabbed his shoulder bag containing the zipped leather pouch with the unused needles and vial of cloudy white liquid. His thoughts had been that his horse would not need juice to win the race. And she hadn't. "But that rear low leg sure broke just the same," he mumbled as he headed for the cabin's door. He bent to the horse's ear, "You got what you deserved, you, RAT."

The unlatched door on the far side of the van shot open then lazily closed. Bud Coleman was gone. He didn't look back.

St. John would not get the photo of the police escorting the villain to lock up. St. John chastised himself for missing Bud's exit. Not one to pout, he jumped atop a stack of heavy duty boxes and trunks belonging to the television camera crew, but could not isolate Bud in the melee. He returned to the vanbulance to interview the vet and the tech.

Luis and Baxter had no badge to flash for right of way into the track as St. John had. Baxter pulled into a welcoming parking area for Thoroughbred owners, his glistening white Escalade drawing no suspicious attention. Baxter pulled Luis from the passenger seat and hurried around the outside fence to an opening for the owners. Security officers were not in evidence. Luis pointed to the vanbulance in the center field. As the two hustled toward the van they saw St. John rounding the vehicle, taking photos.

The radio announcer squinted into binoculars. He leaned to the microphone and told the listening public, "Ladies and gentlemen, two police cars have crossed the track and are pulling up to the vanbulance holding the record breaking winner of the Sterling Bridle Stakes race. No, wait, these are not Tampa police escorts, they are …, they are, yes, I can now read they are from the City of Palmetto. The Palmetto personnel are exiting their vehicles.

There seems to be some excitement at the vanbulance and we will go to station identification."

The second Palmetto cruiser sped to the trainer/owners' parking area, isolating and closing in the Prescott Acres truck and trailer, expecting, but, unable to stop Coleman's getaway attempt.

Luis and Baxter arrived immediately behind the Palmetto authority, breathless and relieved at finding St. John in the crowd of people clustered around the vanbulance. St. John looked up in amazement at seeing the two Palmetto young men. "What are you doing here?"

Luis answered. "Isn't it obvious? Where's Coleman? I'm here to help you capture Coleman. You've met him only once, and believe me, *I* can identify him anytime, anywhere, from any angle. I know his posture, how he stands and I recognize his walk."

The crowd of rubberneckers around the vanbulance thinned. A burly racetrack security officer, feeling his authority, confirmed by his official, black denim uniform jacket, moved across the inside track. "You men need to vacate this area."

St. John flashed his press pass and lifted his self-explanatory camera. Luis straightened his injured back, and despite his arm in a sling, radiated authority with his convincing explanation of representing the filly's Florida residence. The guard did not rebuke him and summarily overlooked Baxter, perhaps assuming this well dressed young man in the triumvirate was the Thoroughbred owner's kid.

The three stood in the vanbulance's shadow and resumed their information swap. St. John described Bumble

B's limping exit from the field and added his apology, "I was certain I'd catch up to document Coleman's arrest." He slumped and dropped his camera to his side. "Well, somehow in all this tumult, Coleman got away. Dammit, I wanted that photo of Bud Coleman in handcuffs. The creep's an accessory to a death."

St. John said, "Oh, maybe you didn't know. Things look pretty bad for Bumble. Looks like she broke her left hind leg. Broke it low, where she always had the green wrap."

Both boys silenced to take in this news. Luis broke towards St. John as if he intended to grab him. "Jonesie are you serious? Are you shitting me?"

Baxter grabbed Luis's good arm. "Luis, just listen."

St. John said, "That's what I heard when I was pushing through the crowd. The examining vet, or maybe it was a tech, leapt from the van with the horse's last tirade and said something about maybe needing to euthanize her."

Luis's hand flew to his head. "They can't just kill her without Mr. Prescott's permission. I wonder how I could find out. What should I tell my mom?"

St. John said, "Cool it, Luis. We can't do anything without Coleman. He's gone. The horse won the race, but her living or dying won't change anything here today. Go home. I have to make a few notes, talk to a few people; the announcer, the vet, you know, the life of a newspaper man, then go back to work to write this up. Front page, stuff Mr. Smitt, I promise you that.

Across the field in the flood of people moving toward the exit, Bud Coleman pulled the brim of his Stetson to the bridge of his nose, and put his head down, his feet kicking through a drift of torn, failed betting tickets. He hustled past the lines of bettors, both the winners and the unlucky. He picked his way through the clot of people who chose to not stay for the final races. They waddled toward the exit gates and parking lots, talking loudly over each other, congratulating and complaining in their slow progression. He overheard the 'tsk-tsk'ing of conversations of compassion and speculation about the poor, lame horse.

Coleman abandoned the Prescott Acres trailer. No need to return for his personal effects. The police would be waiting for him there. Coleman pushed into the crowd. He learned how easy it was for a white, medium build, medium height, middle-aged cowboy to disappear among the thousands of Floridians in the grandstands and parking lots. In the safety of the anonymous crowd, he collegially walked in step, then swung his arm around the neck and shoulder of a skinny teen boy who was calling to friends, to wait for him to jump into the back of their truck. Bud followed and hopped into the truck bed, chatting and melting into this coterie. He leaned over the edge of the truck to pull a few laughing fellows into their ride home. After the truck rumbled through the exit gates of the parking lot, and slowed at the first sharp right turn, Coleman hopped to the black top and ambled past the string of cars heading west. Maybe Baja was a good choice, after all. He'd lose the big payoff, but a new start out of the purview and reach of the US law seemed a more prudent direction. He stuck out his thumb, and he was gone.

Chapter 21

PRESCOTT'S FAME

Static interrupted the announcer and the television picture's fidelity as lightning shot across the April sky in Maryland. "Damned storm better not interrupt the reception of this race," Albert Prescott settled in front of the large TV screen and complained to himself during races two, three, and four, brought to him via his horse racing channel. At race five, he phoned the stable's staff to be sure they were assembled in front of their smaller TV. Satisfied, he bullied his large screen with a threatening, raised, misshapen fist. He rejoiced at the start of the coverage of the sixth race at Tampa Bay Downs. If he'd been able to walk, Mr. Prescott would have been pacing. An impatient man in a motorized chair has fewer options, but rocking in his chair answered his nervousness. He talked aloud to the screen, gave his rebuttal to the announcer's running dialogue, and at last, the race was on!

Prescott pounded his knobby hands against his arthritic legs as he sat alone in his den watching his horse, in miniature, dashing across the screen. The passionate, breathless report of the racetrack's announcer detailed Prescott's Pride's early formidable lead. The crippled Mr. Prescott never came closer to jettisoning himself to standing and jumping than he did when his horse's nose, then eyes and ears, flying feet, then rump and tail crossed the finish line. Prescott whooped to the wide screen, watching his horse ridden by the man he'd picked for the job. "Great God in heaven! I *knew* Ticky Bartholomew was a winner." As Bumble B crossed the finish line, Mr. Prescott sang out, "Oh that beautiful, speedy Prescott's Pride. Her first time out!"

The announcer returned in his enthusiasm to declare the winning and record-breaking time. Prescott cheered aloud to his living room. "Ahhh, my own Sterling Bridle Stakes winner! Two-minutes, six point eleven seconds." Prescott laughed and aimed his scooter to the liquor cabinet and reached for his Bushmills, his special, celebratory Irish whiskey. He poured a generous drink, singing aloud, "Oops, careful! Don't want to spill a precious drop." He tasted the liquid with his lips, his tongue and with his throat. He savored the burn and said, "Next year, the Triple Crown." Prescott rejoiced, congratulating himself on his cunning, his shrewd management of switching the twin horses. The TV coverage moved from a rerun of Bumble B crossing the finish line to a prerecorded story about the history of the women spectators' outlandish and fashionable hats worn to the races, then cut back to the camera focusing on the limping horse being led by her jockey to the inside track. Confident in the victory, Mr. Prescott turned his back to the screen as he savored another sip of his best single malt whiskey. He missed seeing Coleman join the jockey, maneuvering his injured horse into the camera's frame. Animated conversation between the jockey and the trainer was broadcast without sound. The rerun of the footage of Prescott's

Pride's early lead was shown over again. The chestnut filly, number nine, gained ground from the center again and number five, the black, elegant favorite from Tampa Bay, stretched his legs to pass on the far right, threatening the front runner. A cheering roar went up from the locals in the stands again and again with every rerun. The thrill of the win was not diminished by the repetition of showing the horses sprinting for the finish line.

The cable coverage went to real time faces of the spectators, to other horses being walked and readied for the seventh race. Prescott turned his scooter and in exuberance started down the hall to the stables where he knew the trainers and barn manager would be grouped around the TV, all celebrating. He did not see the Florida horse vanbulance driving to the inside field, shown on the screen. He did not see the police car advance toward the emergency vehicle. With the static of the lightning, Mr. Prescott missed the frustration of the screen darkening and returning with a cartoon featuring a raccoon and a fox haggling over a hole in the ground.

Mr. Prescott's front doorbell rang. He was expecting reporters. "Ahhh, yes, the adoring public." A crooked smile snaked across his cheek as he chuckled to himself, "These bastards must have been camped at the bottom of my driveway for the whole race." Mr. Albert Prescott laughed to himself and adjusted his tie, then picked up his old fashioned glass. Careful to not spill a drop, he pushed the directional knob on his scooter's armrest and headed to the vestibule, still beaming, thrilled and proud that *his* horse had shattered the record for two-year-olds. He was exuberant. "Oh, all the planning has paid off handsomely."

He smiled and opened his door to camera flashes from an Asian-American woman photographer. He backed his scooter to allow the door to be fully open. This was the precise fame he had imagined and even predicted. When his vision cleared from the flash of the camera's white lights, he recognized a Baltimore County policewoman standing in front of three other police officers, all neat, in pressed gray and blue uniforms. The photographer and the four policemen stood in a semicircle, like Christmas carolers, around the well-appointed front door, tastefully enhanced by topiary. The lead policewoman lifted her badge, "Mr. Prescott, please?"

Prescott scanned the large audience, made a visor of his hand to shade his eyes from the camera's lights. "Is this about my winning filly today in Florida?" His eyes sparkled. His smile revealed an expensive upper plate of straight white teeth with a glint of gold at the lower molars. "Yes, I'm Albert Prescott." He proudly sat forward, balancing his libation. His confident hand dropped from the front door knob to the scooter's control lever.

"Mr. Prescott, you are wanted for questioning for your part in contributing to two counts of manslaughter and possibly second degree murder."

His head jolted backwards, bumping into his headrest. He croaked, "Two counts of manslaughter? Second degree murder?" He bellowed a loud, "Nooo." His bulging eyes rolled up. He flopped forward, folding into his scooter's handlebars. His forty-year-old Bushmills splashed

232

indecorously across his vest while his whiskey glass rolled from his relaxed grasp. The crash and splintering of the glass activated the congregation.

One of the officers ordered an ambulance to the estate. He stepped forward and aided Mr. Prescott to sit up and breathe. Adding to the immediate confusion, a phone rang in the background, the desperate voice of the vet from the Tampa Bay racetrack was captured on the phone's messages, asking questions no one could answer. With one of the officers seeing to Mr. Prescott's recuperation, the photographer skidded to Mr. Prescott's side and snapped the scene. While the group of county police officers revived and Mirandized the man, a blustery, capricious April storm blew through Long Green, Maryland. The conscientious police photographer peeled off to have a look at the environs and to find the real Bumble B. The officer ran through the beginnings of a rainy shower, following a slate path around to the well-manicured lawns that led straight to the long, low, white stables where a flat, black horse weather vane atop the largest of the picturesque turrets spun in the wind. She stepped into the Prescott Acres stables, to a neatly swept concrete floor.

On seeing the Asian woman in jeans and a leather jacket, holding her camera, and mistaking her for a newspaper photographer, the stable manager gallantly rose from his chair. The woman lifted her camera in greeting. With a winning smile she said, "Yeah, Hi. Congratulations on your horse's win. I'll bet you're thrilled. Listen, I'm here to get some pictures." Billy Goff's replacement raised his hand, wiggling his fingers, inviting the young lady into the barn to take pictures, all the better to increase Mr. Prescott's fame, and perhaps suggest a pay increase for the stablemen and trainers. In a socially correct manner, the trainers backed away from their cluster at the TV to welcome the young lady.

As St. John Jones had snapped photos of the Smitt's barn, this photographer documented Prescott's stables. She noticed two photos with curled corners, tacked to a bulletin board. The first was of two young girls showing all their teeth in braces in big smiles, holding up baby bottles while nestling black foals in their laps. Another picture showed an old man in a wheelchair next to the same foals. One foal had its nose next to the man's ear. The woman snapped the picture, then turned to the vocal horse in the stall across the aisle.

She was greeted by the complaint of an elegant black Thoroughbred. She gasped in surprise at the tall horse and touched the nameplate on the upright next to her stall, and read "Prescott's Pride."

"Well, eureka! Hello, girl. So you're the genuine Bumble B, huh? No need for the masquerade of using your sister's name any more." She whispered, "Your sister's a goner." She returned to her public voice to include the stablemen. "My, my, but this is a gorgeous piece of horseflesh. She looks like the female version of the horse in the Black Stallion movie, but I guess everyone says that."

The horse's hide shimmered like patent leather in the overhead light. She had a symmetrical facial star, and four uniform three-inch-high-bright white socks. "Let me get your picture, you beauty. I hear you're good looking *and* a speedster." She moved closer to get a photo of the stately head of Bumble B. The horse shook her thick mane and backed.

Bumble B turned her head to regard the photographer from her left eye. The woman smiled, whispering continuous compliments of the horse's beauty. "Smile, Black Beauty, I need one good head shot of you." Lightning lit the sky. The stables' lights blinked once as the photographer decided on a closer focus. She leaned over the mesh fence and repositioned her feet. The thunder rumbled. Bumble B responded by flattening her ears and rearing up, moving toward the photographer, rolling her front hooves high into the air.

The young woman gasped and jumped backwards, narrowly avoiding a braining at the whim of Bumble B. She spilled an expletive while searching the floor for her footing. Grasping her camera, her hands were unavailable to break a fall. Her canvas camera supply bag swung up and back in a wide arc from her shoulder. Her smooth black hair covered her face. She hollered, "Whoah. This is a mean horse!" She staggered backwards, falling into the arms of a willing, ready stable man.

He scooped her up to her feet. "Yeah, she's mighty skittery, I'll tell ya. She's fast on the track, all right, but ya don't want to get too close." He steadied the young woman, holding her elbow and helped her to the door, saying too much, like Mr. Goff before him. "At least you got away with your life." With dismissive laughter, he shook his head and held the door open to watch the young woman escape into the April shower with her photos and her life.

Chapter 22

AFTER THE RACE

In Florida, Kirk, Big Russ and Jose buttoned up the barn. Jose ran to the house to refill the cats' and dog's bowls. The men left with the promise to return early tomorrow.

Saturday evening was settling in when Luis accomplished the x-rays, boasted a cast, and a newer, better sling, and received his prescription. Finally, an hour was spent at the police department answering questions about Bud Coleman. Baxter drove his Escalade up Smitt's lane to the farm. Both were surprised to see two unfamiliar cars parked on the ashy ground between the entrance to the barn and the house. The cars' shiny fenders and roofs reflected the overhead porch light.

"What's this?" Luis powered down his window and leaned forward to better examine the bumper of the closer car. A small silver cross topped by the curved word, "clergy" was affixed to the frame of the license plate. The second car had a "Christian Helping Hands" bumper sticker on a pale rainbow background. "Looks like the church people are here. I wonder how long they've been here. Oh, how I dread going in."

Baxter turned to Luis, "Guess you'd better face up to it. Tell my mom I'm waiting, and you can leave your car door open for her." Baxter sat with his arms stiff and hands firmly glued to the steering wheel. He groaned as his feet touched the floor. He looked at Luis's exiting back and said, "Luis, you did a fine thing today. I'm proud to know you."

Luis looked back with an expression of worry and surprise. He nodded to Baxter. There was nothing left to say. He waved his right hand over his head and slowly walked, in equal measures of pain and foreboding to the porch. He disappeared into the house and thanked Mrs. Blackerby for staying with his mom. Jeanette Blackerby gathered her purse and sweater, kissed Patrizia goodbye, whispered she'd drive her to the funeral director tomorrow, hugged her again and joined her son for the ride home. The Escalade sedately departed Smitt's Water Walk Farm, fading into the failing light of the evening.

Two church ladies left after saying consoling words and leaving two casseroles, a salad, a cake, and a pie. Patrizia and Luis escorted the reverend to the door a few minutes later, thanking him, over and over again.

Patrizia turned to her son, "Honey, I know you're hungry. Let's have a little of that comfort food. We could both use it. When I got up this morning I never thought that tonight my dinner would be delivered by the Helping Hands ladies from the church." Instead of putting out two dinner plates, she collapsed into the kitchen chair and said, "I'm sorry Luis, I can't face it." She sniffed back tears, and fitted the church ladies' dinner into the refrigerator.

"Honey, what did the x-rays show?" She smiled a thin, interested smile at her son.

"Fracture of the humerus with bruising to shoulder and scapula. The trifecta. Followup in a week with an orthopedist in Palmetto. Lucky, huh? Another doctor bill, in case you don't have enough."

"Luis, I told you, our finances are under control. What I wouldn't give to have merely money problems rather than a death in the family." Patrizia brought her hand up to her mouth and caught her breath. She turned her back to Luis and pointed behind her. "Sit down honey. I'll have the corn chowder ready for you in a second. Here's the corn bread. Butter a piece for me too, would you?"

Patrizia served the small supper to her son, "… to keep something on your stomach so you can tolerate those pain pills and keep your strength up. Honey, put your dish in the sink when you've finished. I'll clean up later." Patrizia carried her corn bread in a paper napkin and went straight to her bedroom.

Luis made no comment to his mother's instruction. The cats were absent, although Barney sat, pressed into Luis's leg. With his good hand, Luis alternately patted the dog's head and spooned sips of chowder into his mouth, until one of the three overhead light bulbs popped off, startling Luis. He looked to the ceiling. "Now how did that light know to cut off right now? Who would have thought things could get gloomier and lonelier?"

He climbed the stairs and shuffled to his bedroom, turning his head from Miranda's door. He eased his injured body onto his bed and glanced at the University of Miami poster. "It's funny, but yesterday this time that poster excited me. Tonight the whole idea of going to college seems foreign and ridiculous. Who could care about stupid Hurricanes in

Miami? Maybe I won't go. Mom will need me here more than ever."

He glanced at the abstract arrangement of the stacked splintered, ruined wooden baseball card frames next to his trash can. "Huh, my last temper tantrum." He scuffed to his desk. He caressed the brown envelope containing his trussed up, most valuable baseball cards waiting to be registered at the post office before being mailed to the retailer in Baltimore. Luis was sure the money he'd get from selling the cards would help around the farm. He sighed and licked shut the envelope. Odd, his tongue was almost too dry to seal the envelope, yet his eyes overflowed with wetness.

Luis slumped across the bottom of his bed. He wiped at his eyes and sat and stared. He leaned forward with a deep breath, his face twisting in pain, then tackled his boot's laces with his right hand. He'd talk to his mom tomorrow about the outstanding payment due from Mr. Prescott. His thoughts were so loud in his head, he began to mutter aloud, "And Mom had better insist on that thousand-dollar bonus for the killer horse winning the race, like the old man promised on his margin note. That money from Paley's Comet's sale should help pay for the lawyer. I'm sure we'll need a lawyer for dealing with Prescott. I wonder if Baxter's mom takes care of that kind of lawyering. Maybe St. John knows of the best lawyer for Mom to hire. I'll look in on Paley's Comet in a few minutes. We need to talk." Luis's pain pills and spontaneous nap postponed his visit to the barn.

St. John arrived at the Smitt's farmhouse, but saw no porch light, no kitchen light, no bedroom lights on the second floor and noticed the barn was dark. Barney wasn't in the yard to meet the truck. He pulled a sedate U-turn and returned to Palmetto to watch his story roll off the press. His story would top all other headlines.

Chapter 23
AUGUST 1999

Cardboard boxes holding Patrizia's library of books, CDs, and some old tapes, and various knickknacks, were stacked on the floor. Violin sheet music, some flopped open, was not yet loaded into the boxes stacked atop the glass front bookcase. The rolled tasseled rug lay across the couch, chair and ottoman in Patrizia's office.

She organized her two-drawer file cabinet marked Water Walk. A second small file box marked Medical was pushed to a corner of the room. Tissue paper and sheets of newspaper slid from the desktop to the bare floor. Luis interrupted her work. "Mom, suppose you hate Texas. I mean, it's Texas!" Patrizia retrieved a sheet of newspaper and continued wrapping her green glass-shaded banker's lamp. "Honey, I spent four years at Rice University. Married your dad and lived there for a year after college. Weather wasn't worse than Florida's." She closed the lamp into its box, then stepped to the window and addressed both Luis and the orchard. "I have good memories and some old friends in Texas. Honey, hand that balled up newspaper to me to stick into this box. Ellie, my old college roommate's sister is in real estate. She has a few condos and small houses for me to look at next week. I'd say she has a pretty good idea of what I'm looking for."

Luis crumbled a piece of newspaper and handed it to his mom. "Well, what about me?"

Patrizia taped shut the box. "Oh Luis, I'll always have a room for you. Besides, there's only two small states between Florida and Texas. You'll see. Most of the kids at your college will go home to other states for summers and vacations. That's how it is. Eighteen-year-old kids go away from home to go to college. You'll still have a home to come home to, only it'll be a different home. And Luis, you *are* going to college."

Luis touched the open mandolin case where Miranda's instrument lay in its fitted, deep blue velveteen bed. The light from the window touched the golden wood, accenting the decorative arrangement of small pieces of ivory surrounding the sound hole, covered with an old artisan's carved, lacy wood decoration. "You know this mandolin is beautiful. I never looked at it before. It was always just Miranda's. What will happen to it now?"

Patrizia's deep sigh included her shoulders. "I've thought about it. Glancing at the mandolin breaks my heart, but I think in time, we'll call it, 'Aunt Miranda's mandolin.' Maybe one of your kids will play. Anyway, it's valuable in its own right, and beautiful. I'll display it next to the piano in Texas. Hang it on the wall." Patrizia walked to the kitchen. Luis followed. She poured a cup of coffee. "Luis, pull that box of donuts over here and sit down. The Horshams and I are working on a plan."

Luis obeyed and sat and dipped into the donuts. The expression on his mother's face clued him to put off the first bite. He sat in silent sobriety. His leg began to bounce.

"Dr. Horsham, Stan, suggested maybe you'd want to keep a place here in the trainer's bunkhouse."

Luis started to stand. His mom reached out to grab his hand. "Honey, sit down and listen. That's why I had you and Baxter choose the color to paint the inside of the bunkhouse—to freshen it up for you. The tentative plan is, when there's spring break or semester breaks you'd come back here. In the summer and at Christmas, the longer vacations, you'd visit me in Texas for a while, then if you wish, you'll come here to be in your old neighborhood, close to the Blackerbys and to St. John, and to ride Paley's Comet. You can help these people with the water walk business if they want to keep it.

I'll leave my truck here for you. Maybe you can take it to Miami. I don't know if freshmen can have vehicles on campus or not."

"Nope, not for freshmen. Of course I checked."

She patted his head. "Oh, I'm sorry, honey. You'll manage. We all lived through college. Anyway, it's hard to know what all to put into a contract. So Dr. and Mrs. Horsham and I have decided to proceed as if we're family and trust each other and give it a try. But who knows? I might hate being away from Florida, you might hate Miami, all unknowable. The Horshams might hate our farm, but not likely. We're going forward."

"So, he'll buy Paley's Comet?" He kept his head down, but looked up under his eyebrows and listened to the answer.

Patrizia sighed and answered. "It's Paley's Comet who brought us all together. He wanted the horse for his daughter's birthday. I can't afford to board Paley while we're both away, so I think selling her to Dr. Horsham is a good plan. She's a fast horse and wants to be ridden. His girls will be with her every day. Win-win." Luis looked at the untouched donut and realized he had no appetite.

Two days later, Patrizia, Dr. and Mrs. Horsham, and Counselor Jeanette Blackerby leaned over their contract for the doctor's family's one-year rental, with the intention of purchasing, the house, track, the sheds and property. Patrizia swiped at perspiration on her forehead. She spoke her postscript to the contract, "Gingerfoot's owners are agreeable to keeping her boarded here in your care. She's a little work, but brings in a steady income, and she's a darling."

Horsham smiled and said, "Let's add a Gingerfoot clause to the bottom of the contract, Mrs. Blackerby." The counselor nodded and penned a line.

She stood and backed from the papers with her hands outstretched over the paper. "Ready to sign."

Patrizia, Dr. and Mrs. Horsham reread the documents, then flourished signatures. Patrizia poured flutes of champagne and pushed the basket of sandwiches to the center of her desk. Dr. Horsham would continue to commute back to his veterinary practice for a year. The first year's rent would be applied toward next year's expected sale of the farm. Mrs. Horsham carried a paper plate of sandwiches to the porch to join her daughters, awaiting a celebratory snack and to perambulate their new property. Stan sat at the table and read over the contract while Patrizia walked her lawyer to the porch.

Jeanette Blackerby tucked her valise under her arm and started to her Escalade. She hugged Patrizia at the door and said in a confidential voice, "There's a lot going on up in Maryland. Albert Prescott's prosecutor blames Goff's death directly on Mr. Prescott, for forcing him to sign out of the hospital Against Medical Advice. They call it AMA. That's a separate charge from him transporting his dangerous horse to Florida. But if you put the two ill-begotten incidents and their consequences together, you have two deaths resultant of Prescott's intentional, dangerous and malicious actions. Doesn't look good for greedy Albert Prescott. I'll keep you informed. I expect you'll win a money settlement, but don't spend it yet. The court case will drag on, but I think our suit may see light within the year."

Patrizia leaned on the door post, "I'm ragged. I feel torn, and hollowed out. My blood pressure soars each time I think about Bud Coleman. I'll deny saying this, but if he's found, I may kill him myself. I *know* he's responsible for Miranda's death."

Jeanette hugged Patrizia and said, "There's no news on Coleman, but they'll find him. While drunk, Coleman mentioned to Luis his plan to go to Baja, so it's a start. Drinkers make mistakes. Don't worry, sweetie, we'll get him."

Patrizia nodded. "I can't even think about it right now. I ... " She turned away, then returned to face her friend, "Money won't undo Miranda's death, and nothing can cure my shredded heart."

Jeanette put her arm around Patrizia again, "I know, but her death is directly responsible for you moving away and incurring all these new costs. You know better than anyone how much this is costing you." The two stood for a moment in silence. The attorney straightened and said, "I'll make these copies and document today's transaction. We'll get together for dinner at my house before the boys go to college, and before you move to Texas."

Patrizia slugged back to the dining room and opened the café curtains. Dr.Horsham pushed up the window. The warm air wafted in. She took a deep breath and smiled to herself. Stan Horsham leaned on his elbows on the sill and also took a deep breath. After a moment of silence the two looked at each other and laughed. Patrizia asked, "Would you say the dominant fragrance was the orchard or the horse manure?"

"Well, I'm no stranger to horse manure, but I expected the fragrance of the orange orchard." They turned their backs to the window and laughed congenially again. She offered him a sandwich from the basket, and took one for herself. "I suppose it would be smart of me to face up to selling the farm now, but I can't do it yet."

Horsham pulled out a chair and sat at the table. Patrizia continued, "I'm caught between leaving this sod and making a new life, versus the feeling that I'm abandoning Luis. I spoke to him and he agrees to having the bunkhouse to come home to for holidays and summer. It's breaking his heart to leave this home and especially, Paley's Comet. And it's breaking my heart to still be within these walls where I grieved the death of my husband and now my daughter. I simply can't stay here any longer."

Luis, now graduated from his left arm's cast and sling, stood at the doorway and coughed his need to interrupt.

"Mom, I hate to interrupt, but have you two decided if Kirk, Jose, or Big Russ will be retained?"

Stanley Horsham clapped both hands on his knees and stood. "No, Luis, not yet. I have my own stable and grounds man, but he's getting on in years and may not want to move to Palmetto. This property is larger than my present farm, so there are still unanswered questions." He turned to Patrizia, "We'll discuss the business of your men tomorrow."

Patrizia, deflated by the reality of the recent negotiation, answered in little more than a whisper, "My guys and I have talked about it. You know what I pay them, and they know you know. The rest is up to you."

Horsham watched the spent Patrizia Smitt wilt like a wild flower yanked from the earth. He chose a fat sandwich, and after the first bite said to Patrizia, "Did I tell you that I purchased a Guernsey and her calf six months ago? I'll be moving them into your barn in September."

Patrizia laughed and gave Dr. Horsham a hug. "Ah, that's such good news."

On Luis's last Saturday at the farm before his mom would drive him to Miami, he flipped his shirts and jeans into the bureau drawers of the bunkhouse. Baxter joined, carrying a sturdy box of Luis's shoes and cowboy boots, topped by a shoe box holding a small mountain of heaped, rolled socks.

"Here ya go, Bro. Your bedroom is now empty, at least until the Horshams' moving van gets here." Baxt sat on the chair by the Formica table. "You know, I think having the bunkhouse as your proxy home is a great idea. My mother

suggests, and I'm under pain of death if I don't invite you, that you can crash at our place when we're both home on vacations."

The old black phone on the table rang. Luis scooped up the receiver. "Ashley? Oh, hello, how are you?" He put his hand over the mouthpiece, mouthing the name "Ashley" to Baxter. Baxter bobbed his head, crossed his eyes and dangled his tongue to affect a cartoon drunk. Luis continued, "Naw, can't. I've got to be in Miami on Monday. Yeah, orientation. Should be good ... Uh-huh ... Sure ... At Thanksgiving break, then. Good. You can tell me all about Duke. Good luck, Ash."

Luis hung up and stood with a surprised expression still on his face. "Did that just happen? She must have had another fight with poor Matt Harrison."

Baxter asked, "So, who gets Barney?"

"I asked Mom the same question." He responded in a high voice, "'Oh, please. Barney's family. He's my youngest kid. Of course he'll stay with me until he's old enough for college.'" Both boys laughed

"That's good to hear. He'd be brokenhearted without your mom."

"Are you kidding? It's killing her to leave the horses and Donkey Boy. Right now she's agonizing over what to do about the cats. She wants them, but after being working barn cats, I doubt they'd appreciate a move to a small Texas condo."

"Donkey Boy?"

"Horsham gets him since the donkey is Paley's companion donkey." Luis took a deep breath and swatted his leg with his Smitt's Water Walk cap. "Yeah, this will be good. I can ride Paley's Comet when I'm home, and sort of bring these new people up to speed on how the place works. Here, Baxt, help me move this bunk bed to the window wall." The boys worked side by side, shoving the heavy structure. "Hey, I can … " Luis stopped talking to yank the mattress from the top bunk and placed it on the lower mattress, doubling the thickness. "These two stacked mattresses reminds me of the kid's story where a pea goes under nine mattresses. When I was little I was afraid there were peas under my mattress. I figured all peas must be covered in dust, so I never ate them."

Luis sobered. "The vet's arrangement is for the first year, before they buy the property outright. Then, next year, Mom and I have to come up with another plan."

"You never know, the Horshams might allow you to rent the bunkhouse the whole time you're in college. And that fourteen-year-old girl of theirs will be eighteen by the time you graduate. Maybe she'll look good to you by that time."

Luis laughed. "You're crazy."

Penny lugged Luis's bedding and bathroom towels into the bunkhouse. "Who's crazy? Probably you, Baxter."

Luis grabbed a knot of sport socks and beaned the unsuspecting Penny. She screamed and dipped into the socks and before long, there evolved a good-humored sock ball fight.

Patrizia came to the door, flagging a business sized envelope. "Luis, this just came. I'll bet it's news about financial aid, never too late. Return address is the Greater Southern

Scholarship Committee. Hurry up and open it. Does it start with 'Congratulations'?"

Baxter said, "Come on Penny, let's hit the road. Mr. Luis Smitt here needs to talk finances with his mom."

Penny stood, gave both Luis and Patrizia a hug and said, "Don't forget. Dinner at our house tomorrow night." The Blackerby kids left, leaving Luis and his mom standing with his unopened envelope.

Luis tore open the seal, unfolded the thick award letter with its embossed inside address, with a block of names of the members of the board in tiny print. He flitted past the 'Congratulations' and ran his finger through the lines of typed words until his wide, hungry eyes opened wider at the amount of money he was awarded.

He handed the papers to his mother and stepped to the porch, stared ahead, pulled his visor to his eyebrows, and strutted to the barn.

"Come on Paley's Comet, we need a date. Therapy again, my girl." He continued his conversation as he saddled his horse. He kept a patter going in response to Paley's ear twitches, and mentioned, "It's amazing, isn't it, Paley, but I'm feeling happy. After Dad died I never thought I'd be happy again. Then Miranda…"

He mounted his horse and ambled through the paddock to the track. "I'm far from accepting Miranda's death. But it happened. And, well, I don't know what else to say." Paley ran on without a remark, following Luis's signal to accelerate.

Luis pointed out the changing colors of orange tree's leaves in the orchard, and said, "Mom is crushed, but going

to Texas seems to cheer her up. That's a good thing, huh?"
They pushed to a canter for half a mile, then galloped. The
earthy fragrance of the kicked up track was lost on Luis in
his flight, eight feet above the earth. "I know you can't hear
me over the sound of your hooves and the wind you're creating, but Paley, I suddenly have a heap of money to pay for
college. Oh, look at those purple and orange streaks in the
west. Paley, I'll be alright. I *know* that Horsham's daughters
will be here and will love you every day while I'm away."

The wind from the gallop whipped Luis's cap from his
head. He watched the red and black advertisement for
Smitt's farm blow over the shrubs next to the track, bounce
over the fence then tumble end over end, down Smitt's
Lane. Luis laughed aloud.

The end

About the Author

Fairytales read by her mother sparked Karen S. Bennett to a course of fiction. With an eye to irony, after a lifetime of observations and experiences from cello lessons, choir singing, art school, marriage, three kids, divorce, welfare, nurse's training, jobs in prison, travel to Vietnam, Russia, and South Africa, and homes in NYC, Georgia and Maryland, she sat down to write. Her first novel won first place in fiction in the Maryland Writer's Association in 2006, with other novels placing in national competitions. Many short stories have been both traditionally and e-published. Her motto is: From Fibs to Fiction.

Apprentice House Press

Loyola University Maryland

Apprentice House is the country's only campus-based, student-staffed book publishing company. Directed by professors and industry professionals, it is a nonprofit activity of the Communication Department at Loyola University Maryland.

Using state-of-the-art technology and an experiential learning model of education, Apprentice House publishes books in untraditional ways. This dual responsibility as publishers and educators creates an unprecedented collaborative environment among faculty and students, while teaching tomorrow's editors, designers, and marketers.

Outside of class, progress on book projects is carried forth by the AH Book Publishing Club, a co-curricular campus organization supported by Loyola University Maryland's Office of Student Activities.

Eclectic and provocative, Apprentice House titles intend to entertain as well as spark dialogue on a variety of topics. Financial contributions to sustain the press's work are welcomed. Contributions are tax deductible to the fullest extent allowed by the IRS.

To learn more about Apprentice House books or to obtain submission guidelines, please visit www.apprenticehouse.com.

Apprentice House
Communication Department
Loyola University Maryland
4501 N. Charles Street
Baltimore, MD 21210
Ph: 410-617-5265
info@apprenticehouse.com • www.apprenticehouse.com